Lori

Plenty of Time

May you always
have Plenty of
Time

Dee Kelber

Based on a true story.

Written by
Dee Keller

Edited by
Shelby Ayers King

Dedication

To my two sons;
Steven, Jr. and Edward ("Eddie")
You are my strength and reason to keep going.

And

To Stan's three sons;
Matt, Steve and Dave
Know that I will be here for you always.

I love each of you with all my heart.

And lastly…

To Stan
You will be in my heart forever.

Current Day, February 2013

It's Saturday evening, and I'm sitting at my desk at home working on my computer. My dog, Karlee, is snuggled under my feet while my cat, Squirt, sits close by watching my fingers breeze across the keyboard.

Squirt is a three-time orphaned cat that my son left here for me. After our family cat died that we'd had for over 13 years, he felt I needed a replacement. He didn't remember I said I wanted to get a dog once she passed or maybe he chose not to. One of his ex-girlfriends dropped her off at his place, and he figured I wouldn't say no. He was right but not without a fight. I couldn't leave her homeless.

Karlee is a beautiful Dachshund and Terrier mix who I adopted two years ago. She was abused in her last home and has a very skittish personality that comes out when strangers come around. Once she gets to know you, she will love you but it takes her a while.

My desk is in the living room, where I'm enjoying the roaring fireplace, and Rob Thomas singing in the background. It's such a quiet, peaceful evening.

Breaking the quiet, my computer rang, and Squirt jumped, startled by the noise.

It's my older sister, Sue, in Pennsylvania.

As she came into focus on the screen I said, "Hey there, what's up?"

Kevin, Sue's husband, was sitting in the background on the couch. He smiled and waved. "We're just sitting here watching TV, what about you?"

My main communication with my family up north is Skype on the computer. It's great to not only be able to talk to them but also see them from so far away.

Sue and I are two years apart in age. Growing up, we were very close and were the two that got into all the trouble. Our adult life couldn't have been more different. I consider both of us successful in our lives, just in different ways. Sue met her husband when we were very young and having fun. She is the only one of my three sisters who is still married. She met her husband on one of our fun excursions way back then, and they've been together ever since. Sue and I had a few rough years when we didn't get along, but we repaired those wounds and we've become close again. We don't talk as much as I would like, but any time is always nice.

"I was thinking about the past two months of my life. It was as if it was lived by someone else. You know that most of my life has been the same old routine of going to work, going home, working my second job and then collapsing in front of the TV. It's a wonder I've not gained 100 pounds. Visiting the family for the holidays this year in New Jersey was great. It was a long time coming. Can you believe it's been since 1989 that I'd been home for the holidays?"

"Yes, I hear it every year from mother." Sue replied.

I chuckled, "I don't handle cold weather very well. Why else would I be down here in Georgia?"

"I know it's always had been your excuse for not coming up here during the holidays." Sue laughed.

"I don't know why but this year was different; maybe because everyone is getting older, even me. Going to New Jersey always brings me back to my youth," I said, thinking about where we grew up.

"You did need to come up here for the holidays; it has been way too long. You know mother really enjoys your visits."

This year I spent the first half of the holiday with my mom and her side of the family. We had Christmas Eve with my cousins and Christmas day with my sister Sue. The second half of my holiday was with my sister Karen and my dad. It was a great trip.

"Well, I didn't plan things very well because as soon as I got home I had to go to work in California right away. I was supposed to only be there for five days but ended up there for two weeks. That was a long trip and I didn't pack right for it. Then I was home from California four days and then I was off to Vegas for a work/play weekend. Don't get me wrong, Vegas was awesome. You know it was the first time I'd been there, and I had a great time. After a few drinks, I opened up a little with my co-workers and their spouses about things in my past I'd done."

"I bet they loved the stories." Sue laughed, thinking about the times we've had.

"I may have shared a bit too much, but then the stories I told are funny… now. Back then maybe not so much." I said.

"Why, what did you share?" She asked.

"I talked about some of the places I'd travelled to for work and funny stories of things that happened. And then somehow the subject of my book came up. I didn't say much, but enough that one of the girls, Shelby, got me excited about finally finishing it."

I love my job and have a good rapport with my colleagues. The Vegas trip was with my colleagues and their spouses for a three-day weekend. I think everyone got to see a different side of me (and I of them) that weekend. As they say… *What happens in Vegas stays in Vegas.*

I would bet they would have said I'm a bit obsessive with my work before the trip, but afterwards I think they understood what drives me. I've always felt I just need to keep busy. I needed a break from my normal life, I needed a change. And boy, has it been a change. It's strange how you get out of your normal routine, and you almost feel like a different person, refreshed and ready for new challenges. It made me think of the experiences I've had and how they molded me into the person I am.

"She was so sweet and after hearing my story she said she would love to read the book. It felt good hearing someone being interested in the story again." I continued, "I decided to pick up my book again and see if I can finally finish it. I feel like something just isn't right about it, and I'm not sure what to do. There are too many gaps, and I don't know how to put it together."

Sue thought for a moment and replied, "Why don't you tell me about the book, and we'll see what we can do to make it blend together."

"That sounds like a great idea. When do you want to start?" I was excited that she was interested and wanted to see what we would come up with.

"I'm ready to start now if you want." She replied waiting for me to start.

"OK I will start at the beginning." I said and began to read the book to her.

The Time of Youth and Innocence

We lived in a small community located in the mountains of northwest New Jersey. A single dirt road circled around from one side of the mountain to the other to allow passage between the homes. Thirteen privately-owned houses were spread throughout densely wooded areas that divided each property from the other. In the summer, you could barely see your neighbor's home. This was a community that no one moved away from. We had lived there since I was 4 years old. At times, it was difficult to have any private life. Everyone always seemed to know what you did and where you were.

We had an area of cleared land on the side of the mountain but the forest was my seclusion, my way of having a private life, a place to find myself.

My family lived in a three bedroom ranch house on the side of the hill that overlooked the main town. It was a beautiful view regardless of what time of year it was. In the summer, you could see miles and miles of mountains in the distance. The fall surrounded us with the gorgeous autumn colors that filled our enormous living room picture window. In the winter, you could see even farther beyond the mountains and trees. When it snowed, you felt like you were in a ski lodge overlooking the beautiful snow-covered mountains. It was the only home I ever remembered growing up.

I was the third of four girls. Growing up, Sue and I were very close and shared a lot of experiences, both good and bad. We were the middle two and wanted to experience the world and the adventures life had to offer.

Out of the four of us, Sue and I looked the most alike. Most people thought we were twins, which, when she became 18, was a bonus for me. But then that could be an entire other book.

We both had long, blonde hair. She had blue eyes and straight baby fine hair, while I had brown eyes and thick curly hair. But it was our facial features that were so similar, which is why we passed for twins.

Our oldest sister, Donna, was focused on school and was content staying at home. She had always been very shy and a little over weight. She also had long hair but it was brown and didn't have the same features as Sue and I. Donna took after my dad's side of the family while I think we took after mom's side.

I had always wished I had the drive towards education Donna had. Her goal was to be a scholar and make something good out of her life. I was focused on having a fun life and what it had to offer me.

And then there was Karen, the youngest, four years younger than me, and she seemed to be a different world. She also had long blonde hair and you could see a resemblance, but she was a younger version. Karen and I didn't have much in common back then. We were dreaming of different things.

Our parents were very strict and kept us close to home. The mountain and its densely filled woods surrounding our home was our only sanctuary.

When I think back, the woods and their peacefulness and unconditional acceptance gave me the comfort to be alone and to learn to how focus on the things that are important to me, knowing that I had the control to seek and dream for the life I wanted.

Growing up, I wanted to know my dad better; to understand why he did certain things and said the things he did. Even though he lived at home, we only saw him on Sundays and holidays when he took us to see his parents. My dad came home so late every evening and left before we woke in the morning, so we never saw him during the week.

The only sense of a normal relationship I was exposed to were my grandparents from both sides. They had each been married for decades. Each had a unique relationship with strong bonds between them, the kind of relationship I thought of for my future.

My parents, on the other hand, had a very different relationship. They both had significant others in their lives even though they were married and still lived in the same house. I got to know and accept both of their relationships. It was bringing some type of happiness into my parent's lives. And somehow, it brought a strange sense of normalcy into our family life.

Back in the 60's you didn't leave your husband and raise kids alone; things were a lot harder for single women. Because of the strained situation at home, I wasn't close with either of my parents during this time. I couldn't understand why they stayed together while living separate lives. It was obvious how unhappy they were together.

I hoped for more when I got married. I thought it was a partnership that you could share with someone and if you weren't happy, you didn't stay together just because there were kids involved. I saw first-hand how much it affected everyone and the walls it put up in everyone's relationships. It created strained relationships between us all. I knew I could never have or want that kind of marriage. I lived through the confusion it caused and vowed to never put my children through it.

This was when I decided to become financially stable before bringing a child into the world. I needed to be sure that if something did not work out, I could still care for my children and give them the best life I could.

It was the summer of '75, and I was starting my high school junior year in a few months. My first two years of high school had been filled with a lot of visits to the principal's office with my partner in crime, my sister Sue. My parents could see I was slowly going down the wrong path in life.

My dad and I had discussed going to a different high school, starting over fresh somewhere else.

The trouble we got into was never anything serious; I was just slowly losing interest in school and never wanted to go. The high school in our town, the best training you would receive would allow you to become a bookkeeper, receptionist, or cashier at the local grocery store. I wanted so much more. I wanted to be respected and to succeed in my career. I wanted to be able to stand on my own two feet. I also knew that college would probably not be in my future so my options were limited.

My father heard of the new technical high school that just opened in our county. We talked about the opportunities it could give me. There was a nursing program, cosmetology, and computers. He laughed remembering how much I hated the site of blood and immediately rejected nursing. We decided I would major in this new fad called *"computers"*. It seemed to be the direction I was looking for; a place where a few more doors were available. If I stayed where I was, I would continue down the same path. While my life had been fun, it was at the expense of my parents' trust and my grades at school. I was determined to make this change in my life. This was a great opportunity I could not let go of. I could start over and focus on my future.

My dad was very excited at the possibilities it could provide me and hopefully give me direction and skills that would give me a good start in the world. It could mean having a career without having to bare the expense of college, which I knew my parents could not handle. My older sisters hadn't gone to college and I was sure that my chances of going were as good as theirs.

I regretted not focusing on my studies, the years I had wasted. At 15, I was anxious to start the journey of my life.

The new school had so much to offer, a new start, and the new person I could become. I had gone to school with the same group of people my whole life, and this new school would introduce me to a much larger world than what I'd been used to. Even though it took me from all my friends and teachers I knew, I was ready to move on.

At the time, computers were just being introduced to the world and my father had the insight that it would be a good fall-back option. Somehow he knew they would become a major part my future.

"Ok Dee, you've done a good job describing the area we grew up in, but when are you going to get to the point of the story." Sue said.

"I see what you're saying. Let me go on and see if it gets better".

I think about back then and growing up in this secluded area of our town and how disconnected we really were from the real world. Growing up, it was all I knew, so of course, I had no idea of the ambitions to seek outside of our small world. But something inside of me yearned for so much more, so much that I never knew existed.

The fantasies of happily ever after were flooding my head. I had so many dreams and aspirations to be wealthy and happy, that there was a man that would come sweep me off my feet, and we would live in our dream home with our perfect jobs and perfect kids with no care in the world.

I can look back and smile at the dreams I had. My life didn't exactly go that way; but I did get my dream and that's what counts the most; what I cherish the most.

The Beginning
Summer 1975

It was a beautiful summer day and we were waiting in anticipation to see who our new neighbors would be, and of course, if there were any boys moving in. They were the first new family to move into our small neighborhood since we moved in 11 years ago. The mystery had us very curious and looking forward to the changes our new neighbors could bring to the mountain.

There were five of us, my neighbors, Cheryl and Noelle, my sisters, Sue and Karen, and myself. Sue was 17, Cheryl and Noelle were 16, I was 15, and Karen was 11. The three older girls were dressed in their shortest shorts, makeup perfect and hair all fixed.

Cheryl had shoulder length brown hair and was one of the popular girls at school. She had a younger brother and sister that were closer in age to my sister Karen.

Noelle was an only child. She had long curly blonde hair that flowed past her waist. Her family moved into town about 10 months ago, and she had all of the guys in town wanting to know her.

I wasn't allowed to wear makeup or pick out my own clothes yet, so I did the best I could. I had long wavy strawberry blonde hair with brown-green eyes.

Karen was there to be a part of what we were doing. She always wanted to be with the older girls.

The neighborhood was mostly teenaged girls with the exception of their younger brothers, at least three years my junior. This was lucky for Karen; all the guys were her age. The only way to meet boys in this small town was school.

Unfortunately, because of how strict my parents were, my social life was restricted to the occupants of the mountain.

- 21 -

Finally, the moving truck pulled in. The buzz around the neighborhood was that a single guy was moving in with his parents... and he was cute! We gathered together and plotted our way to introduce ourselves the first chance we had, each of us secretly wondering if he would be interested in one of us.

The five of us agreed to meet the next afternoon just above their property and then go as a group together to introduce ourselves. The anticipation about meeting him or if he would be interested in one of us was creating such emotion, we could barely talk to each other as we slowly walked to the house. I could sense the nervousness we all felt, and I wished that the others were not there, that I had had the courage to do this alone. "What if he catches the eye of the older girls; I'm so much younger."

I was so shy, and as much as I wished I was doing this alone, I would have been far too nervous to approach him. I'd never know what to say and felt the only way I would get to meet him would be with the rest of the group.

As we approached, I saw him for the first time working in his backyard and thought he was most intriguing. He was short but nicely built, with dark hair and a mustache that gave him an air of mystery. I was smitten immediately and wanted to know everything about him.

He was installing a new pool in the back yard as we approached. I remember thinking, *what nationality is he? Italian maybe?* He immediately stopped working when he saw us approaching. The older girls took the lead and confidently introduced themselves. Then it was my turn, and I shyly introduced myself. He gave me a big smile and his dark brown eyes lit up when he talked.

Was I imagining it or did he only give that special smile to me and none of the others? No, I convinced myself I must have imagined it.

I loved his laugh and the enthusiasm when he talked. He stood there talking to us for quite a while, laughing and getting to know us all, showing no particular interest in any of us but at the same time being very cordial to all of us. His name was Stan. He said he was an only child and just moved back home after completing his time in the military. He was going to live with his mom and step dad until he got on his feet and found a new job. I couldn't help wishing the other girls would go away so that his gaze would rest on me only. I wished I wasn't so shy, wished I could think of something clever and witty to say. I hated the older girls for being at ease. All I could do was nervously giggle and smile. *What he must be thinking of me? If only I could really talk to him...*

It seemed like seconds, but quite a while had gone by. His dad called out to him from the upstairs window saying, "Stan, you have a phone call and need to come in."

With regrets, we said our goodbyes, and he left to get the phone.

I left wanting to know more about him.

My favorite place was the small wooded lot next to my parent's property and now, next to where Stan had just moved in. The previous owners had let me come on the property because they didn't use it. It was a small undeveloped piece of land filled with trees and rocks. My special spot was in the middle of the property. It was a small clearing with a large bolder in the middle. It seemed like the sun would find this spot each day and light up just this spot in the dark forest just for me. I would sit on that rock and read or just think about what my future would be. I always considered this "my spot". I'm not sure if anyone else even knew about it back then, not even my sisters.

A few days after my initial encounter with Stan, I was sitting in "my spot" and this spunky long haired black and white dog came running into the woods, straight over to me. I heard a shout, "Joby, where are you going?"

I looked up, and he was walking towards me. Joby had taken the lead and proceeded to say hello to me in a very playful manner.

Stan apologized, "I'm sorry, she loves people. How are you?"

I was so nervous. My heart was racing. *"What do I say to make him stay and talk?"* My head was spinning faster than ever before.

"You're Dee, right?"

I couldn't believe he remembered my name. I smiled and said, "Yes, how are you?"

Then, as if he read my thoughts, he asked, "Can I join you?"

Relieved, I said, "Of course. Have a seat."

I couldn't believe that he was being so nice.

He seemed to be so at ease talking, and I could see the excitement as he started telling me small details of his life.

He proudly said, "I purchased this lot for an investment into my future. It isn't worth much now, but someday it will be worth a lot of money, I know it."

I shyly said, "This has always been my special place to sit and enjoy being alone. I apologize for trespassing."

He immediately said, "I can see why it's your favorite spot. You can come here anytime. Consider this still your special place."

Stan was just about to turn 22.

I was just beginning to think about how to be successful, not giving a thought about investing for the future. How could I have left that out of my plans? I was impressed with his plans. Real estate is a great investment.

We talked for almost an hour, and when it was time for me to go, he said, "I hope to see you again soon."

Shyly, I said, "I do to. Goodbye".

I couldn't believe how easy it was to talk to him and how interested he seemed in getting to know me.

Every day I would sit in the woods on the rock waiting for him to come. He always did.

The rock became "*our* special spot." I could see his car come in from work, and within minutes, I would hear Joby barking and then see him running to me as I sat in our spot in the woods. We spent hours there talking of his travels. He had been in the Army and traveled to many faraway places. He loved talking about his travels and his special interest, the stars and constellations.

As with a lot of things, I was so intrigued by him and wanted to know everything. I was curious about his nationality. It wasn't something I normally ask about but for some reason, I couldn't figure out what he was. I had to ask him, "Ok, I can't put my finger on it, but what is your nationality?"

Smiling he said, "Mainly Polish. My Dad is Polish and my mom is sort of a mix of different nationalities."

I responded, "Wow, just like me. My dad is actually from Poland and my mom's family is a mix from all over the U.S."

The more we talked, the more I found we had in common, and the more I wondered how he felt about me.

I knew Stan being Polish would get him good points with my dad. My dad was an immigrant from Poland and was very old fashioned. It was very important to him that his daughters would carry on the Polish traditions, and dating someone Polish would only be a bonus. Maybe he could be the one my parents would approve of. If only our age difference did not matter to them.

My parents didn't allow me to date anyone without their express approval. They were both so strict, I didn't know how I could possibly get them to approve. Needless to say, I hadn't dated much up to that point.

Just a few days after our first rendezvous, he asked, "Can I kiss you?"

How polite of him to ask… no one ever asked before they kissed me. He was such a gentleman, never assuming anything and respecting me in a way I'd never seen before.

I just smiled and leaned in for the kiss.

It was the most sensual kiss I ever experienced. It wasn't one of those shy nervous kisses, nor was it the groping, lusting, smothering kind. It was the kind of kiss that says how special you are. You could feel the passion in his lips. He had a way of making me feel safe and cared for. I couldn't believe that he was spending time with me and not one of the other girls.

Stan opened a new world to me, a world that included unconditional love. Being together was all that mattered.

Days later, while daydreaming of him on my walk home from school; there he was, standing at the bottom of our driveway talking with my dad. I couldn't imagine what they could be talking about.

As I approached them, my dad looked up at me and smiled in a strange way. This made me even more curious about what they were discussing.

My dad smiled again, "Hello there… I guess I'll let you two talk a while… I really need to get back to work. It was nice talking with you Stan." He shook his hand then smiled at me again as he walked away.

As my dad got out of site, Stan smiled at me and said, "I just had an interesting discussion with your dad."

"Oh really, and what was the topic of conversation?" I responded.

"I just asked him for permission to date you." He replied with the biggest grin I'd ever seen.

Nervously, I asked, "What did he say?"

"I must have made an impression coming over and asking him for permission. He said it was okay with him." He said grinning, "We got to know each other pretty good. He's an interesting man, and we have a lot in common."

I couldn't believe my ears; my father had never shown interest in my personal happiness outside of my career goals. We always talked of how I needed to succeed.

My father's approval meant the world to me. He was interested that I was learning computers, and now he approved of Stan. This could finally be something else I could share with my father.

What kind of man was standing before me to have such power over my father, for him to be so accepting even with the difference in our ages? It didn't matter to my father for some reason.

Interrupting my deep thoughts Stan said, "I have something important to do, I'll call you in a little bit."

He walked away leaving me standing there, wondering what just happened. I made my way into the house to begin my homework and found I couldn't concentrate on anything else but what just happened.

Within a half hour Stan called and said, "Meet me at the rock; I have something to talk to you about."

We hung up, and forgetting my homework, I ran out the door to meet him. As I walked into the woods, Joby came barking and running to greet me. I could see Stan sitting there waiting for me. As he saw me approach, he stood up and gave me the biggest smile. He grabbed my hand and gave me a gentle kiss on the lips.

He said, "Would you go steady with me?" He blushed and continued, "I know it's old fashioned, but I want to keep seeing you. I love our time together and want to get to know you more. I know I have to respect your age and won't ever push you into anything you don't want to do."

He was the first to ever ask me. I was overjoyed that the first would be him. I immediately said, "Yes!" and gently kissed him.

Stan took my hand and placed a ring on my finger. I could see the disappointment in his face when he saw it was at least three sizes too large for my ring finger. I smiled at him and said, "I'll find a way for it to fit."

He shared with me the history behind the ring. "I found this ring two years ago when I was in the military stationed in Turkey. There was a quaint jewelry store in the outskirts of the town where I was stationed. I got to know the owner very well, and he couldn't wait to share the history of the ring with me. He said it's a Turkish wedding band. The ring was created by Turkish men to ensure their wives were faithful; the ring would fall apart if taken off your finger. It consisted of four bands entangled together. It's a puzzle that only the men had the solution to putting it back together. They would always know if their bride had taken the ring off for any reason. I bought this ring for the woman who will be my wife, and someday I'm hoping that will be you."

I hesitated looking at the ring, and he smiled, "Don't worry, I will show you how to put it back together, that was an old tradition. I loved that the ring has a story behind it. It gives it meaning. Trust between two people."

I was so touched by the story and how much it meant to him. I didn't think men thought about their future wife and what a gift the ring would be. It was the most romantic story.

When I got back home, I realized my first challenge was to find a way that it wouldn't fall off my finger. My mom came up with a great idea to not only make it fit but to also keep it from falling apart; we wrapped it with a band aid. It made it fit perfectly and became a part of the ring and its history between us. I never took the ring off.

I'm glad my mom was so open to Stan and my relationship also. Finding a way to keep the ring on my finger showed me how much he meant to her also.

We spent every possible moment together, hours at our rock talking, dreaming about the future, where we wanted to go, where we wanted to live, and the family we would have.

Each morning as I was getting ready for school, I would think about him next door getting ready for work. *Was he thinking about me? Was he thinking of our future together?* It was a strange but comforting feeling. He was so handsome and treated me like I was the only person in his world.

We did have our challenges. His mom was the only one not crazy about us dating because of the age difference and especially because I wasn't 18 yet. Even though we had my parent's approval, she still didn't agree with the relationship. At least his step dad and I got along great. He was such a likeable person and got along with everyone.

It bothered us that his mom didn't like the relationship. We hoped in time, when I was a little older that would eventually fade. I hoped I could be close to her one day. She was a special person in his life. I knew she would be a challenge, and I was determined to make her like me. I was determined to get everyone in his world to accept me as he did and let them get to know the person I really was; the person Stan got to know so well.

Stan had a different childhood than I had. His mom and step dad had been together since Stan was one year old, and he didn't know his real father. He said it saddened him, and someday he hoped to meet his real dad. He loved his mom and stepdad, but he always felt something was missing.

His parents had a good relationship. It was nice to see a happily married couple. It reminded me of my grandparents.

Stan was very close with his grandmother and talked about her constantly. He had spent most of his younger years living with her. He took me to meet her once before she passed, and I could see the pride in her eyes when she looked at him and talked about him when he was a little boy. He was her only grandchild and she loved him dearly. You could tell he felt the same for her and see the special bond they had.

You could always tell who the special women were in Stan's life. How lucky I felt to become one of them.

Current Day, February 2013

I look at the screen and can see Sue slowly nodding off. "Hey, go to sleep. We can continue another night."

"I'm sorry; it's been a long day. I remember so much of the story. It's like reading a diary of our lives back then. You did pretty well with the detail."

"Thanks, luckily, most of this I wrote years ago so it was easy to remember. I will let you go to sleep and we can continue another night. I'm tired of talking anyway." I said, laughing. "Good-night and I love you."

"I love you too. Good night."

The screen went blank and I sat wondering, "How can I continue?" There are so many little things, little details that will make our story special, as special as it is to me. I decided I would put the book down for the night and see what I came up with the next day.

I woke up thinking about my father and how much of an influence on my life he'd been. The next part of the book is much of the bond between my father and Stan as it is how I grew to know my father. The things they have in common and the things I never knew.

I called my dad and asked him if I could read this section to him.

September 1976

Stan had a passion for vintage sports cars that was a borderline obsession. He would never buy a new car when he could get an older one for almost nothing and, with just a little time and muscle invested into it, he could have a better car; one he could be proud of. He loved spending his time on cars and the challenge of getting them to work. He also appreciated being able to restore older cars to their original condition.

Stan had a '69 Camaro that had been a race car and not street legal. It had a manual transmission and no power steering.

My dad, being a mechanic by profession, offered to help him restore it back to its original condition. The car was their pride and joy.

When he could, Stan drove me to school, and it drove my classmates crazy. The car was awesome. How proud I was having him drive me to school in it. When we pulled up to the front of the school, everyone came out to see the car.

I felt so lucky, but something reminded me I couldn't lose my head entirely. This was my senior year of high school. It was time to seriously think about my future. I was pretty good with computers by now. The concept seemed to come naturally to me. I could finally start to plan my future, what I would do with myself. Would Stan be a part of my future?

My 17th birthday was approaching fast and I could see my father panicking that he would have to, again, bear the torture of teaching another daughter to drive. One day, as I watched them working so meticulously together on each detail of the car, out-of-the-blue, my dad asked, "How would you like to do us a favor and teach Dee how to drive?"

With the biggest smile, Stan answered, "I'd love the challenge."

I stood there in shock as they plotted out the details of how I should be taught. Stan was so excited that he had found a way for us to spend even more time together while making it seem like it was my dad's idea.

Stan had such patience, showing me the tricks to his car. His easy-going smile and the pride he had in showing me the driving techniques just made it so I was able to relax and learn. He had raced cars in the past, but because his mom was worried about what could happen, he decided to stop. At times, I couldn't believe how much he'd done in his life already.

He kept referring to his racing techniques when explaining how to drive. I thought, if we could survive this, we'd survive anything, even when I almost totaled his beautiful car.

It was a hot summer night, and he wanted to show me another technique he learned while racing. He explained that if you slow down slightly before coming up on a curve and then accelerate slightly while going through the corner, the car would glide right through even without power steering.

There I was trying to follow his instructions in a car I could barely handle and not realizing the next corner was a 90-degree turn. Concentrating on his words, I slowed down as I approached the turn and then accelerated as we reached the corner.

Not realizing the speed I was going and the power of his car, I couldn't handle making the sharp turn. I veered into a parking lot and the car finally stopped just feet away from the front entrance of a chicken restaurant. Luckily, there were no cars parked in the area or we would have been in a big mess.

I looked over at him to see his reaction… I saw a little fear in his eyes but when he saw how upset I was, he broke into a smile and then started laughing.

I asked, "Do you want to take over?"

He smiled and said "No, you got the concept and need to keep trying. Just take it a little easier on those really sharp corners." He always found humor in every situation and put me at ease again.

While I was still shaking, I put the car in drive and continued down the road. I could see him grinning with pride in the passenger seat.

My parents had a rule that we were only allowed to go out once a week. After all, I was still in high school. Stan convinced them that teaching me to drive as much as possible was the only way for me to be a good driver. To me, he admitted it was a good excuse for us to spend more time together, and it worked. We went out driving almost every day. If we didn't go out driving, we studied the driving book together and then we would secretly meet at our rock in the woods to have that special time alone.

The day finally came to take my driving test. I went for the written exam first and aced with only one wrong. The next step was the eye exam, and then if you passed, you got to take the behind-the-wheel part.

As I approached the machine to have my eyes tested, I had a very bad feeling inside. Just as I feared, I failed the eye exam. I failed so bad, the examiner asked, "How can you see?" I'd never worn glasses and was shocked how bad my eyes really were.

Stan was so disappointed but happy I didn't fail because of all our hard work. This put off the test for another month until I could get glasses and reschedule another appointment.

Of course, it meant another month of practicing together. It was a good thing I failed so we still had that excuse of spending more time together.

A month passed, with new glasses in hand, I went to take the test again and passed both the eye and driving tests.

"Now what reason can we come up with to spend as much time together?" Stan asked.

Current day, February 2013

I've been sitting here listening to Stevie Nicks, Heart, Tom Petty and others from their era. *Because of the Night* is playing. It's a boring Sunday night and I turn on Skype to see if anyone is out there.

My sister, Karen, is online and I'm thinking, "I can bore her tonight with the book and see what happens." She answers immediately and walks away.

I hear her in the background yelling, "You caught me feeding my cats. Hold on."

Karen is my younger sister by 4 years. We didn't get along with when we were young, but time and our common backgrounds have brought us close through the years. Karen and I married brothers. Michael, the younger brother, married Karen and they had 2 kids, Michael Jr. and Theresa. I married Steve, the older brother and we had 2 boys, Steven Jr. and Edward ("Eddie"). We are both divorced now and luckily had each other as support through the years of being divorced from the same family. It was unique. I had moved to Georgia and got away. Karen stayed in New Jersey. She did move south to the Jersey shore, 2 hours away from home. Distance from the families helped make things easier for both of us.

Our kids are in their mid-20s and living separate lives. My son, Ed, is in Japan for 3 years. He tried his own website business for 5 years, but then when the economy went south, so did his business. He's in the Navy and doing very well. His brother, Steven, lives in Atlanta not far our home and visits occasionally. Of course, he never visits enough or stays long enough for me. Both of them are doing great and I couldn't be prouder.

Karen's kids have a unique relationship to my sons. We married brothers so they also have the same last name and cousins from both sides.

Through the years, we've become close and talk frequently. Now with the computer age, Karen and I talk even more on Skype. I enjoy being able to spend time with her even if it's only virtually.

As she always does, her camera was pointed towards the ceiling so I did the same. I get tired of telling her where her camera is pointing so this is my tactful way of letting her know. I patiently waited for her to come on screen.

"Ok smartass, I'm fixing my camera. Now fix yours." She says as she finally comes back.

We get disconnected a few times, damn internet.

I fixed my camera and say, "What's up?"

"Nothing much. Just texting Jim." Jim is Karen's boyfriend for the past year.

"How is he?"

"Good, just saying "hi" and letting him know I can't come see him this weekend. He's not real happy but understands." Karen lives about 90 minutes from Jim and they see each other mainly on weekends.

"Well I'm calling to see if I can bounce an idea off you? I was talking with Sue last night and she gave me some great ideas for my book."

The look on Karen's face was priceless, "What did Sue say that would get you so interested in finishing the book? Wait a minute; what do you want me to do?" She said with a smile.

"She suggested a way to make the book blend more together, and just talking with you guys and reminiscing of the past is going to bring back more memories to fill the book. She even talked me into calling Daddy."

"And what did he have to say about it?"

"I read to him the parts about them working on his Camaro. He seemed to like it. I avoided any parts that I felt would hurt his feelings and kept more to the details of them working on the car."

"That was smart."

"I could tell he liked talking about the work they did together and how close they were. Anyway, the part I wanted to talk to you about is if you remembered how much Stan loved talking about the constellations? What a great story teller he was...."

Flashback...October 1976

On a cool summer night, a full sky of big bright stars staring down upon us, as if the clouds cleared above us to lead Stan into his story, Stan and I sat gazing at the sky as he went into one of his magical stories pointing towards the stars he was describing.

"Now Orion is right over there," he said pointing towards the sky. "He was in love with Merope, but with all his hunting down the ferocious bull Taurus, and racing past her with his Camaro star, he couldn't seem to impress her, although she did have a soft spot for his dog, *"Joby"* or *"Jobitrius"* as he was called in Greek."

"And what happened to Orion?" I would prompt him, never quite knowing each time how he would twist the story to make it different.

"Oh, very sad", he would say, kissing my forehead and shaking his head in mock sympathy for the ill-fated hero of the story. "Orion was racing his Camaro against a new Ford Scorpion, again trying to impress Merope, and the Scorpion left the old Camaro of Orion in the dust, it was so fast, and in the cloud of dust, poor Orion couldn't see the turn, and crashed into the Scorpion from behind, getting smashed to a million pieces, right before the very eyes of Merope. That was when she finally realized how she loved Orion, and wept over the pile of junk and debris, which had been the Camaro's. As Merope's tears dropped, the Gods began to feel sorry for Orion, and for Merope who had been left behind, so they put Orion, with his faithful dog Joby, up in the sky where they could live forever and where Merope would be comforted seeing him every night that they were apart. The Gods put her close enough in the sky to Orion so that they could see each other and put all her sisters up there with her to keep her company when Orion was off hunting. And they put the Scorpion on the other side of the sky so that Orion would never get stung again."

I would dream of Orion and Merope. My mind filled with Stan's stories of never-ending bliss, wondering if this would be our future, always in love and filled with happiness; each time I look at the stars I think of him and the faraway places he could take me to with his words.

Stan opened my eyes to a whole universe outside of my young high school world. He would tell me about things I'd never even thought about and how intrigued he was with the unexplainable. One of these fascinations was the techniques for having an "out-of-body" experience. I'd heard very little about it before and at the time, it was looked down upon by most people if you talked about it. He loved the unknown and wanted to open his mind to all aspects of life and experience them for himself, to make his own decisions and create his own opinions before following the crowd or how society looked at life and its complexities.

He would prompt me to close my eyes and he would describe the stars and how to reach out to them. I never was quite able to concentrate enough to successfully have the "out-of-body" experience that Stan was trying to invoke. But it did put me further adrift in my fascination and admiration for him, and further triggered the love I felt for him, which was, in and of itself, a somewhat "out-of-body" experience.

Stan believed that two people who had a strong bond would always be able to communicate and be together, even if they weren't physically together. We agreed that as long as the moon glowed in the night sky, we would be connected through the stars above. If I ever was feeling alone, or scared, or missing him, all I would have to do would be to go out and gaze at the stars, and he would know I was reaching out to him. Stan was convinced he could send his love to someone, even without being together with them. There were times I was convinced I could actually feel his arms around me and sense his presence, even when we were apart.

Stan became very creative to find ways to spend more time together. We worked on his parent's pool together, and we even went on a double date a few times with my dad and his girlfriend, Lee. How strange it was to me, but it was a welcome development in family life; it brought my dad and I closer than we ever had been. My dad had been dating Lee for the past couple of years and they seemed to get along great. I could see Stan enjoyed being the reason my dad and I were getting close. I was finally able to see my dad as a person and not just an authority figure. I really didn't know that side of my dad, and it was nice to get to know him that way.

Most of the time when we went out, we would find a place to just sit and talk. He was still so respectful and never tried to force himself on me. He knew I was young and still scared. "I will wait for you. I know we will be together forever and it's worth the wait." Then he said, "*We have plenty of time.*"

He was also creative in finding places where we could be alone. One day, while we were parking at one of our favorite spots, the overlook off the interstate highway above our town, and getting a bit carried away with each other, I looked up to see a strange man peering in our car window at us. I screamed and Stan jumped out of the car to approach the guy. This terrified me even more, not knowing what type of person he was approaching. The stranger had made it back into his car, the only other one in the parking lot, but pretended he was asleep in the driver's seat. Stan quickly came back to the car to check on me and saw how frightened I was. He started the car and we left immediately. Needless to say, from that time on, we found other areas closer to home to have that alone time together. I felt so safe with him.

We dated almost a year before Stan had given me clue to the frustration he had been feeling. He never tried to take advantage of me; he was always a gentleman and never pushed me.

We were young, and he knew I feared getting pregnant. He had such strong feelings against abortion, and he realized I was too young to have a child. I knew he was mature enough to handle it, but he respected that I wasn't.

I still remember so well the first and only time we ever made love back then. One afternoon after school, he invited me over to his house while his parents were out. He was so excited about this new album he bought and wanted me to listen to it. He walked me to his room and sat me down on the floor in front of his bed and told me he wanted me to listen to this album.

As I looked around the room, he had laid pillows on the floor making a comfortable place for me to sit. As I continued to look, he also had candles lit around the room reflecting a scene from romantic novel. He placed earphones on me and smiled. I could see the happiness in his eyes seeing me comfortably sitting on the pillows he arranged so carefully for me.

I listened through the first song and looked up at him. He was watching me enjoy the music. I reached up to take off the headphones and he stopped me. He said, "Just relax and listen".

I felt bad that he couldn't hear the music but he insisted that listening with the ear phones was the only way to truly appreciate the music. Each time I looked over at him, he was sitting patiently waiting for me to finish. He watched me for almost 45 minutes so I could listen to the entire album. It was the Moody Blues.

When it was done, I took off the head phones and he said, "I love you and will wait for you forever."

I loved him so much, and I knew he would wait for me. I melted as I turned toward him and saw in his eyes that he truly meant it, just like he meant every word he ever said. At that moment it fully sunk in that I could trust this man more fully than I had ever trusted anyone in my life before. The Moody Blues drifting me ever closer to him, we sank further and further into each other, and he showed me that day what it meant to truly make love.

Stan was struggling to get a job that would be a life time career and not *just* a job. In our small town there were very few job opportunities with any future, and he worked for the town park and one of the factories in town. I saw the frustration he was experiencing and wanted to give my full support in any choice he made. Then, one day, he came to me with a choice that made my heart stop. He called me all excited and said, "I have something I need to talk to you about. Can you meet me at the rock?"

As I got to the rock, he moved me over to sit as he knelt down in front of me. He started, "I have something very important to talk with you about and if you could just listen for a few minutes so I can explain." I nodded for him to continue.

"You know how I always wanted to further my career with the military? After being in the Special Forces in the army before I met you, I realized how much I loved that kind of work. I made a few phone calls and now I have an appointment for an interview."

I could see the excitement in his eyes, but something deep down was telling me that his news was not something I wanted to hear. I sat and listened.

He continued, "I made a few calls to some old military buddies of mine and they made me an offer that would not only enable me to use my skills but also possibly make a very good living. It would set us up for life. I could give you the life you deserve, and you would never have to think about working." The thought of that brought on a sense of loss, the thought of not being able to see where I could go with my career. The thought of just being a wife scared me. How, at this time of him being so excited, could I be thinking such selfish things? I quickly brought my mind back to his news.

"Ok Stan, I can tell you're avoiding the details and highlighting the benefits… tell me what the job is." I said.

He replied, "They're interested in interviewing me to join the CIA."

He paused for my reaction, and I didn't know what to say. My mind was racing at the possibility of him leaving me, and that's all I could think of.

I asked, "When would you find out if you got the job?"

He said, "Well, they put you through intensive interviews, background checks and intelligence tests and the entire process takes about a year before they make a decision. You would be out of high school by then, and we could travel together."

The thought of traveling and seeing the world with him excited me while at the same time scared me to death. I'd barely been out of this small town. The biggest move I'd ever made was going to the technical school in the next town, and now, he was offering me the world. Knowing it would take a year before any decision was made, I put my mind at ease for now, and it was something I figured I would worry about later…. We had plenty of time before any of that would happen. We had plenty of time to talk about me still having a career while being the devoted wife he deserved.

Stan started the process of his interviews with the CIA immediately. One of the first steps was a full background check on him and everyone that was in his life. My father, being an immigrant from Poland, threw a slight glitch in his getting approved because he wasn't a naturalized citizen. He became a citizen once he moved to the states in his early teens.

In the 70's, Poland was a communist country and communism was widespread in the news. Stan had to do a lot of explaining about his relationship with my father and what my father's standing currently was with the country. He almost lost the possibility of continuing with the interviews because of it. I had to hide my sense of relief each time he would explain how hard it was during this process.

He finally got the call I feared, they agreed to continue interviewing him about a position regardless of his affiliation with my dad. I knew, deep down, I was hoping he wouldn't get approved. I knew what it meant and I didn't want him to leave me or worse yet, be taken to another country, losing any chance of accomplishment for my own life. How could I be thinking these thoughts? How could I not want him to follow his dream? Why did his dream seem to not include mine?

The next Friday evening as I was anticipating what we would do and what we would talk about, my dad told me that he and Stan had plans to go out to dinner. Because they had been working together, I didn't think it was strange, but I resented my dad for cutting into my precious time with Stan.

I'd loved our time together, counting our minutes as if they were pearls. Stan called me later that evening when he got home from dinner and was in an exceptionally great mood. It made me a little jealous and gave me a strange feeling that he could have such a good time without me and at same time be bonding with my father in a way I never could.

For some unknown reason, from that day on, my dad talked about me marrying Stan and tried to convince me that I would never get anyone better. What hurt the most was his thinking that I wouldn't be able to provide for myself. All the encouragement to succeed as an individual left, and I was to be nothing if I was not someone's wife. What happened to change his view of me? What did I do to make him feel I would never succeed? I never understood where it was coming from but my dad's approval of who I was as a person meant so much to me. I know he was proud of Stan for interviewing with the CIA but how could he feel so strongly about Stan's success and not of mine? I was heartbroken. How could he feel I could no longer succeed in life unless I was married? What changed his mind? His persistence on the subject saddened me in a way that was hard to explain. It was as if he felt my life would be a failure if I didn't marry Stan. That was my only choice in life. I would never be able to survive on my own. His words affected me so much that they completely shifted my focus away from being happy with Stan and into how I could make my father proud of the person I was. I was determined to be successful regardless of the price.

I was driving home from my after-school job a few days later, and my dad signaled me on the CB. My dad had put one in my car so I would have a way to contact him if I ever broke down. The old '69 Volvo I had wasn't very reliable. He said, "Dee, I'm going over to Lee's house. Her girls are very upset, one of their good friends died on the way to school this morning."

I replied, "Tell them I'm very sorry for their loss and my thoughts are with them." I wondered who had died. I was going to a different school than Lee's daughters and hadn't heard about anyone, so I assumed it was someone I didn't know. I asked him, "Who was it?"

He said, "Their friend Jeff. He had just started dating Amy a few weeks back, and they are all very devastated."

I thought about it for a moment and realized I knew who my dad was talking about. I had known Jeff since grammar school, and we had always been very good friends. During the time I hung out with Jeff, he was dating a girl he'd been with since 6th grade, and I'd heard they had just recently broken up after 5 years together. Jeff and I had lost contact with each other because I went to the other high school and we didn't run into each other much anymore. I saw him a couple of times recently over at Lee's house when visiting her and my dad. Amy was a good friend of Lee's daughters and had just started dating Jeff. They looked so cute together, and for the first time, I could see how happy he really was. It was great seeing him again and seeing him with someone who really cared for him.

Barely able to speak, I said, "I know Jeff. What happened?"

He replied, "It was a car accident on Route 46. He was going around that bridge with a the sharp curve in the middle, the one right after passing the grammar school in Great Meadows. He lost control and his car went under a school bus. It happened about 8 o'clock this morning." After a short pause, he continued, "I'm sorry to be the one to tell you; I didn't realize you knew him too. Why don't you come meet me at Lee's?"

Relieved at wanting to be with someone right then, I said, "I'll see you in a few minutes."

All of Jeff's close friends came to Lee's house. Her place was where everyone hung out, so it only seemed natural to meet and talk about Jeff there. They weren't my normal crowd I hung out with, but I knew all of them, and we had always got along. It felt good to be with others that knew him so well and we reminisced about all the good times with him and how he'd finally found happiness with Amy. Everyone knew that the one person who was hurting the most was her, and we all did what we could to be there for her.

Stan and I had our first fight that night. I was telling him about Jeff, and I could see a little jealously in his reaction. I wasn't sure how to react other than being defensive for my good friend who had just died. Stan insisted that he should go to the funeral with me, but I wanted to be with Jeff's friends who knew him well and grieve together. We fought over this, and I couldn't understand his insistence in going with me. He didn't know Jeff or any of his friends, and he made it seem like he didn't trust me to go alone, that he should be there. It was my first funeral of a close friend, and at the time I felt I needed a different kind of comfort that I knew he couldn't give and wasn't giving me.

Stan left disappointed, knowing I would be going with Jeff's friends even though he would see me afterwards.

At Jeff's funeral, Connie, the girl he'd dated since 6th grade, sat in the front row with his family, like she was his whole world. While his true love, Amy was pushed in the back of the room like she didn't matter in his life. How sad I was to see Amy set to the side while Connie was treated like the widow, the grieving girlfriend. I felt it was so unfair that in a time like this, people forgot about what was currently happening in his life when he died. Instead, they put all the emphasis onto a relationship that may have taken more time in his life, but it wasn't the true love that he felt when he died. This was one of the major turning points in my life.

It again made me think of my parent's relationship. What would happen if one of them passed, who would be the one standing next to them at the funeral as their life partner. Both of them had been in long term relationships by now, and I felt sad to think that the special person in their life would be overshadowed just because of legality. I vowed to never stay in a marriage if it wasn't working and always let everyone know who the special person in my life was.

There I was, only 17, my father pushing me to get married. Knowing that if I did and Stan got the CIA job, I would be possibly leaving the country or be alone if they wouldn't let me go with him. I didn't want to end up alone as nothing more than a housewife, with no friends in a foreign place with no career and no comforts of home. I was so overwhelmed with the decision I needed to make about my life, and for some reason that was the time I felt I needed to make it. It scared me to death. What if I made the wrong decision? In time, if I married Stan I felt we would drift apart and possibly hate each other for being so confined to only us in a foreign country.

After Jeff's death, I questioned my purpose, my future, my goals, and most importantly my relationship with Stan. I asked myself, *"What do I really want out of my life?"*

One thing I did know was that I desperately wanted my dad's approval but for my own accomplishments, not because of who I married. The need for dad's approval of me put such a huge wall between Stan and I. Stan never knew the real reason why that wall went up. I knew I loved him but I also knew that just being someone's wife wasn't going to be enough for me. And somehow, I was convinced that marrying Stan would mean kissing any future career and the chance of being my own person, goodbye.

Stan and I met in the woods after I returned from the funeral. I was consumed with the finality of it all; the sadness for Amy not being consoled as his true love, the idea that Jeff would never fulfill his dreams and grow to be the man he should have been.

It seemed Stan didn't want to talk about it; he was still hurt over me not wanting him to go with me, and I couldn't understand how he could be jealous over a funeral. I felt so trapped and frustrated with everything that was going on in my life.

We were sitting on our rock when I finally said, "I think we need some time apart to see what we both really want out of life. We seem to be going in different directions and my dreams seem to have gotten lost somehow."

For the first time, Stan could sense something terribly wrong, and neither of us were doing very well trying to explain our feelings to each other. It was the first time we just weren't able to communicate.

I could tell he was seeing that I needed some time alone, that I needed to find myself and see what I wanted for my future. I knew I loved him but also knew my life's goal was so much more.

I could see the hurt in his eyes as they began to tear up. It was as if he knew what I was about to say. I gently placed the ring in his hand and said, "I need some time alone to see what I want out of life."

While I needed my time, deep down I always counted on the fact that we would be together again, but I also knew right now wasn't the right time for me, even though I knew it was the right time for him.

He was so overwhelmed with sadness that unfortunately his reaction came out as disdain. He looked down at the ring with tears in his eyes and said, "No one else will ever wear this ring." He took the ring, twisted it all out of shape, threw it deep into the woods, and just walked away. His reaction shocked me, but I knew it had to be this way.

I ran home and cried myself to sleep that night. I knew it was the best thing to do. The only thing that got me through it was hoping that someday we'd get back together again. I knew Stan was my one and only true love, and I would never forget what we had together. I thought to myself, *"We have plenty of time.* Someday we'll get back together… when I'm truly ready and hopefully he will be also."

Chapter 2
Life after the Breakup
'77 thru '81

Even after we broke up, we continued to be good friends and kept in touch. After all, it was hard to avoid each other; he still lived next door, and I had to pass by his house every day to go home. I always found myself glancing over just to see if he was there. I often wondered if he watched for me to pass by.

Stan didn't mind me sitting at "our" rock, so I could still spend my quiet time there alone. I think he purposely stopped going there as often to give me my space. Only occasionally would we run into each other there, and he was always so nice. While I, on the other hand, was still trying to prove myself to my dad, and really didn't treat Stan the way I should have. Each time he would make a nice gesture, I would pretend I didn't notice. I knew we both still had very strong feelings for each other, but my frustration and sadness over how my dad felt about me overshadowed everything else in my life at the time and I didn't have the heart to open up and let him know the struggles I was going through. I wanted him to see me as a strong woman and not the insecure person I really was.

Stan and my dad continued being friends for quite a few years after our breakup. Stan even started working with him for a short period of time doing odd jobs at my dad's gas station. It always seemed that my dad was a lot closer to Stan than me, even when we were dating. It was strange to have my father be a friend to my boyfriend while, at the same time, being a stern father figure to me. I could just imagine the conversations they had. They must have been interesting. I know Stan wouldn't tell him any details about our relationship, but I always knew he told my dad how much he loved me. In the years after the breakup, my father and I drifted further and further apart. I could tell he never forgave me for breaking up with Stan, and on numerous occasions made a point to tell me so. This may have been one of the main reasons my dad and I began to drift apart again. I know my dad meant well and only had my best interest at heart but the way he handled it pushed me away from Stan and slowly put a wall in our relationship too. I realize now that his insistence on marrying Stan was simply that he did, in his own way, recognize what a great man Stan really was and how good the two of us were together. Somehow, my dad always knew Stan would make me very happy if I did marry him. I also knew, deep down, my dad was right but I was still struggling with creating my own identity.

Eventually Stan got the job with the CIA, and he left town for places unknown. This left me with a bit of sadness knowing he wasn't next door anymore and could be meeting the woman of his dreams. I had to put him out of my mind and go on with my life. We were both still very young and had plenty of time to get back together.

I graduated high school in June of 1977, and a few years later finally found a great job where I was able to travel the United States teaching others how to use the computer system for the company I worked for. It was the best job I'd had up to that point, and I hoped it would finally give my father something about me to be proud of; something about me and not about Stan.

I moved out of my parent's house after landing the job and was able to get a really nice apartment not too far away. Finally, some sense of success was beginning to show.

Chapter 3
The Missed Chance
Summer of '81

My job took me to places like Hartford, Connecticut, Philadelphia, Pennsylvania, Manhattan, and Albuquerque, New Mexico. The travelling was exciting. I spent 6 weeks in each place and got to see how the locals really lived. It was amazing to see how different each place was; how different the people were; how different the traditions were; how everyone thought I had an accent and loved it.

I was finally feeling successful in my life and loved my job.

It had been a few years of traveling and experiencing a different lifestyle than my sheltered early life when my dad called me out of the blue.

"Lee and I are going to Washington, DC to visit Stan. I'm bringing him his Camaro, and we wondered if you wanted to go." Stan had left the car with my dad to finish the work on it. He painted it for him while he was out of the country. I'd been on my own for a few years now and thought it would be a good opportunity to get to know my dad again and maybe rebuild the bond we'd had during the time I had dated Stan.

"When are you going? If I'm not scheduled for another trip at work, I'd love to go."

When my dad invited me to go on the trip, I was excited both to see Stan again and to show my dad what I had made of myself, now that I was grown-up and living on my own. I hoped enough time had passed and the old walls had dissolved into distant memories.

It was a 4 ½ -hour drive and I rode half of the way with my dad in the Camaro and the other half with Lee in her car. The two hours driving with my dad stretched into an agonizing eternity. He was still caught in the same old story, how I was wasting my life and should have married Stan. By the time we got there, I was so upset about what my dad said. That was the only way I'd ever be a good enough daughter for him. I was so caught up with my disappointment, I couldn't even enjoy the time with Stan. I was hurt that nothing short of Stan was right in his eyes and angry at myself for not having a thicker skin when dealing with my dad, after all these years. I hated that I was still an inadequate little girl to him rather than the intelligent ambitious woman I knew myself to be.

We were going to spend 4 days in DC. My dad and Lee stayed at a hotel, and I stayed with Stan at his apartment just outside of DC.

Our first day there, Stan showed us around town and that night we all went to dinner. My dad and Lee excused themselves very early, leaving us alone. We had a great night together, but I couldn't get my dad's words out of my head. I still didn't think that being married was the most important thing to me. I was just starting out with a great job and wanted to make something of myself first. Only then could I finally be a valid part of a relationship. I wanted to be able to give to my husband as much as he was willing to give to me.

When Stan and I got back to his house, he asked if I'd like to see some pictures of places he'd been. Stan always loved taking pictures; he always captured his favorite moments on film. We were looking at his photo albums, and we came across this picture of him and a friend. I didn't have any pictures of him and asked if I could have that one. Of course, he said yes…. It's the only one I had of him for years.

That night, I was just about asleep on his bed, and he came quietly into the room. The gentleman that he always was, he slept on the couch the entire time I was there. He sat on the floor next to me and gently touched my face. I could tell he wanted to talk, but I pretended I was asleep. I didn't know what to say to him and didn't want to hurt his feelings by telling him I still wasn't ready. I didn't feel it was fair to ask him to continue to wait for me.

After he left the room, I cried myself to sleep. I was so torn between my feelings I still had for Stan and the frustration I felt about my father and my life.

We spent the rest of the trip site seeing in DC with Stan being our personal tour guide. We would try to talk but neither of us knew how to start. Our conversations became more of him playing tour guide and we avoided any personal conversation between us. This was the only time in our lives we had difficulty talking. He never knew why. He didn't know that I just wasn't ready yet, that I was still looking for that approval before I could commit to him fully. I knew I had to be happy with myself before it would really work for us. When I left, I felt so empty, so alone.

I could tell Stan was ready to finally settle down and was surprised he wasn't seeing anyone at the time. It made me wonder if he was still waiting for me. It made me wonder after this weekend together and how I acted whether he would still want to wait for me.

It was the spring of '82, just 8 months after our awkward visit together. Even though I was still trying to find myself, I always thought we would someday get back together.

That evening my dad called me out of the blue and said, "Hey kiddo, guess who I had dinner with last night?"

Knowing my dad and how it could have been anyone, I asked "Ok dad, who did you have dinner with?"

He responded, "Stan and his new wife."

I was so shocked, I couldn't speak. He continued, "They got married in February and are expecting their first child. She's really nice but not who I would have expected him to marry. You know, Dee, it could have been and should have been you. I just don't understand why you broke up with him; he was the best you will ever find."

Again, my dad's words went through me like a knife. I knew finding out that Stan was married and had a child on the way, that chapter of my life was over.

I knew how he felt about wanting kids and how he was against abortions and divorce. He'd always told me that neither would be a part of his life. I knew I could never think of contacting him again. I knew deep down that both of us would always hold the love we felt, but he'd moved on without me. It saddened me that I never had the chance to tell him how I really felt about him. I felt such a loss that I could never really fill. Stan was always in my heart, and now I had to forget about any dreams and wishes I wanted for us in the future. I had to realize that we really didn't have plenty of time to be together, it was over.

Chapter 4
How life really was….

My parents finally divorced in December of 1982, and I hoped that each of them would be able to have that special relationship I knew they both deserved. My dad was going on 8 years with Lee at the time of their divorce. I really thought she would be the one who would settle him down. Unfortunately, they split up and went their own ways a year later.

My career was really taking off, and I finally started feeling like things were falling into place for me.

It was an average Friday night. I had just returned from another one of my work trips. This time I was in Denver, Colorado and after being there for 5 weeks, was glad to be home. I loved my job and I got to see a lot of military history that trip. It was fun, but I was so glad to be home.

When I arrived home Karen was there, and I could tell she wanted to talk.

"How was your trip?" she asked.

"It went really good. I met a lot of people but could never see living there. It is a beautiful place and I hope to be able to visit one time that I'm not working. I sure wished I'd had my skis with me this trip." One of my hobbies was snow skiing. I loved it and went every chance I had. Unfortunately with my job, it was getting less frequent.

"Did you have any plans for tonight?" she asked.

"No, was thinking of staying in. Why? What are you doing?" I asked curiously.

"I met this guy at work that I'd really like to go out with, but there's one problem. He said he would go but wanted me to find a date for his brother. I just thought, if you didn't have plans, would you like to go?"

I could see she really liked this guy but wondered what I would have to put up with, and why his brother couldn't find his own date. I was still curious and bored and ready to get out.

"Sure, why not. I have nothing planned. What's this guy look like and why does he need his younger brother to set him up?"

She smiled and said, "You are going to love this guy. He's tall, blonde, blue eyes and has a body that is built like a rock. He works at the factory where I do. All the girls would love to date him, but for some reason, he hasn't asked anyone."

And this is how I met Steve one late August night of '82, on a blind date that my younger sister Karen had set up.

He was a very nice looking man, as she described, and had a great laugh. We enjoyed our first evening, but I didn't think I would see him again.

The next evening, as I walked in the house, the phone was ringing and it was him, "Hi, it's Steve; would you like to go to a party with me? Mike is having a get together at our house and I would like you to come."

I hesitated and thought; last night wasn't that bad and again I had no plans. "Sure, what is the address?"

I no sooner laid the phone down when it rang again. "Hey Dee, how have you been? It's Dave."

Dave was a guy I dated occasionally for the past few years. It was a strange relationship. We only went together for office parties, his or mine. We would go like we were a couple and then not see each other again until the next event. Sometimes, it would be months between seeing each other. He was tall, solid man with blonde hair and the most beautiful blue eyes. He was so handsome and at times I wondered why he picked me to be his date for all the important events in his life.

"Hello there. I'm doing really good. Work is keeping me out of town a lot and your timing is perfect. I'll be in town for a few weeks and would love to see you."

"I'm glad you said that, I have been invited to a party tonight and wanted to see if you would like to go," He said.

"If you had called me 5 minutes sooner, I would have been available. I just made other plans for tonight, but we need to get together as soon as we can." I was disappointed to have to say no. I always enjoyed going out with Dave but I also knew it would never lead to anything. I used to love to take him to my office parties and show him off. He was so handsome and I know it kept all the other ladies wondering why he was with me. He always treated me like I was his lady in front of everyone. While we both knew it was only for the night.

It was a nice arrangement, no ties and to always have someone to call last minute and go out with when no one else was around. He was always available, and I never understood why. And I'm not sure why I never asked him.

I arrived at Steve's house and walked slowly to the door. I was thinking maybe I should call Dave and change my plans. No, I couldn't be like that to someone. It would be a nice evening and I could see Dave soon. I knocked on the door.

Steve opened the door and, to my shock, there was Dave standing right next to him. Of course, Dave walked over and gave me a big hug and a kiss. Not our normal kiss, just a quick peck. He looked great. He smiled and said, "This is the guy you turned me down for?"

I could tell Steve was boiling inside. I smiled at Dave and said, "Yes he is. But it is great to see you also. Hi Steve, so this is your home?"

Steve grabbed my arm to stop me from moving into the room and said, "Let me know now, who do you want to be with?" That was my first experience with his temper and jealousy.

I didn't know how to respond, his tone frightened me a little, and I knew Dave was there if he turned out to be a creep, or worse. I responded, "As I told Dave, I already made plans with you."

There was a nice turn out for the party, and everyone seemed to be having a good time. Dave stayed for a while but avoided me the rest of the time he was there. The next thing I knew, he had left.

The rest of the evening went surprisingly well with Steve. I'm really not sure what attracted me to him.

Karen began dating his brother, Mike, exclusively, and we did a lot of double dating the first few months. Both of us questioned whether they were right for us but for some reason we kept dating them.

A few weeks later, I went away with my aunt for a long weekend to Canada, to get away and think about where my life was going. We went to see family I hadn't seen since I was a child. It was great reconnecting with them, even though the trip had been very short.

On our way back we spent an afternoon at an orange orchard and picked oranges. We talked and had a great time. Before we knew it, it was time to go home. As we were approaching the border, there were signs everywhere that you could not carry any food across the border of substantial quantity.

We had about 4 crates of oranges and didn't want to give up one. I piled all our coats and luggage on top of the fruit and we breezed right through the security checks. Who was going to question two women who were visiting their elderly aunt? We laughed so hard, harder than I had in a long time.

It was then I decided I would break up with Steve when I returned home.

Karen called me as soon as I arrived home. She said that Steve and Mike were in a very bad car accident the day before. Both were at home but weren't doing very well.

I went to see Steve and seeing how hurt he was, I just didn't have the heart to break it off and thought once he got better and stronger, I would. I just couldn't kick him while he was down.

Steve asked me to marry him while he was recovering from his accident. He hadn't even completely healed, and I just didn't want to add more troubles to his plate. I felt bad for how much in pain he was in. What do they call it - *Florence Nightingale syndrome*?

Even though I was not even close to that point in our relationship, I wanted a change so badly… I thought, *why not? Stan is married, so that dream is gone, why not? Someone give me a reason, please.* I said yes.

We got married at the end of November of '82, only 3 months after we had met. Karen married Mike 6 months later, and both of us had the same last name again.

I went into my marriage thinking that if it didn't work, I would just get a divorce. I knew I'd never stay in a bad marriage, even if I did have kids. Thank goodness that was not the reason we got married.

The life I thought I would have would no longer be a reality and for some reason I felt I needed to grasp any type of happiness and relationship I felt I could get. I really didn't have my full heart in it but took the plunge anyway. Most of my friends and acquaintances thought it must have been because I was pregnant, but it took another 2 years for my first son, Steven, to arrive. No one knew the truth of how I really felt. No one knew how bad it was. No one really knew that I knew things would not work out. But I kept trying.

Steve and I lived in New Jersey for the first 4 ½ years of our marriage and when my second son Ed turned 6 months old we moved to North Carolina to work on our marriage. I was determined, for the sake of my boys to give our marriage the best shot I could and made that my focus.

Two more years went by, and our marriage hadn't improved. We had a lot of problems and neither of us tried very hard to get along anymore. We were drifting further and further apart. I wanted stability, and he wanted to live day by day without any planning for the future.

His temper was getting worse and beginning to scare me, more for the boys. I didn't want them to grow up with that kind of influence in their life. I wanted them to be happy, and I knew as each day went on that happiness was not going to be a part of our marriage. I knew I could never put my boys through what I went through growing up. It would be hard, but I would do it for them.

Eight long married years, and I decided to move to Georgia, alone with my boys. I wanted so much more for them. Growing up in a home full of fighting and all his drinking was getting out of control.

I had done some research and found in Georgia you could be divorced in 30 days and off I was packing. Steve and I both knew it was over, and it would be the best thing for the boys if we split up.

I kept thinking of all those years my parents stayed together and were miserable. I just couldn't do that to my children or myself. I didn't want to take the chance that I would take my unhappiness out on my boys.

We got divorced in April of '91 and my boys became the main focus of my life and the drive that kept me going.

After my divorce was final, I moved into an apartment complex that seemed to have nothing but single moms living there. It was a great atmosphere for my boys. There were lots of kids for them to play with and I made a lot of new friends that were in the same situation as me. This is when I met

Lisa, my best friend. She was also a single mom with one daughter. We immediately bonded and became very close. The mom's at the complex all looked out for each other and all of the kids. We became one big family.

I thought about Stan through the years, what he was doing and what would my life had been like if I hadn't been so stubborn back then. I wondered often about the "what if's" that would have changed the course of my entire life. I began to wonder what he was doing and if his life was happy.

Lisa and Janet, another good friend from the complex, decided to drag me out on my birthday to celebrate. The three of us had spent the last month celebrating our birthdays which were within a month of each other. We celebrated every time we could line up a baby sitter between us. This was the "official" celebration on my real birthday, and they said there was no way I could back out. It was September 28th, 1993, my 34th birthday. This is the night I met Billy.

Lisa never liked him from the moment we met him. I should have listened.

Billy was small but very strong man. I could see some of the qualities I ran from in Steve that were a very big part of Billy's personality.

I always seemed to attract the same type of man. One who wanted me to be the sole person responsible for paying the bills and taking care of the kids, while constantly putting me down and telling me what I was doing wrong with my life. It seemed I attracted men that treated me a lot like my dad had always done. My ex-husband had been the same way to me. Lisa immediately knew it wasn't going to work for me and Billy, but it took me years to realize how right she was.

A few weeks after Billy and I met, I had an accident at work. A partition wall fell on my back. It had torn one of my lower disks and also gave me whiplash in my neck. I was in so much pain. It was so bad; I had to sleep in a lounge chair. When I tried to lie down in bed, the pain was so excruciating I couldn't sleep. The choice I had was sleep in the chair or take pain killers the rest of my life, I chose the chair. The only other choice I had was to get fusion surgery. I had no choice but to come up with another solution. The only thing that helped was sleeping in a lounge chair.

I felt so trapped in my life with no way out. I struggled to get my health back.

Billy wasn't much support during this time and had no sympathy for the pain I was in. He made me feel like I was alone, and I had to fight this issue the best way I could. I knew that if I did go for surgery, I would be laid up for quite a while and I would have needed someone there constantly to take care of me. I didn't want to put anyone through that and also knew that Billy wouldn't be there to take care of me. I had no choice but to continue without the surgery.

I've always been the one to take care of others and it was difficult to imagine having to ask for the kind of help I would need.

I wanted to spend more time with my boys and hopefully recover enough to work a full-time job again; I decided to start my own business. I could be home after the boys got out of school and do most of the work from home. This saved a lot of money on babysitters and hopefully helped fill the absence of not seeing their father very often.

Unfortunately, after our divorce, Steve didn't spend much time with them. Once he re-married, they didn't see or hear from him again for almost 13 years.

When I met Billy, he had been separated from his wife for 3 years, but he hadn't taken any steps towards getting a divorce. It was always one excuse after the next and mostly the lack of money. He always seemed to have money for everything else but that. Even though I knew he wasn't with her, it still bothered me that he wouldn't take that step. I always felt it was his way of not being able to make a commitment to me.

After 7 years of being together, I realized we would not be what I was looking for. It was a good thing that we didn't marry. I thought back at what had been so important to me when I was young and now, the one thing I avoided back then, being someone's wife, I realized, was something I really wanted.

We stayed together for almost 9 years, and 8 ½ years of it, he was married to someone else while living with me.

Age 40 was fast approaching and I think I hit my mid-life crisis. It was September of 2000. I was at the end of a failing relationship with Billy. He still hadn't gotten his divorce, and we weren't getting along very well. I really wanted to buy a house, and I could tell it would never happen between us. I knew that if I waited for Billy, he'd never make that move with me. He didn't seem to have any goals or plans for the future. He was happy just living day to day. How much it reminded me of my life with Steve.

Other than raising my boys, buying a home was one of my biggest goals. I wanted to give my boys some security and a place to call home before they eventually moved out.

I came home one day and Billy told me he quit his job and is joining my business.

The next day I began looking for a full-time job. I knew that we could never be in business together. I would be doing all the work.

I closed my business the day I found a full time job with a small software company in Roswell, Georgia. It was a family-run company that had just been purchased by a major firm in New York. Everyone treated me like family, and it was the first job to pay me decent money.

I was finally able to start seriously looking for a house and move on with just my boys.

One of my favorite clients from when I had my own company asked me to continue working with him on a part-time basis even after I closed the business. I knew I could always use the money, and it was easy work that I enjoyed, so I decided to continue working with him.

He was a doctor, writer and entertainer. I was computerizing his business to help do his taxes each year, and he got me involved with some of the projects he was working on. It was always something new and interesting. I worked each Saturday morning, and it really helped bring in the extra income I needed to get the house I wanted.

At that time, I also fit in a third job that I did from home. It was working for a collection agency building a database system to track their correspondence with clients. I worked mostly nights and Sundays from home. And then, at the same time I was trying to get my computer certification so I would have some type of document to prove what I know. Life was very hectic for me at that time.

Shortly after I turned 40, late November of 2000; I received the first correspondence from Stan in years. It was an email message. He said he had "*googled*" my name on the internet and got my email address. I was still with Billy but loved hearing from Stan again. It was such a nice surprise. I was so interested to hear what he'd been up to through the years, including if he was still married. Apparently they had just split. I wanted to hear about his job but knew that subject would have to be left up to him to bringing it up. I knew a lot of his work details would be confidential and off limits to me. As much as his job always interested me, I was really more interested in the outside-of-work details, like him being single again.

He signed his messages "YOBF" (your old boyfriend). I teased him to not use the word old in any correspondence so he changed it to YFBF (your former boyfriend). I told him about Billy, and he told me about his wife. It was so great to talk to him again.

I started working towards buying a house the first of the year in 2001.

During that time, Stan and I kept in touch just via emails. He respected that I was with someone even though he knew it wasn't going very well. We kept the conversations more about generic topics, like our families.

He told me about finding his real father and that he found out that he now had 2 younger brothers. He was so excited to find his real father and was overjoyed to learn about having brothers. He was no longer an only child, and the thought of being a big brother thrilled him. Here are some of our emails....

From: Stanley S
Sent: Fri 3/2/2001 5:54 AM
To: Dee Keller
Subject: Hi Dee...

I was at work and my son called asking me to come home because of an ear ache, so I did, now he's asleep, so I figured I'd drop you a line or two.
I know what you mean about us old bodies, but you know, somehow I still picture you as 17...I can't seem to put the years on you in my mind. In fact, I found an old slide of you sitting on a rock in those woods behind my parent's house. It seems we spend our youth wishing we were older and our later years wishing we were younger...oh well.

On kids leaving the nest...I guess that day is closing in on you for your oldest. I can tell you from personal experience that you get a strange mix of emotions when they leave. I was elated that my son Matt would be going to college, no one in my family ever did before him including my newfound brothers. But at the same time, he was my bud, my fellow sci-fi and sports enthusiast, fishing pal etc., and in that sense it was a sad day when he left. And of course you worry about them being on their own for the first time. But I guess one can get used to just about anything, and he does call from time to time. He's due to come for spring break next Saturday by the way and is itching to drive that Camaro...he's been driving a '92 Topaz and says he hates it 'it just doesn't have any style Dad'....kids today eh? Spoiled rotten.

Anyhow, aside from the see-sawing weather...I'm talked out for the moment. Always good to hear from Dee, write when you can!

Stan

I loved hearing from him. He always had a way of cheering me up, whether or not I really needed it. He would always be a special part of my life, and the bond we still had showed with our conversations. We periodically kept in touch just let each other know we were doing well but still thinking of each other.

From: Dee Keller
To: Stanley S
Sent: Wednesday, June 27, 2001 8:58 AM
Subject: hey there

Well its been a while, how've ya been. I've been working my tail off trying to get caught up with everything and I can really tell my age lately. Nothing new is going on, just work. I'm hoping I'll be working from home more often soon cause of all the hours I have been putting in. They are buying me a new computer for the house and I'm gonna have DSL put in on July 12th.

Maybe I'll be able to keep more in touch with people. So, how's life? My oldest is talking about moving out already. Boy, time flies... I remember when.... Oh well. Sorry I seem to be just throwing out thoughts... I had a dream about you last night and just had to drop you a note. Hope to hear from you soon.

Dee

From: Stanley
Sent: Wed 6/27/2001 9:33 PM
To: Dee Keller
Subject: Re: hey there

Hi Dee,

Amazingly, I was at work last night waiting for my computer to crank out some data and for no apparent reason, I started thinking that's it's been a long time since I wrote to you and planned to drop you a line or two tonight. Lo and behold, there's a letter from you!! Maybe all of that astral projection stuff we used to talk about all those years ago had an element of truth to it? Anyway, it was great to hear from you.

I had been considering DSL myself but decided against it because the companies seem to go in and out of business too often resulting in downtime and in some cases, complete loss of connectivity. High speed internet through cable T.V. systems was the next choice...performance was similar bandwidth-wise, price was comparable, but reliability was far better according to the comparison made in this magazine article. The next steps up are those T-2, T-3 and something called Starlink or Star[something anyway] ($700.00/month for commercial users like Hollywood film making companies). At any rate, I haven't made the switch yet myself, just thought I'd let you know what I've seen on it.

Not too much happening around here. I seem to make a lot of plans, but they don't pan out for one reason or another...sometimes work, sometimes the weather. We've been having some really crazy weather lately...heavy winds, micro bursts, mini-tornadoes, hail; you name it we seem to be having it. (Didn't the bible foretell something like this? Ha, ha ... I think!). My oldest son Matt has been home from college since May 14th, so the family is mostly whole. He got a summer job working at my place which he has mixed feelings about...he likes the money and 'atmosphere' but feels like the summer is slipping by without much 'fun'. I kind of agree there...we need to make more time for some good times before it's over.

The latest plan is to visit my Mom and Dad next week over the 4th and into the weekend. It's been about a year since they've seen the kids and I guess we're due. I also want to get to the beach at some point. Matt's last day of work is August 4th and doesn't have to be back at school until the 22nd so maybe I can squeeze a few days in there somewhere.

Don't worry about throwing out stray thoughts...I'm an old friend after all, not some chairman of the board, so feel free! I've had my share of those too.... sometimes I think I have my thumb on the pulse of things, other times I'm completely lost and feel like a kid in need of 'my mommy'. I guess life can overwhelm the best of us on occasion, but so far I've been able to deal with things pretty well. I don't have any social life to speak of though, guess I miss that to a degree...my boys take up most of my time. I think you mentioned it was pretty much the same with you.

Well, it's about time to get ready for work...AGAIN! Ugghhh!! Write soon! -Stan-

---

I felt a little guilty with talking with Stan even though Billy and I were still together. Stan would always be a special part of my life that I knew Billy would never understand. If Billy found out we were corresponding, I knew he wouldn't like it so I kept our emails to myself. Stan only had my work address, and I knew that Billy was checking my computer to see if I was talking to other people, even women. For some reason, Billy was always checking up on me even though I never gave him a reason. I always felt deep down that I couldn't move on to a new relationship until I finished the one I was in. To me, being faithful was the most important thing in a relationship, regardless of how bad it really was.

I didn't feel talking with Stan was cheating on Billy because we truly were good friends that cared for each other. Stan and I had both moved on and married. Stan respected my feelings and knew all about Billy. He never made any inclination that he was trying to get back together, just that he truly wanted to keep in touch because of the special past we had shared together.

From: Stanley S
Sent: Tue 9/4/2001 2:53 PM
To: Dee Keller
Subject: Hi & Sorry 'Bout That...
Hi Dee,

Just a quick note to say hi and let you know I'm back on-line. I don't know if was able to send you a warning but I (or rather my computer) had become infected with not one, but two viruses. One was a backdoor.trojanhorse that snuck in through AIM and the other was an e-mail attachment that I stupidly opened. The last one went into my address book and sent itself out to everyone in there, so if you got a funky e-mail from me, it wasn't really from me, but I **apologize** anyway if it infected your system. Anyway, all is cured via Norton Anti-Virus 2001 ($39.95 at COMPUSA). With your computer savvy, I'm sure you have all of the safeguards against this sort of thing.

Anyway, it's been awhile since I heard from you...hope that dream you said you had about me in your last note wasn't a nightmare! (heh,heh)..So sit down when you have time and tell me all about your summer.

Your Old Bud, Stan

Hey there – let's see – the dream....it has been a few weeks and I am getting old ... got me on the spot with that one must have been a good one 'cause I always remember the bad ones. great hearing from you to, working hard – still working 3 jobs so time is not on my side much – my oldest is bugging me to help him get a car and then help with college and its just, well you know, don't get me wrong this is probably sounding really bad – just timing isn't really good – trying to do too much at one time... well need to get back to work but I'll write soon
Dee

I never did remember the details of the dream, but somehow I knew it had to do with us seeing each other again. Life went on, and I didn't hear from him again for almost a year. It was always good timing when he did write me. I was still in a failing relationship and wondering why it was lasting so long. Billy and I knew after I got the house that it was over but we held on for some reason anyway.

I didn't hear from Stan again for a while... the tragedy of September 11th came and went, and I wondered if he was involved with anything to help. I wanted to email or call him, but if he was doing something with the government I figured it might not be a good idea contacting him yet. He wouldn't be able to tell me anything anyway. He wrote me one more time just before his life was about to change. He was about to go through his most tragic and painful experience of his life next to the split of his marriage.

From: Stanley S
Sent: Mon 6/10/2002 12:57 AM
To: Dee Keller
Subject: Re: Hi & Sorry 'Bout That...

Hi Dee, I hope this reaches you...I'm using an old note you sent me last year so it should get to you unless you too have changed your e-mail address. When I 'upgraded' to DSL, I neglected to tell you...anyway, it's stanley.s@mail.net

Not much new here, all the boys are home for the summer driving me crazy, well, at least the 16year old is...they can be so demanding at this age. My oldest (Matt-20) has got the old Camaro just a headliner away from being perfect again, you'd love it. I do have more to talk about, but in case I'm sending this out into the ether, I'll cut it short for now. Hope to hear from you!
Stan

Chapter 5

Getting Reacquainted

August 2004 thru May 2005

During the next few years I became very close with my mom and Ben. They still lived in the same house I grew up in, the one next door to where Stan's mom and step-dad still lived. My mom and Ben were still together after all these years, and it was great to see her finally happy and with someone who treated her the right way.

Billy and I finally split up after 9 years, and it was a very painful breakup. It took me a few years to get over the hurt and deceit he put me through. Trusting someone again became a very big issue with me, and having another relationship was the last thing I was thinking about. My mom helped pull me through this time and kept in constant contact with me. Even Ben was there for me when I hit rock bottom financially, and he pulled me out of it. I don't know if I would have survived without them being there for me. They not only helped financially but emotionally too.

When Ben passed away a few years later, my mom and I became even closer. I will never forget the day he passed. Ben had been in the hospital from a massive heart attack he'd had a few months before. He had just been moved to an assisted living center for his final treatments before being released to go home. I just got to work one morning and received a call from Ben's oldest daughter, Fran. Apparently, the nurses at the center couldn't reach my mom, so they called the next name on the list of contacts. Fran tried to call my mom, but there was no answer at her house. Frantically, she called me to see if I could reach her.

I had to break the news to mom over the phone. It was the hardest thing I'd ever done. When her work phone was answered I said, "Hi this is Dee, Carol's daughter. Is Phil there?" Phil is my mom's boss who has known both of them a very long time. I thought he would be good support until I could get someone in the family over there.

"No, Phil is out of town this week. Can I help you? This is Cindy."

"Cindy, Ben has passed away, and I have to break the news to my mom. Could you please stay with her until I can get my sister there?"

"Of course we both will. Joanne and I are here. Hold on, I will go get her and I promise we won't leave her side." I could hear Cindy's footsteps and then her saying, "Carol, you daughter Dee is on the phone."

It took what seemed forever, but it was only a few moments when mom came onto the phone. "What's going on? You never call me at work."

"Mom, its Ben. Fran just called and said he passed away this morning."

Luckily my mom worked at the same place for over 20 years, and everyone there knew both her and Ben very well. I hated telling her over the phone but felt some comfort in knowing that she was surrounded by good friends.

I promised my mom to call my sister Sue and that she would be there as soon as she can.

I took the first flight to New Jersey I could get on.

I thought about when my friend Jeff who died all those years ago, and I worried that because my mom and Ben never married, his family might treat her like she had been nothing in his life.

I finally arrived around 10:30 in the evening to find my mom and sister Sue sitting alone in the house. Mom was sitting in her recliner in shock.

As I walked in she smiled briefly, and I walked over to her and gave her a big hug. The three of us spent the evening talking about Ben. We laughed, we cried, but we couldn't sleep. Why is it when someone passes, sleep just isn't important? Or is it that your mind takes over not allowing sleep to come?

Sue and I helped mom make the arrangements for his funeral, and I was so relieved to see how his kids treated her. They knew she was the most important person in his life and didn't take that from her. They all welcomed us and treated us like family. It meant a lot to me that she wasn't denied her place in his life. I know it helped her during the grieving process to know she had the support from all of us.

My mom became my best friend, my confidant. She had a very difficult time when Ben passed away; they had been together for over 30 years, and it was the most devastating time in her life. I tried everything to keep her spirits up, to help her get through the loneliness she felt. I had no idea how devastating her loss was.

Somehow, I hoped just being there to talk to was enough, anything to keep her from being alone. I hated that I was over 800 miles away, so it was all I could do to keep her spirits up. We spoke on the phone almost every day.

One day in early August 2004, during one of our daily calls, she mentioned she saw Stan's step-dad, as she was driving past their house. He told her that Stan had been having a very bad time the past few years and had been very sick. He thought it would be nice if I contacted him.

I immediately emailed him. It had been 2 years since my breakup with Billy, and I was finally ready to move on. I wasn't thinking of rekindling anything with Stan at the time, but I knew talking with him would definitely help bring me out of the isolation I was in. He always had a way to make me smile and brighten my day. I wanted to see how he was and if I could help.

Here is the email I sent him.....

From: "Dee Keller"
To: "Stanley S"
Sent: Thursday, August 05, 2004 5:59 PM
Subject: Hey stranger

I was cleaning up my emails and found your address yesterday....
I really hope this is still the right one. My mom said you had a
tough time this past year; I wanted to see how you are doing? I'm
sorry to hear about your health problems. I can't believe it's been
2 years since we wrote, time has just flown by. My oldest son is in
his second year of college and my younger one is a senior in high
school. Talk about feeling old. How is everything going? You
need to send your phone number and we can talk, of course, if
you want to. It would be nice to hear from you again. Hopefully
this will make it to you.
Dee

From: Stan
Sent: Fri 8/6/2004 4:44 PM
To: Dee Keller
Subject: Re: Hey stranger

Dee!!

What a wonderful surprise!! Yes, it made it to me...I've had
several computer crashes and virus attacks since we last wrote,
and long since lost your address...and I forgot how I found it in the
first place. I could REALLY make use of your IT expertise
sometimes. Of course you can have my phone number....hell
girl...with our history??!! Anyway, it's 301-333-5555. I'll instruct
my boys not to hang up on you...they know your name, but may
have forgotten it. (They've been "programmed" to hang up on
unknown callers...sales folk ya know?). But be careful...I may talk
your ear off!!

Yes, it's been a rough year...actually a rough millennium so far
starting with my marriage going south (no pun intended) and most
recently, this damn cancer. But somehow, I've managed to keep
a positive attitude for the most part. My boys were a big part of
that especially during my darkest moments. The cancer was
esophageal and stomach by the way and it was kind of accidental
in the way I found out. It started with simple indigestion and acid
reflux that I was being treated for with Nexium and other stuff...but
the drugs just masked the real cause of my pain. I was also taking
a lot of Excedrin (which thins the blood). I had been feeling
unusually tired for a couple of months and decided to go have a
check-up. The doc cleared me, but hadn't had a return from the

blood work yet. He called me on an October Sunday (the 13th...3 days after my 50th birthday) during a football game (which scared the heck out of me) and said he didn't know why I was alive because my hemoglobin count was so low. I was bleeding internally, but there was no obvious evidence of it...so, he scheduled me for a GI exam. I was expecting an ulcer, but the results showed fairly advanced cancer. Needless to say I was pretty devastated. But to make a long story a bit shorter...I went through intense chemo and radiation treatment, then major surgery in February followed by post-op chemo during most of this summer. I lost 65 pounds and all of my hair. That brings me to now...I'm still recovering, but have gained 25 pounds back, my hair is coming back nicely, I've started working out again, and most importantly the cancer appears to be gone. The enormous medical bills are another story, but even that end of it is starting clear up.

So that's my story of the year. The boys are doing well...Matt will be 22 this November and will have his degree by next Spring after going through this 5th semester, Steve is 18 and starting college in the Fall and Dave will be 16 in a week and concentrating of getting his drivers license. Yes, a lot of time has passed. I'd love to hear your voice again, but I may be a
bit nervous at first...writing is one thing, but talking was never one of my strong points (ha, ha). Anyway, sounds like things are going well for you...I hope it will always stay that way.

Your old friend,

-Stan-

I called him immediately after getting his phone number. We talked for over an hour and a half. It was like no time had gone by, and it was the same old Stan who was so easy to talk to. The years had definitely faded any ill feelings we both may have had. We realized how much our lives were very similar during the years apart, and how, deep down, we were still the same people we were all those years ago.

We talked about our boys and how much they meant in our lives, how our entire world seemed to be consumed with them and everything they were going through. It felt so good to see that his boys were his main focus like mine were to me. He had 3 sons, Matt, Steve and Dave. I had 2 sons, Steven and Ed. They were all around the same age ranging from 17 to 23, and the more we talked, the more we realized how much the boys had in common; especially both of our Stevens. They were both into sports and body building. Ed seemed to be a combination of Matt and Dave's personalities. Matt was into computers, seemed pretty shy with girls and stayed home a lot just like Ed, while Dave was a scholar in school just like Ed. I couldn't wait to meet his boys and for Stan get to know mine.

I wondered what his boys looked like. My Steven is the exact image of his father when I first met him; tall, blonde and very fit. Ed was a combination of both his father's and my side of the family. He was a little shorter and during high school he struggled with his weight. He also has blonde hair and blue eyes like his dad but his build resembles the men on my side of the family.

It was so easy opening up to Stan and sharing what I'd gone through. I normally didn't share my personal life with people. My life story normally made me feel like a failure while with Stan it was opening up and letting him in and allowing him to hear about the struggles of my life. He never made me feel like a failure. I told him about my marriage where we had fought constantly and about his drinking problem, how hard it was to deal with and how it was affecting the boys. I was getting scared at what could possibly happen. The mixture of a bad temper and a serious drinking habit was not a good combination. I was able to tell him what my original reason for moving to Georgia was, to get a divorce, and he did not judge me for it.

My aunt lived in Georgia, and I felt I would at least have some family around to help get me through the divorce. We had done research and found that the state of Georgia will grant a divorce in 30 days if both parties agree. Most other states you needed to be legally separated for at least 12 months before one would be granted. I knew he wanted the divorce too and felt this was the best move for me to make at the time. After my divorce, I wanted to give the boys some security in their lives, and I ended up staying in Georgia.

Stan opened up to me too, telling me about his failed marriage. He explained how they had been drifting apart for years and weren't communicating at all. He took his share of blame for it, and he felt his job may have contributed quite a bit. His wife, Shelley, met someone else and decided to give that relationship a try. She moved to South Georgia and left the boys with him.

I wondered how she could have done it. Leaving my boys would have broken my heart, but he told me that she was in contact with them all the time and kept up her relationship with them. It was good to hear that Stan and Shelley had a better relationship than when they'd been together. They could talk again and even discuss why it didn't work out. He said that they both took equal share in the blame for not working hard enough on it. Both of them realized and accepted the marriage was over and it was time to move on.

He also had told me about the slew of doctors he now has on file for various parts of his body. The cancer treatment he'd gone through had put his entire body through hell, and he now had specialists in a lot of different areas that were very familiar with his case. It made me feel better knowing that he had medical support after hearing the details of the type of cancer he came down with. Normally, it would have been fatal and a full recovery was rare in most cases.

I hated saying goodbye on the phone, but I knew I would hear from him again soon.

I'd done pretty well in my career and my sons were almost grown; that job was almost done. I was finally to the point in my life where a relationship could be number one in my life and not a career or even approval of my parents. I'd finally got myself to the point that how I accepted my life was more important than how others saw it. I wondered if happiness could finally be found with Stan.

We kept in close contact, talking about seeing each other again and how we could possibly schedule it between both of our hectic lives.

This was the first time he signed with love. From the day we started talking on the phone, he changed his signature from "YFBF" to Love. It touched me so much that he easily signed the note with love for me after all these years. He made me feel like I'd always been in his mind and he never forgot what we shared together so many years ago. It also made me wonder how he felt about me now. He told me he always cared about me and never forgot me. To have a man think about me for so many years and care for me after all this time touched me so much. I couldn't wait to hear from him again and looked forward to every moment we could talk.

The next few months we tried to talk on the phone at least once a month and emailed as much as possible. He sent me 4 pictures of himself where he placed a caption underneath each one. He started with about 5 years ago where he looked the same he did when we dated all those years ago. Although, from the picture, I could see where he'd gotten even more defined and well-built, it was the same smile I'd always loved. The only difference was his hair style.

The next picture was one from after his chemo where he'd lost a great deal of weight and had gone totally grey. He didn't even look like Stan. Underneath that picture he wrote, "Going on 80?" He explained that when he returned to work after his chemo, he had lost so much weight and looked so different with grey hair that they made him get a new ID badge for work because his old one didn't look like him anymore. It was so true; it didn't even look like him. The loss of weight made the difference astounding.

The last picture was a little more recent where you could tell he was on his way back to his old self again, including his thick dark hair.

I loved his sense of humor and how he could laugh at himself. He had warned me that one of the pictures reminded him about a commercial that was running on TV for *Six Flags Amusement Park.* It featured a guy dressed as an old bald man who danced around trying to entice people to come visit the park. I couldn't believe how much he looked like that character in the picture, and Stan's silly personality reminded me of that guy. I could easily see him dancing around having a great time. Whenever that commercial came on I could only smile and think of Stan.

He worried the pictures would bother me. I told him, "At least I will know what you are going to look like when you get old." It made me feel at ease that maybe he would accept the changes and flaws in me. With Stan, I knew it had always been what was inside that I was attracted to, not the outside. He was a great looking man but his personality, morals and just how he treated people was what drew me to him. He was one of the most caring people I ever met in my life. His good looks were just a bonus in the package.

Hi Dee, thanks for thinking of me...I'm still doing pretty good.
Things have just been a bit hectic these past couple of weeks
with my son Matt getting ready to go back to Memphis, and my
other sons getting back into their respective schools. Also, I
bought a new truck...I may have mentioned that I was planning on
it when we talked last. It's a 2004 Chevy Trailblazer. It's the first
brand new car I've ever owned (not counting a Pinto I bought in
'79), and it's a real rush!!

Anyway, I still plan to give you a call, just be patient with me, I'm
getting forgetful in my old age...maybe tomorrow?

Love, -Stan-

I was shocked to hear about him buying a new car.
He'd always loved getting old cars and fixing them up. I
teased him about getting old and how he couldn't keep up
with his old hobbies. He hated to admit that he just couldn't
do everything he used to, and the new car gave him a
different feeling of excitement.

I always had new cars other than the first one my dad
gave me so many years ago. That old relic taught me what it
was like to be stranded on the road alone. Being a woman, I
would rather have something reliable to count on. I explained,
"When I had a used car I never knew how much I would
spend a month just to keep it on the road. At least with a new

one, I can schedule the car payment into my budget and always know how much I need each month."

From: Dee Keller
To: Stan S
Sent: Friday, September 24, 2004 2:24 PM
Subject: email

Just wanted to send you my personal email address because I may not have access to my work one until I return to work on wed. They're making changes this weekend that may shut off my account.

It was really nice talking with you last night. It feels like hardly any time has passed. It would be nice to see you again sometime. We'll have to work on that.

Dee

From: Stan S
Sent: Sat 9/25/2004 1:31 AM
To: Dee Keller
Subject: Re: email

Thanks for the e-mail address...it's officially added. Now, if you give me your snail mail address, I'll send ya stuff...like pictures. I've included a pic of the Camero...but I'll take some better ones for your son.

I enjoyed talking with you too, and you read my mind about it being nice to see each other again, I'd love to. It boggles my mind to think that it's been 25 years since I've seen you and 29 since we were going together. Breaking up is always difficult, but I prefer to think of some of the good times we had, and I remember when you first started coming over...helping me with my parent's pool and lots of other mental snapshots. Pardon my reminiscing.

Anyway, as you say...we'll work on it.

-Stan-

p.s. My address:

25 Poolesville Road
Poolesville, Maryland

I loved seeing the picture of the car after all these years and knowing he still had it with him. It was the same car he had used to teach me to drive all those years ago. We reminisced about those times we'd had in the car, and I had to keep reminding him when his boys were within earshot that he needed to stop. He liked to reminisce the most about the times we got a little carried away with each other, especially in the Camaro. He said, "It made me feel young again to remember and talk about those times we used to sit and talk and well… you know." He had a way of bringing me back to 16 again.

We started talking about the trip I was going to make to New Jersey to see my mom. After Ben died, I tried to go see her each year around her birthday in May. We made annual plans to go watch the Kentucky Derby together because that was one thing her and Ben did religiously each year. I tried to fill the void Ben left in my Mom's life as much as possible with little things like enjoying with her the things her and Ben loved to do. Even though I knew I was only a distraction, I really know I was a welcome one. I asked Stan if he'd like to go, and he was very open to the idea. The only thing that might get in the way was his son Matt graduating from college. He didn't know when, but he was sure it was sometime in May. I hoped it wouldn't be during the same week.

He mentioned that it would be nice if I flew up to DC and then we could drive together to New Jersey and visit both my mom and his. Our parents still lived next door to each other, and I thought it would be a perfect trip. He could stay with his mom and I'd stay with mine, but we could still spend a lot of the time together and there would be no pressure on either of us to stay together. We could play it by ear and see how things went but still have a backup in case things didn't progress further.

From: Dee
Date: 01/02/2005 Sun PM 05:49:36 EST
To: "Stan S"
Subject: something to look forward to

It was really nice talking with you again last night. I couldn't believe how fast an hour an 1/2 went.... thank goodness I have free long distance on my cell phone :) (I have lots of roll over minutes left over so if you ever want to talk, let's use them up)

It is nice how we haven't an awkward moment of nothing to say or how I feel I can say anything to you. If you only knew how my life has lacked that and just to have someone to talk with that isn't judging me or correcting me in every move. Thank you for giving me that. Talking with you has helped get thru a lot here... it has been a very tough year. Hopefully this one will be a lot better.

I did some checking and the flight up there really isn't that bad... might have to think about doing it a little sooner. :)

I'm really looking forward to the trip in May and I mentioned it to my mom and she's excited to see you again also. It should be a fun trip. As always, she is starting to fill the time and of course, you're included. I guess you will need to reserve some time for your family also :)

Actually, she mentioned us going to dinner on Friday and then if you would like to join us to go to the track on Saturday. She is going to be bringing her friend so I guess we'd be double dating with my mom. Of course, I don't want to assume that your time would be with us, but I do want to extend the invite.

From what my mom and I decided, I'd be coming up for the weekend of May 7th. I thought it would be nice if I flew up to DC on the 5th (Thursday, May 5th) and spend the night there. Then we could take our time getting there on Friday. I figured I'd make my flight back for the following Wednesday so we would have to leave on Tuesday to get back to DC. This way there is no rush.

Well... what do you think? That's the game plan for now and hopefully everything will go as planned...

Talk to you soon.... Dee

I was getting excited thinking about seeing him again. He brought me back to my youth and how happy we were together. It was such a great time in my life. It was a happy time that I could always think back to.

We were getting along so well during our talks, and I loved getting his emails. I felt like we were really getting to know each other again. I thought about the idea of us getting back together, but I didn't want to get my hopes up too much. I knew I'd changed a lot since back then and had gained a little weight the past few years. I definitely wasn't the fit and trim 16 year old I'm sure he was envisioning. It was really nice just getting to know him again, seeing that deep down he was still the same man with the same values and morals I remembered from long ago.

I kept an eye on the prices for flights just in case we could schedule something. Every once in a while I'd send him a little reminder that the time was approaching and I wanted to be able to save as much money as possible by making the flight arrangements as far in advance as possible. In a way, I wanted to also schedule things so I'd finally have something to look forward to. I had no doubt we'd get along, I just wondered if the physical attraction would still be there.

From: "Dee"
To: "'Stan S'"
Sent: Monday, January 17, 2005 6:42 PM
Subject: prices are rising

Well... just checked again and the prices are going back up... hope this isn't a trend. They've gone up $50 since last week and I'd like to lock in the tickets before it gets too high and I have to cancel altogether. Actually, I am beginning to wonder if you've changed your mind. I was hoping to use this time to get re-acquainted before we got together again, but not hearing from you much is making me wonder if you've changed your mind. I

know you've said you're a bit apprehensive and I understand, it
has been a long time.
Just wondering....
Dee

From: Stan S
Sent: Tuesday, January 18, 2005 3:51 PM
To: Dee
Subject: Re: prices are rising

Hi Dee,

No, and no. I haven't changed my mind at all, and I completely
understand your point about going up to see your Mom anyway in
time for the races. I'm not miffed or hurt or anything, so there's no
need for any explanations... although I really do appreciate you
being concerned for my feelings...makes me smile...I haven't had
anyone concerned about that in a while. The only hang-up
remains my son Matt's graduation date...he tried to check on it
yesterday, but couldn't get through to the admin office there. If
you give me a couple more days, I'll have an answer for ya. I'm
tempted to say just go ahead and book the flight...I'm about 80%
sure that the graduation is mid-May, but I also know my luck. The
apprehension is more like anticipation. I'm really looking forward
to meeting again. I'll even chip in since this plan is for the both of
us. I apologize for not getting back to you sooner...the usual
rigors of life just caught up with me I guess. I have my 3 month
check up with the oncologist tomorrow...I suppose I've been
consciously and unconsciously sweating that. Anyway, I'll be in
touch tonight or tomorrow night.

Cheers, -Stan-

From: Dee
Sent: Tuesday, January 18, 2005 5:48 PM
To: 'Stan S'
Subject: RE: prices are rising

First, no I will pay for my ticket and really feel I should chip in on
gas for the ride up to NJ. This is a trip I would be taking anyway
and I would feel really bad taking any money for it. I've gotten
very independent in my old age and pretty head strong about
supporting myself and I do have a hard time accepting any help.
Just ask my mom :)

I'm glad I didn't hurt your feelings, after thinking about what I
wrote; I was hoping that it didn't come out the wrong way. I have
been told that I can be quite dry when I'm writing. I don't mean to

be but it must be the old technical writing I've done thru the years where I was taught, straight and to the point, no fluff :)

I'll be home tonight but make it about 9. I have to go to the grocery store and then after dinner I normally take my shower and I'll be settled for the night by then. That's why I normally say after 9, this way I'm settled in for the night and there won't be any interruptions.

Talk to you later or tomorrow, whichever is good for you, I'll be here.
>Dee

The plans to get together in May of 2005 fell through because his son was graduating from college the week we were going to spend together. I was so disappointed but hoped we could find another time.

I planned on going to see my mom for her birthday anyway, but I had to cancel those plans also. My oldest son got sick with a Staph infection, and we were afraid I would possibly be a carrier and give it to my mom. Her health wasn't at its best and everyone agreed, including her doctor, that I not take the chance of going up to see her. I was so disappointed at the whole sequence of events for my trip. It was something I looked forward to each year. And this year everything fell through.

Stan and I talked and agreed we had *plenty of time* and would schedule something else soon. The next few months we kept in contact but didn't make any definite plans to get together. Our lives seemed to get consumed with our own separate day-to-day issues and after time we stopped discussing getting together.

Chapter 6
The New Beginning
June 2005

In late May, I had some money to burn, and my friend Lisa and I had been discussing what I could do with it while not being a waste of money.

I met Lisa after my divorce was final and we'd been best friends ever since. She was married to a good man, Kevin, who would do anything to help a person out.

When I bought my house, there was no attic space or much storage space. I had a great space above my garage but it had no floor. It was on my "wish list" of things to do in my new house. While I was making more than enough to pay my bills, any type of structural change to the house took a great deal of money, money I had to save for or stumble into. I had my tax return and the bills were paid, so we talked about the things I wanted to do.

"It has to either be the attic in the garage, put in a fence or repaint the house." I said.

"Repainting the house will take a crew because of the height of the house. Putting in a fence will be quite a bit of money. Why don't you check into the attic instead?" Lisa responded. She was always there to give me great advice and the more I thought about it, that was the best idea.

Of course, Lisa's husband Kevin offered to put the floor down in the attic to my garage.

I desperately needed the extra storage space, and Kevin had a background in construction. He offered to do it for me as soon as I could afford to buy the supplies needed. It took me 3 weeks to come up with the money for all the supplies he needed.

Kevin refused to take any money for his hard work, so I decided I had to come up with something in order to show him my appreciation for all he had done for me. Something that would not only give him some type of payback for his work but also to make it up to Lisa that she had to be alone during the time he was at my house working so hard.

Lisa was such a great friend to me and I felt I owed her something for borrowing her husband during his time off from his normal job. It should have been her time with him. It took him 2 full Saturdays to complete the job, and I couldn't have been happier with the job he did. Kevin was the type of man that would treat any job like he was getting paid a lot of money to do it. He had such pride in his work. He put details into the job that showed me how much he cared. He cared about the stability and even the resale value it would add to my house.

He not only put down a floor but he also installed a pull down ladder so I could get up and down easily. He did a great job.

After careful thinking, I got online to see what shows were playing in the area. I knew Kevin loved comedy shows and thought that might just be the best way to give him something back. I also thought giving them a night out together would be the perfect gift. On the day that Kevin was finishing the job, I got online and paid for the tickets. I knew once they were purchased, Kevin couldn't refuse the gift. I found tickets for "*Larry the Cable Guy*" from the *Blue Collar Comedy Tour* on June 18th down in Columbus, Georgia. I called Lisa to see if Kevin would travel to see the show, and she was very surprised at my offer.

"Dee, that is so generous. You really don't have to do this."

"Are you kidding, wait until you see the job Kevin did in the garage. I have to do something special." I answered.

She knew he would love to go, and we both thought, because of the distance, we could make a weekend out of it. Hearing how happy she was gave me the satisfaction of knowing this would show them both how thankful I was.

I bought 4 tickets, not even thinking who I would take. I went into my garage to let Kevin know about the tickets. I was so excited to see his reaction, and he didn't disappoint me at all. I smiled and said, "I know you didn't want anything from me for doing this favor but I hope you don't mind that I did something anyway."

He stopped what he was doing and said, "What did you do?"

I responded, "I got us tickets to go see Larry the Cable guy, but I hope you don't mind; it's in Columbus Georgia.

The first time that day, he smiled and said, "Thanks… that's a great idea. We could go up the night before and make a weekend of it."

As Lisa and I were making plans for the show, she suggested Stan could be the 4th ticket holder.

It still makes me wonder why she thought of him. Years earlier, after Billy and I first broke up, Lisa and I were discussing how to find a good man that I wanted to be in my life. She had told me that, when she was younger, her mom asked her to make a list of the things she wanted in a man and even include what he might look like. Lisa recanted my list that she remembered, "You had said to me that you would want to find another man like Stan, a man who would treat you like you were the most important person in their life, someone who was emotionally strong and had good morals, someone that would make you happy."

I remembered the conversation and some of the things I had said I wanted but didn't remember mentioning Stan specifically to her. It was strange that she remembered the details of a conversation that took place so many years ago. It brought back all the good memories of him and the way he used to treat me. Somehow, no one else lived up to the way he had treated me. No one else had made me feel the way he had. No one else had ever made me feel like I was the most important thing in their life.

I thought about it and agreed it would be a great excuse to finally see him again. I was hoping with it being a short weekend it would give us a chance to see how things would go without committing to too much time; just in case it was awkward or didn't work out. Our phone calls and emails were great, but a face-to-face meeting might be different. I called Stan that night to see if he would like to join us. He said he wasn't sure if he could, but it did sound like a great idea. He needed to check on a few things, and he would get back with me. I wasn't sure if he was really interested or not.

I didn't hear back from him for almost a week, so I emailed him to see if he was still thinking about it and what I could do to help convince him to come down. I really wasn't sure if it was financial or why he would be hesitating... maybe he wasn't sure if he wanted to come see me. He finally emailed me back and said he would love to come. He made plans to fly in on Friday afternoon of June 17th and leave on Monday the 20th. He said that he wasn't reluctant in wanting to see me again; it was simply whether he could schedule the time off from work. He moved around his schedule a little and was able to come for the weekend.

I was nervous but at the same time couldn't wait to see him again. When talking on the phone, I was so at ease with him, but face–to-face, I wondered what the feelings would be. I wondered if the old sparks would still be there. I wondered if they would be there for him. I immediately took that Friday and Monday off from work so I could spend as much time as possible with him while he was here.

I was a little worried we wouldn't recognize each other after all this time, even after him sending me recent pictures. His most recent picture looked like he was gaining his weight back and looking like his old self again. Even his hair was getting dark again. From his pictures, other than the

- 98 -

hair style and beard, he looked the same as he did 30 years ago. I never sent him recent pictures so he only had the one from when I was 16 to compare to. I feel I aged gracefully, but definitely was different than way back then. I wondered if he would still see the 17-year-old I once was when he looked into my eyes.

I asked Lisa to come with me to the airport to pick up Stan. I still wasn't expecting us to get back together, but at the same time, I wanted everything to be as perfect as possible. The drive to the airport seemed to take forever and we finally arrived about 10 minutes before his plan landed. I thought Lisa would be a good buffer in case he was disappointed with me, and he wouldn't have to feel confined to just being with me. I felt as giddy as the school girl I had been when Stan and I first met.

As we waited for him to arrive, Lisa and I laughed and joked, and she kept calling him Ralph. She said she didn't like the name Stan, and I could tell she was trying to ease the nervousness I was feeling. She teased me and did everything she could to try to make the best of the situation. I was thrilled he was coming to visit and apprehensive at the same time, but I still couldn't wait to see him again. I told her she better be nice when he did show up and not call him Ralph. I wasn't sure how he would take it. Of course, being the friend she was…. she was on her best behavior when he finally arrived.

We were standing by the baggage claim when he came around the corner. I immediately knew it was him. He always had this way he walked with a certain swagger or confidence; I knew it could only be him. He immediately recognized me also and gave me the biggest smile. It was like in the movies, moving in slow motion towards each other. As we reached each other he gave me the biggest hug and kiss. The same old sparks were there between us; I could feel it in his hug. It made me wish that I'd come alone. When I looked into his eyes and saw the same loving man I'd known so long ago, it made me wish no one else was around.

I think Lisa could tell I was still a bit nervous and, of course, with her sense of humor she broke the ice with Stan by saying, "So, you're the guy Dee's told me all about?"

I could tell she immediately liked him. The three of us joked and had a great time while waiting on his luggage to arrive.

The drive to Lisa's house from the airport was quite comical. Lisa and Stan were just chatting away totally forgetting that I had no idea which direction I needed to drive to get to her house. I had to constantly interrupt their conversation for directions. It was really nice to see them getting along so well. Lisa never held back her feelings when she didn't like someone; I remembered her reaction to Billy, she didn't like him from the moment they met, and she wasn't shy about letting him know. But when she likes someone, she'll talk their ears off, and it was hard to get her attention.

Lisa has such a unique house; I couldn't wait for him to see it. The front yard of the house is a huge cactus garden she and Kevin started planting about 10 years ago. Some are now so large they tower over their single-story house. They must have close to a hundred cactus plants that bloom all different times of the year.

Another hobby Lisa also got into is miniatures and crafts. She converted her daughter's old bedroom into a craft room. This was where Lisa and I would spend hours talking, laughing and working on crafts each Saturday afternoon. I could tell Stan enjoyed seeing all the work Lisa had put into her little shop and was impressed with how talented she was. She could take just about anything and turn it into art. There is no such thing as garbage to her, everything can be recycled.

We spent the time listening to him reminiscing of his past. This was the first time I found out that Stan had been hostage during the Iran crisis. Of course, he couldn't go into many details, but I could see that Stan and Lisa had found a very strange connection between them.

Lisa asked, "Do you know anything about Air America?"

Stan smiled and said, "A great deal, why do you ask?"

Lisa grinned and gave him a look of understanding, "My dad was one of the pilots."

The subject quickly turned to Stan asking about all of the Indian memorabilia that Lisa had displayed around her home. Somehow, I knew the subject was not going to be continued. It was something neither of them felt the need to discuss further. I could see that their relationship had changed.

Days later Lisa told me to watch a movie that had been released a few years ago called *"Air America"*. She explained that her father had flown the plane during part of the time they were describing.

I watched the movie and *Air America* was the plane that flew the hostages' home from Iran. The same time that Stan had been released from being a hostage.

I always knew Lisa had an interesting childhood from what she told me about her dad being in the service and all the places she'd lived. She never really discussed many of the details, and now I understood that there were things she could not discuss. It was nice hearing details of my friends' life brought out by Stan. And it was nice seeing the smile on Stan's face when they talked and the connection they made. The possibility that her dad could have been the pilot who brought Stan back home created an unspoken bond between them. I could see then they felt a connection from the things they had in common.

After visiting for about an hour, we left to go to my house before the Friday afternoon rush hour started. I couldn't wait for him to meet my boys and see the home I'd made for us. I wanted him to see what I had accomplished with my life. To show him I did make something of myself and was proud of what I'd done with my life. The drive home went so fast, and we didn't have a moment of silence. I could tell he was as excited to see me as I was to see him.

My oldest son, Steven, didn't stay for dinner; girlfriend plans. He had enough time to pop his head in and introduce himself before scooting off. I was disappointed that he didn't get to really spend time with Stan.

My youngest son, Ed, popped his head in to introduce himself and then excused himself back to his room. He'd been working on a website from home, and he was still in the middle of a big section. He promised to join us for dinner.

After we settled in, he told me he had something to give me. It was a copy of the same Moody Blues cd that he had me listen to all those years ago. I immediately wondered if he also remembered that that had been the one and only time we had made love. I put it on for us to listen to, and we spent hours on my back deck talking about the past, where we each were right now and where we wanted to be in the future. We were rapidly finding out that, deep down, we both wanted exactly the same thing for the rest of our lives. We both wanted someone special to share it with. Money didn't mean much to either of us. Sharing our lives with someone is all we both wanted.

We started reminiscing about the past and he asked if I remembered the day we met and how his step dad had called him inside because of a phone call. Of course, I told him I'd remembered. He said, "He actually called me into the house when he saw all the girls in the back yard talking to me. He was worried my mom would come home and find us and get a little upset." We both laughed thinking about the times so long ago.

We talked about our failed marriages again, how he had never been able to connect with his wife about the special interests he enjoyed like the stars; she had apparently no interest in them and would roll her eyes at him when he would try to tell his stories. Stan asked if I'd remembered our talks about the stars.

"Of course I do, we spent hours sitting staring at the stars, and I'd always wondered about those stories you would tell me." He smiled knowing those times were as special to me as they were to him. It made me feel so good knowing that was one of the special unique bonds that were just between the two of us.

We starting talking about my dad and the relationship they'd had back then. He asked if I remembered the night the two of them went to dinner alone. I barely remembered, but he told me that there had been a purpose for the dinner.

He said, "The reason for the dinner was to ask your dad for your hand in marriage. Your dad had just taken a sip of his drink when I asked him. He about spit it all over me. We laughed, and your dad said he was very happy for us and couldn't wait for us to get married." Stan always did things the old fashioned way. I was so touched, but at the same time realized where my father's persistence in marrying Stan back then came from. I had always wondered where my dad got the idea, never thinking it had come from Stan. I knew he loved me back then, but I never had thought he was serious enough for marriage or ready enough to ask me. He'd always told me we would get married, but I had taken it more for in the future, years from then but not anything that would happen during my teenage years. The thought of knowing he wanted to ask me made me sad, knowing my life could have been so different if only he'd had the chance.

I was then able to finally tell him the pressure my dad had put me under during that time to get married, how I'd never understood where it came from when Stan never had asked me. I explained how trapped I'd felt back then and that the only way to get my dad's approval was to marry him. I finally admitted to him how I'd needed to be satisfied with myself before I could ever be a full part of a lasting relationship.

I could see the disappointment in Stan's eyes but at the same time I also saw deep sadness. He said, "I really wish you would have told me back then; things would have been so different for the both of us."

It made us then think about how our lives did turn out, and both of us agreed that the love we had for our children made our time apart worth it. If we had married back then, the 5 boys we had wouldn't be here, and the thought of that for both of us made us realize it was for the best. Nothing could replace having the 5 of them in our lives.

He asked me if I'd remembered the trip to DC all those years ago when we brought him his car. He asked, "Had I done something wrong, you seemed to be in a different world and not really with me that weekend?"

I was finally able to tell him what happened during the ride down and how bad my dad made me feel. I still felt bad telling him I just wasn't ready yet.

He asked, "What would have been your reaction if I'd made a move?"

"I really don't know. I was so upset and confused about what to do; I really feel that I probably would have turned you away that weekend," I responded.

He frowned and looked into my eyes as he spoke softly, "I really thought you had just moved on and didn't want to be with me anymore."

It's funny, but I really don't know what I would have done. I felt bad that through all the years Stan had always thought that it was really over between us and I had moved on when it was so far from the truth.

Stan then told me about an encounter he had with my sister back after we had split up. He came over to my parent's house one afternoon to meet my dad, and my sister was outside washing her car. She stopped when he got out of his car and started to chat about nothing in particular. He said she asked him out of the blue why he had dated me for so long when I wasn't the easy type.

He said, "I told her it was because I loved you." Knowing the type of man he was back then and beginning to see that he still was, telling me about that time made me feel so special.

He continued, "For some reason, we kissed that afternoon. I don't even remember what lead up to it, but it felt like I was kissing my sister, and that was as far as it went. I could tell she felt the same about me."

I had asked my sister about it and she didn't recall the incident. I'm not sure if she just said that to spare my feelings or if she really didn't remember. It didn't bother me at all finding this out; I knew it would never have happened if she had known that I still had feelings for him.

I then asked him to tell me a little more about when he was a prisoner. He said, "It was the first time in my life I thought I would die. The second time was when I was going through my cancer treatment. It made me think about a question one of my teachers asked me in high school. They asked, "*What do you want out of life?*" I remember my response to his question even now. It was to just be happy."

He looked sad when he said it and then I told him, *"I haven't had that in years."* It's funny how that's what both of us always wanted but never fully achieved.

I finally got up the nerve to ask him, "Do you remember that the cd you brought me was from the one and only time we'd ever made love?"

He smiled and said, "Of course, I remember that day vividly. It was a very special day for me that I will never forget. It was a day that has been in my mind for all these

- 105 -

years. I remember planning all day for that afternoon to be perfect. I wanted it to be memorable but never dreamed it would turn out to be one I could never forget."

I was so touched that that day had meant as much to him as it did for me, that, even after all these years, he had also remembered the details of that day. To see that I'd been a special person in his life, even after all these years and that deep down he'd always thought of me the way I had thought of him overwhelmed me. I felt a closeness to him that I had never felt before.

We both had been through a rough breakup with our marriages, and it had been years for both of us since we'd been happy with our lives. It was so nice to be able to talk so freely with someone who had experienced a lot of the same hurt and pains I had gone through. For both of us, the pain from the past had finally begun to heal, and we were both ready to move on and let go of what happened in our past. I could see the door was finally open to let someone else in. It wasn't until this moment that I realized I was ready to let someone into my life again. But I knew deep down there was only one man who could do it, and that was Stan.

I told him about my back problems, and he was so concerned. I recounted, "After my accident and the choices I had, I knew I would just have to deal with it. The therapist I was seeing explained that at night, when you are laying down, your disks fill with fluid. Each time I laid down my disk would fill with fluid and tear it even more. It was easier to just sleep in a chair. It's a lot to ask of someone to take care of you, so surgery was just not an option."

He smiled and replied, "You do have someone: me."

His immediate offer to take care of me touched me so much. I told him, "I couldn't put anyone through that, but I'm very touched by the offer."

It was our first time in over 25 years being together, and he immediately wanted to take care of me again. He made no gestures assuming we would be together as couple, just a genuine concern about getting me better. I tried to change the subject, but he kept returning to my health. How with all he'd been through in the past few years (and I could tell he had not recovered from 100%), he still thought about nothing but taking care of me was very special to me. No one had ever offered but Lisa.

He couldn't wait to show me the video he made for me of his home and the Camaro. Because I only smoke in my bedroom, we decided to watch the tape there. It began with him taping the outside of his house and a few rooms inside. He quickly got a shot of Dave and Steve in their rooms and then Matt driving up in the Camaro.

Dave had curly reddish hair and a small build. Steve had short blonde hair and was very muscular. And then there was Matt, long black hair and looking more like Stan than the other two.

They made a little movie for me, even including a shot of him taking off into the horizon. He also recorded special pieces of his life in Maryland, including their family dog, Buster. I could see the pride in his eyes as we watched the tape.

When it was finished, he went to his luggage and pulled out the slides of me that he took when I was 16 years old sitting at our rock. They were the old 35mm slides that you had to put up to the light to see them. He had taken them just after we started dating 30 years ago. There were 2 slides; one of me sitting on our rock and one standing next to a tree in his woods. I couldn't believe after all these years he still had them. He told me that through the years, he had shown off my pictures to his boys.

He brought a whole bunch of other pictures to show me of his house and the boys growing up and also his new-found family, his real father and two younger brothers. It was nice to see how much he still documented his life. I had very few pictures through the years and even, at that, most of them were school pictures of my boys. We, unfortunately, didn't have the memories I could see Stan had; we never had the money to travel and take vacations like they did.

We talked about so many plans and the things we had missed out on in life. He had so wanted a little girl and still did. I couldn't believe he still wished he could have another child, even at his age. I had, at one time in my life, regretted not having a girl, but as he talked, I thought of how hard it would be to do at my age and how difficult it would be to carry a child with my back problems. This was the one and only difference that I could find between us, while he would still love to have more children, I was ready to move on to the next chapter of my life, and having another child just wasn't what I had thought of when planning my future. My boys were getting old enough to leave and be on their own, and I was looking forward to just finding someone special to spend the rest of my life with. Starting over with another child scared me to death.

He asked, "Would consider having another child?"

I said, "I would have to be married before I would even consider it."

I could see a little disappointment in his face, but he understood how important the commitment was to me and for the child. Children needed both parents, and I struggled alone to raise the two I had. I just couldn't even consider going through it alone again.

We again talked about the trip I had made with my dad back in '81 to see him and how sad he felt when he thought I had moved on. How that's why he didn't make a move towards trying to get back together that weekend. I felt so bad talking about what had really happened and how I needed to be more than just someone's wife in order to feel good about myself. It's so funny how through the years all I had wanted was a career that I could be proud of, but it turned out that I had always overlooked one of the most important things to me all along, which was a good relationship that would last a lifetime.

The first evening we had dinner at my house. From all the bragging he had done about his gourmet cooking, I had to at least try to cook for him once during his stay. I figured steak was a safe bet since grilling had always been one of my specialties. We went food shopping together, and I let him take the lead. I could tell how much he loved it. I had always hated shopping and always put it off as long as I could. But when I was with him, his enthusiasm for the grocery shopping experience was contagious, and I suddenly realized I was actually enjoying myself, despite the fact that our activity was cruising the aisles of the grocery store.

We cooked dinner together, and it was so much fun. I made the steaks, while he prepared a dish with fried onions and peppers to top off the steaks. Ed joined us for dinner as he promised, and we had a great time. I hadn't told my boys too much about Stan, mainly because I didn't know what I could say and what I needed to keep to myself because of his job.

So, one of the first things Ed asked him was what he did for a living and Stan replied "I'm a spy."

Ed's reaction made us both laugh, "Yeah right, I'm 18, not 8 years old".

Ed looked over at me, and he could tell how amused I was at his reaction. I said, "He is telling the truth. I just never mentioned it to anyone because I knew it wasn't something I should talk about for his security."

Once Ed realized that Stan had been and still does work for the CIA, he became very interested in his travels and things that had happened in his life, not to mention what he was still doing for them now. Of course, Stan couldn't share too many of the details, but did share a few funny escapades that he had been a part of.

After dinner, I told the boys to go relax in the living room while I cleaned up.

They left the room smiling, and I could hear them laughing in the other room. Ed and Stan talked for quite a while and got along great. I decided to take a few extra minutes cleaning to give them time alone.

Ed had never had a strong male figure in his life and it was really nice to see how well they got along. I could tell that Stan genuinely wanted to get to know Ed and see what he had planned for his future. It was great to witness that kind of close male bonding happen so easily between them. He spent a lot of time talking to Ed about the government and the job opportunities he would have if he applied with them and even how he could help get him an interview. I hadn't seen Ed interested in a government job before, but after hearing Stan talk about the benefits and security he had with his position, I could tell it opened up a new avenue for Ed to think about.

I finally ran out of things to clean in the kitchen and decided to join them.

Stan smiled as I came in, and I could see that Ed was having a good time.

Stan said, "Now that you are here, I want to tell you about an episode that happened one year on Halloween when I was in a different country doing my spy thing."

He smiled and winked at me, "I had gone to a party with a lot of diplomats. I can't tell you what country or why I was there but some of the events of that night I can discuss. I was dressed as the *Hunchback of Notre Dame* and had gotten pretty drunk that night. I decided I would walk back to my hotel instead of taking a cab. Being as drunk as I was, I was staggering down the street trying to keep from falling down on my face when a man came from behind a corner and said 'Mr. Stan, we need to take you back to your hotel.'

"I immediately knew who the man was, even in my drunken condition. Knowing I was always being watched, I went with the man, and the hunchback stumbled safely back to where I should have been." He laughed as he reminisced about his adventure and how similar it was to the movies at times. I could see the story teller in him hadn't changed as he went on about his travels.

The three of us talked for hours, and everyone seemed to get sleepy at the same time. It was late and I setup the couch downstairs for Stan and then gave him a quick peck on the cheek before heading upstairs. I wasn't sure what he was feeling and wanted to give it some time. I was so intimidated by the feelings from years ago that were returning. It was very hard leaving him that night, but I didn't want to push him away. I wanted to keep talking and getting re-acquainted with him all night but was torn about what he would think of me.

It took me hours to get to sleep that night, and it was one of the most interrupted nights of sleep I hadn't had in a while. I had to fight the urge to go downstairs and be with him. The next morning, I woke early and found him awake downstairs. He told me my son's cat harassed him all night playing with his arms or legs, whichever came out from under the blanket. I felt so bad because he hardly got any sleep. We were both suffering from a lack of sleep that night.

The next day we sat and talked and talked, catching up on the years we'd been apart. I couldn't believe after all the time on the phone and emails and even the day before, we weren't running out of things to say or talk about. We had so many dreams and plans for the future that were still the same.

He talked about more details of his failed marriage, and I was impressed with how he took as much of the responsibility for its failure.

We talked about the "what ifs" and how deep down, we really were not sorry for the way things had turned out. After all, we wouldn't have the 5 great boys we have now if we had gotten married back then. I could tell that his boys were as important to him as mine are to me. They'd been our drive during the rough years and our reason for living. It was interesting how both of us moved our own happiness aside and found our misplaced happiness in our children's, how their futures became more important than what was happening in our own personal lives. We both centered our lives on them and made that our only goal and purpose.

He described to me meeting his real dad finally at the age of 48 and how excited he was to be an older brother to the two brothers he never knew about. He was so amazed that searching his last name on the internet gave him those details and even how to contact them.

One of the things that really amazed him was that he found out that his dad was one of three brothers, he now was one of three brothers, and he ended up having three boys. Little things like this just fascinated him, how generations can have so many similarities while having no knowledge of each other or their family history. He always looked deeper into the whys and how to's of life.

He talked about the sad times that came with his job. "I didn't really have the opportunity to make close friends because of my job. The closest I had was a good friend from work, Terry. But even with him, our knowledge of intimate details of each other's jobs couldn't be shared. He is about the only person I'm really close to. My boys were my main confidants, but that's not always the same as a close friend."

"I know what you mean. For different reasons, I really only have a few very close friends." I said.

"I'm just getting to know my real dad and brothers. Again, I can only share so much, and it's hard to get really close." He said frowning as he thought about the past. "My job put up a wall so no one could get really close, at least not as close as you and I were back then. I don't share too much about my life with anyone. When I think about it, all those years of privacy could have a lot to do with the failure of my marriage. There were only so many things we could share, and my daily life wasn't one of them."

One of Stan's new hobbies he was so excited to tell me about was how he learned how to cut stones. He met this older man in Arizona where he lived for a few years before he got married. The man taught him how to carve stones into beautiful pieces of jewelry.

"I would love to make you a stone and mount it into anything you would like."

"I actually do have something I would love you to look at. My mom gave me this ring a few years ago, and the stone fell out of it. It was one of my favorites, and I'd love to be able to wear it again."

"Let me see it." Stan said.

I brought him the ring. It had an oval shaped opening where the missing stone had been with 2 small diamond chips on one side and one on the other. One of the diamond chips had also fallen off and was lost.

He was so thrilled, and asked if he could take it home and cut me a new stone for it and then mount it for me. "I know I have a diamond chip to replace the missing one for you. If not, I will order it."

Of course, I let him take it. I handed it to him right away. I knew I would get it back with a beautiful stone and I couldn't wait to see what he would do with it. I was thrilled to think that my favorite ring would again have a stone in it. The ring would be a gift from my mom and a stone cut from his hands.

He asked, "What kind of stone had been in it?

I said, "An opal."

He asked, "What color was it?"

I was so surprised at the question, and said, "I didn't know that opals came in more than one color. The one it had was off-white."

Thinking he would do this for me was so special. Anyone can buy a gift, not everyone is willing to spend time to make one.

The second night, being the undomesticated woman I am, I took him out to dinner. He teased me how he was going to teach me to cook, and we would spend hours together in the kitchen. He kept saying how he was going to fatten me up… how scary that was. I'd been successful all my life to keep my weight under control, and he found such pleasure in saying how he'd fatten me up.

After dinner, Stan and I went to *Stone Mountain* and watched the laser show. It was so romantic lying under the stars with him reminiscing about the past 30 years and all he'd been through. He would look into my eyes and he'd just smile. I felt so warm inside, and I wished we weren't in such a public place. We brought a blanket to sit on and sat together watching the show. He let me lean on him, and I felt him kiss my head like he used to on the rock. I turned and gave him a small kiss back… after all we were in public. I was wondering if he was feeling the same as I was, if the old spark was still there for him as it was for me. As much as I was enjoying the moments with him at the park, I couldn't wait to get back home and be alone with him. After the show, we walked back to the car hand in hand and he mentioned waiting for all the traffic to go before we left. I almost wondered if he wanted to sit and maybe park for a while, but in my excitement to get back home and be alone, I told him it should go pretty fast, and luckily it did. I could tell he wanted to stay a little longer, but my anticipation on getting home and being alone made me want to leave immediately. We got back to the house within a half hour.

During the drive home, I offered to let him sleep in my bed upstairs. I knew I would be sleeping in my chair, and he could have the bed. I could tell Stan was the same respectful person he'd always been, and I had no worries about him sleeping in the same room with me. He was never the type to take advantage of anyone, especially me. Besides, I felt bad he had to go outside to smoke the night before, and I was hoping it would make the night last longer.

We were sitting there watching TV, and he came and sat on the floor in front of my chair. He turned to me and asked if he could kiss me. It brought me back to the first time he asked 30 years ago. I knew immediately when he asked he wasn't talking about a small peck, he was referring to the kind of kiss you give someone you care very deeply for. It was a long and passionate kiss, one that brought me back 30 years, one that brought back all the feelings I had felt for him 30 years ago. He told me he had been waiting since he got off the plane to do it and wasn't sure how I felt about him. The kiss showed the both of us that all of the feelings were still there, and maybe this time, it would be the right time for us to finally be together.

While still holding my hand, he said "I have something to give you."

He put his hand in his pocket and pulled out a ring. He placed it in my hand, when I looked down to see what it looked like; I saw it was the Turkish wedding band he had given me 30 years ago. He said, "After you left the woods that day of our breakup; I went back and searched for the ring and couldn't believe I found it. I carefully straightened it out and put it away in case I ever saw you again."

He put the ring on my finger and said, "I never gave the ring to anyone else; it was and always will be the symbol of the love we'd always had for each other."

I knew from that moment that we were going to be together finally. I realized what that ring meant to him and what it now means to me. That was the one symbol of how much we still care and love each other for all these years. With all we'd both gone through, we never stopped caring for each other. That night, I think we both realized, even after all the years apart, our feelings for each other still were just as strong.

That night, we made love and it was a night I will never forget. Stan had such a way of always wanting to be sure I was taken care of and happy. He told me just seeing my reactions and feeling the closeness we had was all he needed. He was so gentle and caring but at the same time, he was very much a man. I could tell how surprised he was that I wanted to be with him as much as he wanted to be with me. It was one of the most romantic evenings of my life. I think we barely got 4 hours of sleep.

On Sunday morning, we drove to Kevin and Lisa's house to get ready to go to Columbus, GA to see the show. I could see Lisa was anxious to see how we were getting along and couldn't wait to get me alone a moment to talk. Luckily, Kevin and Stan were getting along, and it gave her and me a few moments to talk. I told her about the night before, how special it was between us and how he seemed to be feeling the same towards me.

I showed her the ring and told her the story behind it. She smiled, gave me a hug and said, "You deserve this in your life after all you've been through."

We decided to take separate cars because Kevin had to return early Monday morning for work. Stan and I planned to stay at the hotel until it was time to take him to the airport for his 11:00 flight.

Lisa had done some research to see if there was anything else we could do that day because the show wasn't until 7:30 at night. She found a place that was a drive-through safari.

We stopped off at the safari first before going to the hotel. The safari was set up where you rent a van, ride in a bus with a group of people or you could even take your own car, and you drive through acres of land where the animals run free. We looked around and there were quite a few kids running around so the four of us decided to enjoy the time alone, and we rented the van. No one wanted to drive their own car because of the damage that might occur from the animals. We were right not to have taken our own vehicle.

The drive through took us over an hour to complete, and we laughed the entire time. Lisa seemed to have attracted the animals the most, and she kept jumping onto Kevin's lap to get away from them. Lisa took lots of pictures and Stan, of course, brought his video camera.

A lot of the animals were very bold and would come right up to the van and stick their head inside trying to get food. We ran out of food about three-fourths of the way through and kept getting stuck behind other vehicles feeding the animals. This brought their attention over to our van, and most weren't happy with us not having any food. We were jumping back and forth from one side of the van to the other depending on where the animals were.

As much fun as we'd had, seeing the end of the tour was a relief. We all agreed we should have purchased more food.

We got into our separate cars, with Stan and me taking up the rear. We drove straight to the hotel to freshen up before the show.

After we checked in, Stan and I went to our room to be alone for a bit. We contemplated being late for dinner but decided not to be rude to Lisa and Kevin, and got ready for dinner.

It was so nice seeing Stan and Kevin get along so well. Kevin and Lisa have been very special friends of mine for over 12 years, and it meant a lot for them to like each other.

I really hadn't told Lisa or Kevin what he did for a living prior to his visit, again not knowing how much I could say. During dinner, Stan and Kevin talked about some of his escapades, and Lisa later admitted to me that she asked Kevin if he really believed him. Lisa had always been very skeptical of other people, but I know it was only out of worry for me.

Because of some of the tales he told, I could see why she was skeptical; it was a life that not many people had led, and some of it was what you would expect to come right out of a movie. Kevin did believe him but until Lisa and I got to talk alone, she wasn't really sure. Lisa and I had always shared everything, so the fact that I'd never mentioned he worked for the CIA to her before made her a little doubtful about the whole thing. I had to explain to her about why I didn't mention anything, and she understood.

After dinner, we went to the show and had the best time…. We had great seats and never laughed so much. The entire day was a success, and I felt Stan had a good time with all of us.

That night, when we got back to the hotel, my back had been hurting from all the sitting, between the ride and the show. I was so disappointed that I couldn't cover up the pain I was in. I didn't want to ruin the evening, but my back always had the worst timing.

I could see in his face how bad he felt for me and said "I just want to hold you and take care of you."

We stayed up talking instead.

He said, "I'm afraid to start a relationship because of my bout with cancer two years ago. I was very lucky to have even survived. I'm just afraid that I'm not going to be here very long, and I couldn't put you through that kind of hurt."

I responded with tears in my eyes, "Let me make that decision, and besides, it's a little late for me to turn back now. I already know I want to see where this will go."

He smiled, "I'm glad. It's too late for me too."

It was so great that we both wanted to see where this relationship would lead. We both knew it was going in the same direction.

I kept my ticket as the beginning of what I hoped would be lots of small memories we would share of our special times together. The next morning, as hard as it was, I drove him to the airport. We talked about the next trip we would have together and how he couldn't wait to tell his oldest son, Matt, about this trip. I had to remind him not to go into too many details, and he just smiled. I could tell the details were definitely on his mind, and he would have a hard time hiding them.

We got to the airport early, but he insisted that I didn't spend any more money, even on parking. He said he'd just go wait at the terminal. I watched him go in and left when he got out of site. I felt such sadness as I drove off and overwhelmed with the feeling of wanting to turn back to the airport. The weekend went too fast, and I couldn't believe how leaving him affected me. I didn't want the time to end.

I thought about stopping by and seeing Lisa on my way home so we could talk about the weekend but I was still tired and decided to go home. I decided to take a nap and had a dream he called me from the airport. He called to say that he'd changed his mind and was going to stay a while longer. I was so disappointed to wake up and realize it was only a dream.

It turned out his flight was delayed an hour, and he ended up spending three hours alone at the Atlanta airport. If only he would have called, I would have come back and waited with him. I yelled at him that if he'd only had a cell phone, I would have been able to spend more time with him. But then, it would have been harder to say goodbye again.

He called me as soon as he got home and we started to make plans for our next rendezvous. Neither one of us wanted to wait. The time apart was driving us crazy already and we tried to think of ways to shorten the distance between us. We lived over 600 miles apart, and making a last minute trip wasn't that simple. It was a 10 ½ hour drive each way, and we knew we would need more than a weekend for a trip like that. With me working most Saturdays, we were very limited.

A few days later, he mailed me a jar of joint vitamins for my back that he wanted me to try. He was very big into vitamins now and really wanted to do anything to help get me out of pain.

He also sent Lisa an empty cigarette carton for the brand he smoked. They were called *Jacks* and looked like a *Jack of Clubs*. When she had seen the brand of cigarettes he smoked during his visit, she immediately asked him for an empty pack just to see what she could make with it. I think he was just as interested to see what she would make as I was. Instead of just a single pack, he sent her the empty carton which had a much bigger picture. And, of course, this was made with cardboard instead of the flimsy paper from the pack he had given her already.

It was so great how he always thought of details for everyone and remembered just little comments that people would make. It was like he would make a mental note to himself and would always surprise people with his sincere little gifts and thoughts. Here is the note he sent:

Hi DEE,
PRomise ME you'll TAKE THESE
EVERY DAy! ☺
(THE 'JACKS' CARTON iS FOR LiSA
LUV, ME

Every time we spoke after that, one of the first things he asked was if I was taking my pills. He wanted to know if they were helping, and he said he would keep getting them for me if they did. Of course, with the way I am with taking pills, the only time I remembered was when he called and reminded me. The month's supply he purchased lasted me three months. Not taking them as I should, I really didn't feel the effects he had described. I'm not sure if they actually helped my back, but every vitamin I took was a reminder of Stan's love for me.

A few days later, another package arrived. It was a bag of raw stones for my ring. All of the stones were uncut, and I couldn't believe all the beautiful colors. I carefully opened the bag, put the stones on a white paper plate and took it outside to really see the colors of each of them.

I called and teased him, "You know that was cheating. I wanted you to pick out the stone for me."

He just chuckled and said, "But what if you don't like what I pick?"

I told him, "I selected three of my favorites and will mail them all back to you." Not knowing what was really involved, I figured in case the one I liked wasn't big enough, it would be easier to give him a few choices to select from. I mailed him back the stones and tried not to think about the ring. I had no idea how long it would take and didn't want to hurry him.

I thought a lot about the things we talked about that had happened in our lives during our time apart and how much he had done with his life. Even with all the hurt he'd been through, he had accomplished so much. He was set for the rest of his life because of his careful planning and saving. He still owned the land between his mom's and my mom's houses and had invested in some stocks. He had been with the CIA just eight months shy of 30 years, and once he reached it, he was going to retire with a nice pension.

He had so many plans for his retirement and how he would spend that time. He wanted to travel more and show me the places he had been and take me to the places he always wanted to go to. I was so proud of the man he had become and could tell that he loved the person I turned into also. We had gone through the rough years with other people and now it was our turn to be happy together. I knew this was the start of something very special between us.

Chapter 7
The Spontaneous Rendezvous
July 2005

I immediately made flight arrangements to go up to Maryland and meet his boys on the first weekend it was affordable for me. The first flight wasn't for a month, and we both couldn't wait for the time to pass. We talked on the phone every day and decided that we wanted to see each other before then. With the distance between us, we needed to find a spot somewhere in the middle where we could meet and it not be as much of a distance for either of us. Stan got online and found the halfway point for us. He originally started looking on highway 95, thinking it would be the easiest route to meet on, but I had told him about another route that I used to take whenever I would drive to visit my mom in New Jersey many years ago. It went through the Virginia Mountains and was a beautiful ride. I thought it would be a nice, romantic atmosphere for our visit.

He found a small town called Whytheville, Virginia which was about halfway between our homes. It had been two weeks since we saw each other, and it would only be another two weeks before my scheduled flight to Maryland, but neither of us could wait to be together again. We had planned to meet sometime on Friday night and leave on Sunday to return home.

My original plan was to go to work and then drive up at four when I got off. After thinking about it, I called in sick Friday and left by 10AM to meet him. This was the first time in years I had called in sick, and I felt guilty for only a few minutes. My desire to be with him overshadowed my guilt.

I talked him into borrowing his son's cell phone for the trip so we could keep in touch during our drive. Once I got on the road, I called his house to see where he was. His oldest son answered the phone and said he had gone to the store and would be right back. I was a little disappointed he wasn't on his way yet, but then realized I could get there before him and get cleaned up before he arrived.

The drive seemed to take forever, and I found myself doing over 80mph quite a few times. It was a beautiful drive through the mountains that I remembered so well. It had been at least six years since I'd driven that route and it was refreshing to see how much I did remember. The scenery was breathtaking, and I couldn't wait to share it with him. I felt like a teenager again; the anticipation of being with him made me glow. I was the happiest I'd been in a long time, and Stan was the reason.

He had made reservations at a Holiday Inn just off highway 81. It was the perfect halfway point because he was taking 81 South, and I was on 77 North, when the two highways intersected, the hotel was right off the exit. It was just above the Blue Ridge Mountains.

I got to the room and decided to take a shower and then lay down for a while until he arrived. I called him to let him know I was there and had checked in. He arrived about an hour after I did, and he was so disappointed that I had gotten there first. He said he had wanted to prepare the room for me. He showed up with two bags, one with clothes and the other was a cooler with some special things he had bought for the weekend. He looked around for a refrigerator, but the hotel didn't have them in the room.

I asked why and he smiled… He said, "I left the cooler in the kitchen while I was packing and had bought some whipped cream and honey to have a little fun with. Matt and Dave looked in the cooler and asked what the whipped cream was for. I just smiled, and they knew without me saying anything. They were disappointed that I was taking it. It was one of their favorites. They said, "I guess you're not bringing any back with you then."

I was so embarrassed that he told them what it was for, but then again, they were happy that their dad was finally with someone again. I had to warn him, "When I visit your house, you better not have any whipped cream in the fridge. Do you know how embarrassed I would get if your boys mentioned it?"

I could tell how much he was enjoying sharing his happiness with them, even if it meant sharing some intimate details. I actually think he enjoyed sharing some of those intimate details, but luckily, he did have a line of how much he would share.

The first night, we had dinner at the hotel and then spent the night alone in the room.

We decided to watch a movie first, and both of us had a hard time concentrating on it. We rented *National Treasure*, a new movie starring Nicholas Cage. During the movie, there were some references about the government, and I'd glance over and ask, "Is that real?"

He'd just wink and smile to let me know there may have been some bit of truth but never gave away anything he really knew.

I had made some of my own special plans for the weekend and couldn't wait to surprise him. He had a way of making me feel like a woman. The way he looked at me and held me sent chills through my body. No other man had ever made me feel the way he did. I borrowed a couple of outfits from Lisa to wear in the evenings, just to see what kind of reaction I would get from him. I had never felt comfortable enough with Billy or even my ex-husband to wear anything promiscuous; they had such a way of making me feel cheap. I never got that feeling from Stan; he only made me feel like a woman.

I decided to wear this very sexy long night gown with lace in just the right places. When the movie was over, I had excused myself to the bathroom for a few minutes and said as I was leaving the room, "I have a surprise for you."

When I came out of the bathroom, he had been in the middle of saying something to me but as he turned to look at me his eyes lit up, and he stopped mid-sentence. I could tell by the look in his eyes how he was feeling, and it was one of the most exciting evenings we had ever had. I don't think we slept three hours that night. It was an evening he mentioned quite often after that trip.

The next morning we got up and we were starving, but we were both very much in need of a shower after the long evening before. I was very surprised when he asked, "Would you like to have some company?"

I'd never taken a shower with anyone before and was easily convinced to give it a first try. I smiled, kissed him and said, "I'd love some company."

Let's just say that we went through a lot of hot water during that shower, and it was the first of many we had together. After that, showers just weren't the same and never will be.

That weekend was so special. We walked, talked and spent all the time alone. That was going to be our special meeting place. The small town really didn't have much to do, but that was what we both wanted. The weekend before had been July 4th, and the town must have had a pretty big celebration with all the decorations we saw in the main square. That weekend, it was like a ghost town. We drove down to the main street and parked the car. We decided to walk around and see the town close up. We ended up in the town's small park and sat for hours on the bench just watching the people go by and making plans for our future together. We both loved the mountains and talked about where we would like to live in the future.

That night we rented another movie in the room. Of course, we had another very special night together again. We both knew that this was what we had been waiting so patiently for all our lives. Stan started talking about marriage, and I could tell he was trying to see how I felt about it.

All I could say to him was, "You can't really ask anyone until you have gotten your divorce."

After I said those words, I wondered if I would regret it, but I knew deep down I couldn't even think about it while he was married. I wondered if it would stop him from ever saying those words to me.

He said, "My marriage is just a piece of paper and doesn't mean anything to me anymore."

I asked, "Is that all it would mean between us?" I knew how strongly he'd always been against divorce and how much he never had wanted that to be a part of his life.

He said, "I don't need a piece of paper to say how much I love you."

He walked over to me and held me. I said, "But with you it's different and I would want everyone to know how special we are to each other."

He smiled, kissed me gently and said, "I would have always been proud to call you my wife."

We got up the next morning and turned on the TV. They were predicting tornadoes in Atlanta, and we realized it would be best for my safety that I should leave by 10AM to try to beat the storms before they arrived. As we were packing, he put the honey in my suit case and said, "Save it for our next visit. I won't need it without you."

The whipped cream was gone and he said he would get more.

We showered together one more time and as I was dressing and putting on my jewelry, something didn't feel right to me. Since the day he gave me back the ring, that was always the first one I put on each day. For some reason, that morning I picked up one of my other rings and put it on first. I remember thinking to myself *"I didn't put his ring on first like I had been doing."*

I'm not sure why, but it felt so strange for some reason.

I hated to leave so early, but he helped me pack my car. He stood outside and watched me pull away. I saw him walk back into the hotel to get his own things packed. He called me not too long after I left and said that the hotel had put the charge on my credit card, and he wanted me to know that he made sure it was moved back to his. I had to laugh, he always felt he should pay for everything, and I kept telling him I was in this as much as he was and wanted to give as much as he did.

My drive home was the loneliest I had ever gone through. It was ripping my heart out to leave him again. I knew I wanted to be with him and could tell he felt the same for me. I called him as soon as I got home to let him know I was safe and had beaten the storms. If only I had known, I really could have left a few hours later than I did, and I still would have beaten the storms. Darn those weather men; as always, they can never be counted on…

When I called, he was still on the road from all the traffic he ran into and said he would love the company. We were on the phone for the remainder of his ride. We talked about the weekend and how hard it was to leave each other. I couldn't believe how close we had gotten in the two visits we had and that he felt as strongly for me as I did for him.

When he arrived home we finally hung up. I had gone outside for a cigarette before I started getting into my normal routine again and noticed that some debris was on my property from a neighbor's tree. I picked up the pieces and put them into the trash on the side of her house. I went inside and started a load of laundry and then started to unpack. While I was unpacking, I thought I better take off my rings before I lose them or lose a stone out of one. To my horror, when I looked at my hand, the Turkish wedding band was gone. I figured it must have slipped off recently because I could still feel its presence where it had been on my finger. I searched everywhere with no success. I couldn't believe it was gone!!! I felt such a sinking feeling in the pit of my stomach. Stan had kept the ring for over 30 years and here I lost it within weeks of him giving it back.

I knew I had to tell him; this was something I couldn't keep from him. My next visit would be in two weeks, and he'd notice it was gone. I was hoping that telling him would somehow help bring it back to me. I was devastated. Although he took the news pretty well, I could hear how disappointed he was. I told him I wouldn't stop looking for it. I cried for days…. I somehow felt that if we didn't make it this time it was because of my carelessness. That was the most significant symbol of our relationship, and I knew I had to find it somehow. I retraced my steps and couldn't find it anywhere. I even called the hotel just to be sure I hadn't left it there.

This was the first time he said he loved me…. That he never stopped from all those years ago. I wanted so much to tell him I felt the same, but I had to remind myself that he was still married; I just couldn't say it to him yet. Even hearing how he felt, didn't help the loss I felt about the ring. It was a very strong symbol of how we still felt for each other, even after all of these years. He promised me we would find other symbols of our love that I could cherish just as much as I did that wedding band.

He still had not gotten a divorce from his wife, and after my experience with Billy, I was having a really hard time with knowing he was married. He tried to ease my fears when he explained the whole situation between them and why the divorce had not happened yet. He told me that after his wife left him, they skirted around the issue for the first few years, mostly out of it being a very uncomfortable subject. They kept in close contact because of their three boys and both of them felt that, regardless of what their relationship was like, the boys were the most important. When he came down with cancer she didn't want to bring up the divorce because he was so sick, so it just hadn't happen yet.

They remained friends for the sake of their boys and had a close relationship, even though he said there was no chance they would ever get back together. He said he loved her but in a different way, more like a close relative than a spouse and that she felt the same way about him.

He told me after they'd split up he found some emails she had written to other men telling them how she couldn't stand to have him touch her anymore. After that incident, he said he could never feel that way towards her again.

I tried to put myself in her shoes but could never imagine not wanting him to touch me or be with me. I had never felt that way towards him even back 30 years ago when I broke up with him. I always loved him and wanted to be with him. It was just that I had to make something of myself before I could commit.

Stan asked me again if I would consider having his child. I knew he wanted a girl so badly, and he really felt we would be together for the rest of our lives and wanted to share that special bond with me. We talked about it, and I let him know how scared I was, especially because I wasn't sure if I could physically carry a child. I also let him know that I couldn't even consider it without being married.

He smiled at me and asked, "Do you think your sister would carry it for us? I'm worried about your back and health issues."

I responded, "I can't ask her until you get your divorce."

But at the same time, I felt so close to him and knew that I wanted to give us a chance. That evening I emailed him and told him that I wasn't the type to sleep around and when I made the decision to sleep with him that first time, it wasn't just for a one night stand. I wanted to see where our relationship could go.

His said, "I wouldn't take the chance of losing what we have for a one night stand. That is all it could be with any other woman."

We both agreed that we wouldn't see anyone else.

The next week I called Stan's house and Matt answered. Before I had a chance to say it was me, he said, "Hey Dee, I'll go get dad for you." I heard him in the background, "Dad, Dee is on the phone."

When he finally got to the phone, he told me he'd been working on the stone for my ring. He was so happy to hear my voice and couldn't wait to tell me about the stone he picked out of the ones I sent back to him. He was working on the most colorful one that I had picked from the group. I couldn't wait to see it. He told me he wanted to have it ready for me when I got there in a few weeks.

We talked and emailed constantly, and neither of us could wait for the next time we would be together. Here are some of our conversations:

----- Original Message -----
From: "Dee"
To: "Stan S"
Sent: Tuesday, July 19, 2005 2:38 PM

I guess you were a good boy and went to work today.... I was thinking that in case you did need to reach me during the day, here's my work number: ***-***-**** x ***** I normally leave my cell phone in my purse deep inside one of my drawers and can't always hear it. This week is dragging on and on... somehow I think the weekend will fly right by. Isn't that always the case.

Just thinking of you... love,
Dee

-----Original Message-----
From: Stan S
Sent: Tuesday, July 19, 2005 6:35 PM
To: Dee
Subject: Re:

I did, but I came home early to take Buster in for his hair cut...never got around to it yesterday because of the plumber. Jeez is he funny looking!! Thanks for the phone number...I'll give you my private line at work when you get here...don't want to send it out over the air waves or internet for obvious reasons. Only my immediate family has it, and now you qualify. :) I know...the week is dragging, but I've had a lot going on and that's helped (me anyway). Still, I seem to be always thinking of you...when I'm grocery shopping, it's with you in mind. When I see someone I haven't seen in a while, I want to tell them about you. Guess you're a part of me now. Well, dinner is in need of cooking....lamb chops, asparagus and rice...just a simple meal tonight. Not much else planned...probably make it an early night so I can get into work earlier and conserve some hours.

Anyway, see you soon honey!

Love, -Me-

I received a call from my dad just before the trip. He said he needed to talk with Stan. He wouldn't tell me what about, but I told him I would give Stan his number, and it would be up to Stan whether he would call back.

Then my father said, "I did a lot for him back then and I hope he can help me out with something."

Not knowing what this was about and knowing how my dad can get when he wants something, I felt obligated to tell Stan of my apprehension and that I was a little uncomfortable in him helping him. I didn't want to take any chances with our relationship this time. It was too soon in our relationship to start asking for favors.

I had no idea what my father would request, but I knew it was Stan's nature to oblige and be as helpful as possible to everyone. I really wanted things to work out this time.

I wasn't sure why it bothered me so much how, deep down, I felt wary of anything that could possibly get in our way this time. It felt so unreal, that our relationship could be snatched away from me in a heartbeat, and I feared that getting together permanently would never happen for us.

Lisa was my transportation to and from the airport for my first flight to visit Stan in Maryland. She was supposed to pick me up at my house that morning, so I could leave my car at home.

When I realized she was late and I might miss my flight, I called her. She had overslept, so I raced to her house instead. Luckily, she lived on the way to the airport and I left my car at her house for the weekend.

Lisa was as excited for me to go see Stan as I was. I could tell she really liked him and wanted to see it work out for us, even if it meant me moving away.

Chapter 8
Meeting His Boys
August 2005

It was fascinating how cooking was such a big part of his life now. He explained to me how his passion for food came about.

"With the assignments we had, we couldn't talk to anyone about them, not even the guys we worked with. We had to find something we were allowed to talk about and food was the tradition in the CIA. It became a competition between us to see who the best cook was. I guess I took it to an extreme and became a master chef." He said with a big smile. "I love cooking. I've gotten my boys to try so many foods they would never have dreamed of."

With the traveling he'd done, he'd gotten to know the cuisine from different countries and the styles of cooking from each. He and everyone he worked with became gourmet cooks. Cooking contests became their big sport. He bragged about the chili contests he won and how that was his specialty. He couldn't wait to have me try it.

I thought of how my cooking wasn't much to be desired. But I did have at least one thing I could out-do him on, and that was my mom's homemade cheesecake. He wasn't into making desserts. Stan loved making big meals. So the desserts, we decided, would be my job. I made two cheesecakes for the trip, one for our dinner together and one they could freeze for another night.

With the heightened security at the airports, I was wondering if they would even let me fly with them. I wasn't sure what they considered "undesirable" baggage to be. I called the airline, and they said that I might have to leave one as a bribe in order to get them onboard. I emailed the airport security also, and they had the same response. I guess they still have a sense of humor.

Luckily, when I went through security, they didn't ask the contents of my bag and both of them made it safely onboard.

My first trip to Maryland was wonderful. It was a four-day weekend that seemed to fly by too fast. When I got there, Stan was waiting by the baggage claim for me with the biggest smile. It felt so good to be in his arms again. He didn't let go of my hand until my baggage came.

His house, he had said, was about a half hour from the airport, but it took us over two hours to get there. Of course, part of the time was spent shopping at a grocery store for him to pick out a few things for dinner. That was the first time he admitted to me how much he really enjoyed food shopping and how he went every day. He never froze his meat; it always had to be fresh. He was like a little kid in a candy store when he was shopping; he really enjoyed it. I stood a little behind and watched him carefully pick our dinner for that night.

We hit traffic going back to his house, and I remembered our dessert. I worried that the cheesecakes would spoil. The road to his house took us through a place called Germantown that was quite built up and had a lot of stores and malls on each side. I remember noticing how built up the area was and thinking to myself that I really didn't think I would like living there. It reminded me too much of home.

He finally pulled off the main highway onto a narrow road with a sign, *"To White's Ferry"*.

I remembered him telling me about having to take a ferry ride each day to get to work, but I never imagined how small and picturesque it would be. We drove down this winding road that barely fit one car, but he laughed saying everyone considered it as a two-lane road.

We passed this mansion on the left that reminded me of the homes in *Gone with the Wind*. The large front yard with trees planted in just the right spots, still giving a beautiful view of the large home set up the high behind them.

The narrow road took a sharp right and down a hill where you could see the loading dock for the ferry and the beautiful Potomac River. There were a few cars ahead of us and everyone lined up as if they all knew what to do.

In the distance you could hear the engine of the ferry roaring across the river. As it approached, I saw this small simple flat boat that fit about 20 cars each trip across the Potomac River.

Everyone patiently waited for the cars to come off the ferry before the captain directed everyone waiting to a position on the ferry they would have for the ride across the river. He positioned the cars in two rows across and 10 rows deep.

We stayed in the car during the short 10-minute ride across the river.

The scenery was beautiful and I couldn't believe how peaceful it was. It was a gorgeous, sunny afternoon. Even with the engine of the ferry roaring us across the river, it seemed so peaceful. We sat holding hands and staring out the windows. It reminded me of a Norman Rockwell painting.

I caught him looking at me and I smiled, "What a beautiful ride. I feel like we are going into a different world."

We arrived on the other side of the river, again the captain directed everyone off the ferry and Stan drove off when it was our turn.

As we drove up the small embankment, I saw a small country road filled with big, beautiful and very expensive homes. Each property had acres of undeveloped land surrounding them. He slowed down to show me all of his favorite homes. There was one in particular he asked if I liked. It was set back deep into the property and looked like a cabin. He said, "I had thought about buying it for us to live in."

I loved how he was looking around and making plans for our future, while at the same time throwing out hints to see what I would like.

When we arrived at the house, we were greeted by his youngest son, Dave. He came over to greet me with a hug, but my hands were full, so he grabbed my bags instead. I felt bad I missed that chance and didn't get it again that weekend. Dave didn't spend too much time home that trip.

He was smaller than I expected but very good looking. He was about my height, a small muscular build and short curly reddish hair. His build reminded me of Stan's but the red hair must have been from his mom's side.

I was then greeted by his dog Buster, also known as Butt. He was a short dog with graying hair and had the sweetest personality. He fit in so well with Stan and his sons. I could tell how big a part of the family Buster was, and he warmed up to me immediately.

Stan had a beautiful two story house with 6 bedrooms. It had two entertainment rooms, a dining room/living room, a nice quaint kitchen and two car garage. The first thing he mentioned about the house was the long hallway to the bedrooms that they called the bowling alley. It was long enough to be one. At the very end of the hallway was his room. It was a big room that was twice the size of any of the other bedrooms in the house. He explained, "It has sky lights but I blocked them off with wood. It was too light in there to be sleeping during the day when I worked the night shift."

He then pointed to a beautiful painting of this cabin above his bed. He said, "I always dreamed of living in a house just like that. We could be so happy there."

I loved how he kept referring to our future together and how confident he was that it would happen. He continued to show me the rest of the house with such pride.

The bathroom off his bedroom had a huge old fashioned free standing tub, separate shower stall and was about the size of my bedroom in my house.

As I looked around, I thought the house still had too much his former wife's style. It was very clean and everything in its place. I was very impressed for it being a house of four men. I soon found out that Stan was the neat freak and had to have everything in its place. I quickly learned it wasn't his wife's style I was seeing; it was his.

I briefly met Steve, his middle son, the first night. Steve was a little taller than Stan, short blonde hair and a very athletic build. He smiled and gave me a hug. "I'm so glad to finally meet you. I've heard about you for a long time. I apologize for having plans already, but I will be sure to spend some time before you leave."

I hugged him back saying "I'm looking forward to it."

He had a date and left after hugging his dad goodbye.

So, on the first night, it was Stan and Matt, his oldest, joining me for dinner. Matt insisted on going out to dinner, so we met at their favorite seafood restaurant.

When we walked into the restaurant, Stan pointed over to a table in the corner saying, "There he is."

Matt couldn't have looked more different than his brothers. Matt definitely got his looks from Stan. He had long beautiful black hair that he tied in a ponytail, and he almost looked as if he could be Native American Indian.

He stood to greet me and gave me a big hug. "I'm so glad to finally meet you. Dad has talked about you for years."

I could tell I was blushing, thinking of the things he might have told him.

Dinner was delicious. I order a salmon dinner while the two of them order an all-you-can-eat seafood platter. I learned quickly why they gave us such a big table for just three people. Before I knew it, there were platters of seafood filling every inch of it.

They both ate so much I got full just watching them. The conversation seemed so easy between the three of us. Every once in a while, I had to stop Stan from reminiscing too much about our past. He would just laugh and wink at Matt, making all three of us laugh. I could see the special bond that the two of them had. Stan was so comfortable sharing his memories with Matt.

He proudly said, "I taught Dee how to drive in the Camaro. We had a lot of special memories in that car". I again blushed as he winked at me, knowing full well what he was referring to.

"Ok, we don't have to go into any details about the memories in that car." I had to remind him again. I think he was trying to embarrass me a little but could also see the happiness in his eyes when he reminisced about us.

We had such a lovely evening, and I really liked Matt.

We finished dinner and decided to have dessert at home. Matt drove his own car and followed us to the house.

Stan said as he started the car, "Matt really likes you."

"How can you tell?" I asked.

"Well, he normally will eat real quick and then duck out with his friends. He's following us home. He never does that."

As soon as we arrived at the house, I went straight to the kitchen and cut each of us a slice of the cheesecake, making sure that Matt got the biggest piece. It was the quietest time we spent together.

They devoured their pieces and then Matt asked, "Is there enough for me to have another? That is the best cheesecake I'd ever had."

"We know who will be making desserts for us now." Stan smiled.

I took their plates to the kitchen and cut them each another slice.

When we finished dessert, Stan took me downstairs into his garage and showed me his stone cutting tools and all the stones he already had cut. He showed me one stone that he said he was going to make into a necklace for me once he could find the right setting for it. I could see in his eyes the pride he had in his work and how much he wanted to make me something that I could keep forever. He then took my hand and put my mother's ring back on my finger. He had finished it and didn't tell me.

Even though his stone was done, the ring was missing one very small diamond chip. "I have the diamond chip on order, and it should arrive in a few weeks. That will make the ring complete."

I was so touched by him wanting to make it perfect for me.

He asked, "Do you want the ring now or can you wait until the chip arrives?"

Missing the wedding band he gave me, I told him, "I think I'll take the ring now and will give it back when the diamond arrives. The stone is so beautiful. Thank you." I moved closer and gave him a kiss.

I couldn't stop staring at the ring. I loved it.

He said, "The stone has a slight flaw in it if you look closely under the light. But that's what gives it its authenticity."

He was right, it is the most unique stone I'd ever seen with different shades of green throughout it depending on how the light shown on it. You could only see the flaw he was talking about if you held it a certain way in the light. I loved it, and knowing how it was a special gift from both him and my mother, I knew I would cherish it always.

He then added with a smile, "I am going to cut the two other stones that you had liked for the ring…. Just in case something happens…"

I felt bad, thinking about the ring I'd lost and how nothing will ever be able to replace it, even this one, how I didn't want him to think I was careless. Both my mom's stone breaking and losing his ring were an accident, but I still couldn't feel anything but totally responsible for both of them.

I hadn't even mentioned to my mom about the opal ring's stone being gone, I didn't know how to tell her until now. It was so easy to tell her once Stan replaced the stone, it had been one of her favorites also, and I couldn't wait to show her what he'd done with it.

That night we were watching TV, and he got up saying "I'll be back in a bit. I have something I want to do for you." Then he walked out of the room before I could even respond.

After a few minutes had gone by, he came back into the room and grabbed my hand, "Come with me."

As we walked the long hallway to his room, I wondered what he had done. We walked into his room and he led me into the bathroom.

He had prepared me a bath. He had purchased my favorite bath salts before I arrived and had everything ready for me. I could tell he had spent a lot of time planning for my trip there. There were lit candles throughout the bathroom and bedroom. I undressed as he stood watching me and slipped slowly into the water. As I settled into the soothing hot bubbling water, I asked, "Would you like to join me?"

He smiled, got undressed and joined me.

I don't think I'd ever taken such a long bath, and we both looked like prunes when we finally decided to get out. That was just the beginning of our special night.

I also had made special preparations for my trip and purchased some massage oils to give him a back rub as a surprise. After our bath, I gave him the longest back rub I'd ever given to anyone. Time just seemed to pass so quickly and when I looked down, I realized I was putting him to sleep; he was very relaxed. Of course, he didn't fall asleep; he was just storing up the energy for me. It was one of the most romantic evenings between us.

The next morning was Saturday, and it looked like it was going to be a beautiful day. He hurried and took a shower then rushed to the kitchen. That morning he made me blueberry pancakes from scratch with bacon and fresh squeezed orange juice. I told him, "You're going to make me fat."

"All the more to love" was his response.

He then added, "You're too thin anyway, and I like a little more meat on my woman."

I laughed and said, "I'll fight you the whole way. I love the way you look at me and never want that to fade."

He kissed me and said, "That could never happen regardless of how big you got."

The first thing Stan had planned for the day was a drive in the Camaro.

Matt and Stan were always working on the car to keep it in good shape. I walked around it just to see if I could spot any differences from the last time I had been out for a drive in it with him those many years ago, but it all looked the same. The only thing that caught my eye was the door locks. They were skulls and I teased him that I bet that was Matt's contribution. Of course, they were.

Stan couldn't wait for me to drive the Camaro again. The car still had no power steering and I was worried to drive a stick because of my back. We decided for him to drive instead.

Stan got into the driver's seat and he took off like he was driving in a race. I could see the pride in his face, showing me how it still drove as well as it did so many years ago. We went for a long drive in the countryside near his house. I felt like it was 25 years ago and he was taking us to one of our special places.

It brought back great memories. The car was in great shape for how old it was. I couldn't believe that I was in the car I learned to drive in and had so many special memories in from so many years ago.

We were arriving back into his neighborhood, and he said he had a stop to make. Of course, I knew where it was: food shopping.

Again, I let him take the lead, and I so enjoyed watching him pick out each item like it was the last meal he was to cook, and it had to be special. He occasionally caught me watching him, and he would just smile knowing the fun I was having too.

Stan spent about two hours preparing dinner for us that night. Dave and Matt joined us for a dinner of stuffed chicken and a special sauce with a medley of vegetables and a lovely potato dish. After he summoned everyone to the table, Stan served everyone their meal. It was like watching a gourmet chef at work preparing every step of the meal right down to the gorgeous display on the plate.

I was surprised to see the boys sit there smiling as he served up their plates. They knew how important each step was to their dad, and I could tell they enjoyed it also.

The conversation during dinner was about the boys and what they were doing at school and with their friends. We laughed and enjoyed every entrée served to us.

After dinner, Dave excused himself, as he had plans with his friends.

Again it was Matt, Stan and I left to enjoy the evening. The three of us stayed at the table talking for a while.

Matt got up and offered everyone some wine that he wanted me to try. "It's our favorite red wine." He said as he held up a bottle called *Vampire Red.* It was very good and different from any red wine I had tried.

Once the wine was served, Matt said, "Dee, I just wanted you to know that I'm speaking for all three of us and we approve of your relationship with dad and wish you nothing but the best. We hope to keep seeing you around. I can see how happy you make Dad."

I was so touched and stunned that I didn't know how to respond. I felt the blush come over me, but I managed to say, "You don't know how much that means to me."

Matt stayed with us most of the evening and talked my ears off but at the same time asked me a lot of questions about myself. I was so touched he was trying to get to know me better.

He asked if he could show me some of his drawings and metal work he had done. Matt left the room with a smile.

"He's so proud of the work he has done and I really hope he can make a career out of his artwork." Stan said.

Matt came back in the room with his hands full of different items he had made. The first thing he showed me were these beautiful masks made out of scrap metal. He showed me a sketch pad that he had drawn the original designs on and explained how he turned it into the finished product. I couldn't believe how talented he was.

That night we spent watching TV while Matt showed me the rest of his drawings, and we talked about how he could use his talents toward making art into a career. One of the paintings Stan was most proud of was one Matt did of Stan from a photograph that had been taken years before. It was amazing how immediately recognizable it was. You knew it was Stan. Matt captured the special features in his face and the smile that was uniquely his.

Matt had been drawing for years and had kept a nice portfolio of everything. Both Stan and I encouraged him to find something that would allow him to incorporate his talents into a nice money making venture. At least he would always love to go to work.

Later that evening when we were alone, I asked Stan what prompted Matt's statement after dinner and he said, "It was as much a surprise to me as it was to you. I knew the boys were sad that it would mean the end of my marriage with their mother, and I was very touched that Matt cared that much for my happiness. Besides, that must mean they really like you."

The next afternoon Steve stayed home and spent time with us. It was nice that even Steve couldn't wait to share with me his tapes of him playing high school football. With all the tapes they had of him, you could tell how proud Stan was of him.

That evening I got to know how special each of his kids was to him, the special bonds he held with each of them. They were so talented but unique in their talents.

I learned the special talent that Stan loved the most about Dave was his musical talents. Dave could pick up just about any instrument and play it like a seasoned professional. I could see that his boys were as special to him as mine were to me. You could see how much of his life he put into them, even if they didn't see it.

Saturday night, Matt talked me into watching a movie called *Van Helsing*. Stan was thrilled that we were all getting along so well that just sitting around watching a movie together was enough. All I had known about the movie was that it was about vampires. I felt guilty watching it with them because my sons had tried for months to get me to watch it with them. I just didn't think it was my kind of movie, but it turns out I enjoyed it.

Stan mentioned that his brother-in-law, Josh, stayed with him occasionally and he might stop by one evening. Stan and Josh had a good relationship even though he was separated from Josh's sister. Stan explained that Josh had hit some hard times and needed a place to stay occasionally and with Stan's generous nature, he couldn't say no. Besides, Stan really liked Josh. He smiled as he described him, "He may look a bit rough around the edges, but you'll never find anyone with a bigger heart. It was just dumb luck and unfair deals that wore him down through the years, and unfortunately, you can see it." You could tell that regardless of the bad luck Josh had through the years, Stan would always be there for him.

The three of us were about 45 minutes into the movie when Josh came home. When he first walked in Stan and I were sitting very close to each other on the couch and he had his arm around me. I thought Josh would be a little uncomfortable, but it didn't seem to bother him at all. Stan had said Josh never understood what had caused the split and didn't want to take any sides.

Not moving away from me, Stan introduced us, "Josh, this is Dee".

Josh smiled and shook my hand. "It's a pleasure to finally meet you. I've heard so much about you."

I blushed and said, "It's nice to meet you too."

While Josh was there, it was as if Stan wanted Josh to see how much we did care for each other. He didn't hide anything from Josh or his boys. I felt so welcome from everyone, even Josh. Stan invited him to join us to watch the rest of the movie.

He sat down in the recliner to watch the movie but fell asleep within 15 minutes. Poor guy had just gotten home from a 12-hour work day and was exhausted.

I began to look forward to food shopping time and the things I learned about how to shop for certain foods, what he was willing to skimp on and those items that had to be nothing but the best. A lot of those preferences were also mine; everyone has those certain items they just can't skimp on. I could tell a lot of his budget went towards food. His refrigerator was always full, but he always had a little list to fill, giving him the excuse to shop again.

Stan never grabbed a big carriage at the store; he always took a hand cart. He only wanted to get what was needed for that night. This enabled him to come back with another small list every day.

Stan and I had a lot of serious conversations that weekend about the past and present. We did comparisons between my failed marriage and his; we had very different relationships with our ex's.

Of course, my ex and I did not have a good relationship, while he had a pretty good one with his under the circumstances. I was dealing with an alcoholic; his ex had been through so much with her parent's divorce, they decided that the kids came first and made an effort to get along with each other. How I wished mine had been that simple.

We talked about my relationship with my father, and I explained how I really hadn't heard much from him after we had split up, how I always felt that my dad never really forgave me for not marrying him all those years ago, and we really weren't as close as we had been while I had been dating him all those years ago.

He asked, "Would you quit your job and come live with us? I'm making a decent amount of money that could easily support you, Ed too."

I was so stunned I didn't know how to respond.

"Do you think the amount of money I make is enough to make you happy, do you think we could survive on that amount?" he continued.

I explained, "Money isn't the issue. My ex-husband and Billy felt that it was fine for me work two jobs while they stayed home. I had worked at least two or three jobs at a time since my boys were born, and I couldn't do to you what had been done to me. I want to give as much to our relationship as you are able to. I only have a small retirement built up and just a little bit of equity in my home. I would have to depend on you fully to survive if I came up right away."

I added, "Besides, you have a little matter to take care of before I can make any permanent changes."

He smiled and said he understood. He needed to finalize his divorce first. We would work out how to make it work. I wanted so badly to be with him, but we both agreed we needed to do it the right way.

The day came when it was time for me to leave, and Matt and Steve made sure they were there to say goodbye. I let the boys know how welcome they made me feel. Matt said, "Come back anytime. You put my dad in great mood and he deserves that."

I gave them both a hug, and they picked up my luggage and carried it outside to the car.

I had to look anywhere but at them; I was fighting back the tears. I didn't want to leave and knew I was about to cry.

The ferry ride leaving his town was even worse. We held hands, but neither of us could talk. It felt like this was the dividing line between his world and mine. As soon as we got off the ferry's main road, we were back into civilization. No more beautiful scenery and the feeling of peacefulness, just the feeling of leaving home.

We were still quiet as we arrived at the airport. I got out of the car and walked towards Stan who was unloading my luggage. When he finally looked in my eyes, I could see his were tearing up also.

He smiled and said, "You better go before I don't let you." We hugged and kissed goodbye.

I slowly walked over to the ticket counter and then finally glanced back outside. He was still there… I wanted so badly to go back to him and just forget about getting on the plane.

Something told me, "I can't abandon my life just yet" and I walked to security. I contemplated missing the plane until the time came to get on it. I knew I had no choice but to leave. It was heart breaking knowing that the distance between us meant it would be a while before I could see him again. I knew financially we couldn't keep this up much longer and the visits would become further and further apart.

When I got home, I couldn't stop thinking about my trip and how lonely I felt leaving him. Wondering what he was doing and if he was thinking of me? How were we going to be able to afford to see each other as much as we wanted? I couldn't believe how much I missed him and struggled with knowing I couldn't just leave my life here to be with him.

I was frustrated and had to think of something else. I started thinking about the talk we had about my dad and my boys' father. I felt he didn't understand my feelings. He made one comment that he thought I ran away from things instead of facing them.

He said he couldn't understand why I didn't want my ex in my life.

I tried to explain that I felt the boys were adults and there no longer needed to be any contact between the two of us. I knew he still had a drinking problem, and I didn't want that in my life.

Stan explained that he didn't get that impression because I wasn't willing to bring my ex back into my life. What really made him think that was because of my feelings about my dad, that I felt we needed to keep some type of distance from him, at least for now.

Stan always thought the best of people and felt everyone should get a chance, even a second or third chance, while I'd become very guarded and anyone who had hurt me in my past I kept at a distance as much as possible.

I tried to call him but got no answer, so I sent him this email message instead:

----- Original Message -----
From: "Dee
To: Stan
Sent: Wednesday, July 27, 2005 9:18 AM

I was hoping you would have called me back last night. I wanted to talk to you about a couple of things you said Monday night that really have been bothering me.

I'm wondering if you think I've exaggerated the things I've said about my life. It's actually the exact opposite, I've really down played what has happened and haven't even told you a small portion. You saying that I'm running away from my ex is so far from what it really is. He did leave me a message that night and I returned his call last night. As I thought, he apologized for the message he left and said he didn't remember what he said because he was so tired and had had a few drinks. (aka. he was drunk) He does want to come down and needs a place to stay. If you had ever lived with an alcoholic you would understand the stress and fear that come with every minute of it. I'm not sure why you would even want me to bring that back into my life. If you want to continue to have a relationship with Shelley even after your divorce, that is your decision, but I do not want the same with my ex. The situations are very different and I'm not willing to bring that garbage into my life again. I've worked too hard to get away from that kind of life and have no intention of getting back into that nightmare.

I hope we can talk about this.
Love,
Dee

I didn't know you called...there wasn't anything on the answering machine.
The boys and I were on the phone with Shelley during that time and I didn't hear you beep in. Sorry about that. : (

Whew!! I think you misread a few things I said on Monday... about your ex. I was just offering an opinion and I think I said on Monday that I was sorry I had advised you in the way that I did because I really don't know the situation. I was basing my opinion on how I thought it would be better to face this thing down, but I was wrong and speaking out of ignorance. I don't know what it's like to have a spouse who has a substance abuse problem, but I have had some close contact with those people. As you said, I don't know the half of what you've gone through, and whatever you do about your ex is a decision that only you are qualified to make...I understand that. In Shelley's case, things are so different...I suppose I have a problem with the term "relationship"...it suggests something deep. All I want as far as she's concerned is a friendship and for her to be able to maintain as much contact with the boys as they want. I want to keep the peace and avoid animosity, and (perhaps selfishly) I don't want any bad feeling to develop that would affect her willingness to help out financially from time to time...on her own, without being forced into it legally. We will be divorced though and soon if all goes well. I'm half expecting her to bring it up first. I guess it's just as hard for me to fathom how bad it was and is with your ex as it is for you to understand this business with mine. But you said you were trying to understand, and I promise I will too. No, I don't think you exaggerated, and I don't need proof of what you say to me ever, I just like to bring forward all options and I'm OK with any disagreement you may have with my "alternatives"?

I'm sorry this has bothered you so much, but I'm very glad you said something. Anyway, I'll call you tonight and we can talk about it all some more if you like.

Love,
-Me-

He called me that night and we talked about it. After talking with him I regretted assuming he didn't understand. Really it was me not understanding what he was saying to me. I could tell the distance between us was taking its toll, and we decided to only talk of the future and not the past.

I emailed saying I was sorry and would work on encouraging better communication between us rather than jumping to conclusions. This was his response:

From: Stan
Sent: Monday, August 01, 2005 12:10 AM
To: Dee
Subject: Re: thinking of you

Dee, you never need to apologize to me for the way you feel. One of the things that makes our relationship special is the fact that we can listen to one another's problems without judging or criticizing, and hopefully help the situation...whatever it is. I know you're not used to having a "support system" , but you'll get used to it. Glad I could cheer you up a little, and I'm glad Lisa could provide you with a little distraction. :)

Not much happened today worth mentioning...I was just thinking of what was going on last Sunday. A strange duality....seems like yesterday, but at the same time it also seems like a long time ago...hard to explain. I miss you and it's been so long since I've had such strong feelings that it's hard to interpret the effect it's having on me. You might think I don't feel it as strongly as you, but I do...I just may not be expressing it in the same way. I just know that you're constantly on my mind and in my dreams. Well, I'd better get off to bed. I'll call you tomorrow evening, about 5:30 or so?

I love you!!
-Me-

The distraction he referred to was a night out with Lisa at the local night club in my town. Lisa and I only went when she could get us VIP tickets. It allowed us to stay in the private areas of the club away from all the crowds. It was a nice evening out but the entire time my mind was 600 miles away.

Chapter 9
His Family Vacation
August 2005

I had been having a few medical problems that I didn't want to tell Stan about, but during my visit I slipped up and told him. With all he was dealing with, I didn't really want to tell him or worry him, but he had a way of bringing things out of me that I really wasn't sure I wanted to share or burden anyone with.

I had found a lump a year before that I had removed, and at the time thought it was nothing to really worry about. Unfortunately, it returned even bigger than the first time. I felt it was still nothing, but Stan pressed that I make an appointment with my doctor to get checked out. I promised him I would and called the doctor to make an appointment. I emailed Stan to let him know that my appointment had been set, and tried to downplay any concerns the doctors had.

----- Original Message -----
From: "Dee"
To: "'Stan S'"
Sent: Wednesday, August 03, 2005 6:10 PM

Things are all set for Friday... don't worry about anything, it looks like it's a routine procedure and I'll be just fine. I gave Lisa your number at the house and she'll leave you a message on how everything went.

Talk to you soon... Love,
Dee

During my short visit, we both totally forgot about him giving me his work number.

Stan decided he needed to give me the number immediately. So, he had split the number and put them in an order I only knew how to figure it out. It was actually fun and brought a little fun to our relationship. His little notes and thoughts meant so much to me that I could barely get enough. Even at this stage of our relationship, I wanted more than we already had together. It made me love him more that he always knew what to say and do to help me get through missing him so much.

Each year Stan went on at least a one-week vacation somewhere with his boys. Shelley started going with them again to help rebuild her relationship with their boys. That week, he spent packing and getting ready to go on vacation.

This year, they were going to the *Outer Banks of North Carolina*. It was a beautiful stretch of land off the coast of North Carolina. He told me this would be a good opportunity to bring up the divorce, especially because he preferred to have that conversation alone and in person.

I hadn't heard from him since the email I sent, and I later found out about all the preparation he was going through for the trip. Of course, cooking was the number one item on his packing list.

I wanted that to be what we shared and was a little jealous he was sharing it with her and I wasn't a part of the plans.

The house he rented was supposed to have a full kitchen, but he had to pack his special items. It was hard hearing about all the plans he was making.

At the same time, I was going through my own fears about my surgery. I didn't want to damper any of his plans for the vacation with his sons, so I didn't reach out for his support.

Days went by with no word from him. He finally called the night before my surgery. It was going to be just out-patient surgery to remove the cyst, and I was more uncomfortable than sick but still needed to hear his voice. He sounded so worried, but I could tell he was also preoccupied with the plans for the vacation. He said he would call before he left to check on me.

He called the morning they were leaving and then when they arrived at the place to give me the phone number in case I had to reach him. I missed him so much and wished I was going there, while at the same time understood that he had a purpose for his trip.

-----Original Message-----
From: Stan S
Sent: Thursday, August 04, 2005 12:06 AM
To: Dee
Subject: Re:

I'll stop worrying when I hear you're OK on Friday, and that the docs got all of it. Looks like you called a couple of times today...sorry I missed ya...I was at the grocery store the first time, didn't hear the second time, and fell asleep after dinner. I'll buzz you tomorrow...or you can call me at work up until about 1pm, and at home after 2pm. The last part of the # is 4001.

Hope you sleep well honey....

Love you, -Stan-

Lisa took me for my surgery and luckily, it had only been a cyst and not cancer, which the doctors had warned was a possibility.

I was a little upset with Stan for not contacting me after my surgery. He had always been so caring. I started to question his feelings. Did the trip with Shelly turn into reconciliation?

It was frustrating because I wanted to talk to him every day and become a part of his life, but I was beginning to realize how much he really disliked talking on the phone. It seemed that communication on the phone with him was starting to fade, and instead, I only heard from him via emails.

I don't know why, but it was never enough. I knew deep down my insecurity was coming from him spending his family vacation with Shelley when I so wanted to be there instead of her.

Stan finally called me the Friday night after Shelley left. "Please come out for the weekend. I should have asked you earlier, and you should have been the one here anyway."

I explained, "The drive is over ten hours, and I can't take the time off from work with such short notice."

We spent an hour on the phone talking about his trip and how it hadn't turned out as he'd planned. I could hear the disappointment in his voice. He said he was afraid that it was the last family trip they probably would take. I could hear his tone change when he described the places he'd been that week and how empty he had felt when he thought of me. Each special place, he said he had felt uncomfortable there without me, knowing that I should have been there with him instead.

He told me about the conversation they had about the divorce and how she was receptive to the idea. He said it had gone very well and even tears were a part of the conversation, especially when they reminisced about the past and the boys.

Again, I felt a little jealous. The day of my divorce, my ex and I actually had dinner and had talked and cried about the mistakes we'd made. That was the only thing that made it a little easier to hear about how it had gone with Shelly.

We said goodbye, and Stan promised to let me know when they arrived home on Sunday. Not knowing what time they would arrive home from the trip, I told him to at least be sure and email me when they got home.

From: Stan S
Sent: Sunday, August 14, 2005 7:38 PM

- 158 -

After he returned from his vacation, I was feeling a little unsettled, even after he told me they had agreed to get the divorce. I guess I was looking for details or plans instead of just a discussion. I was beginning to wonder if he wasn't quite over her and still wanted more time to see if it would work. I hated the feeling of insecurity I was beginning to feel but also wondered if it had more to do with my fear, that my past with Billy would be repeated again, than any legitimate concerns.

Stan had told me that his marriage was just a piece of paper and I had heard that from Billy also. I let Stan know that it meant a lot more than a piece of paper to me and could sense his surprise at this. Years ago, it had been me that didn't want marriage, and now it seemed it didn't mean as much to him.

Shortly after he got home from vacation, a package arrived in the mail with gifts from Stan. He had gone to the gift shop at work and got both boys a CIA t-shirt and key chain. Both of them thought they were pretty cool and they loved them.

He had called me the night he mailed the package to tell me about its contents. He didn't mention exactly what he purchased for me, but he did say that it wasn't much but it was the type of gift you would give your 16-year-old girlfriend, and he had thought of me immediately. He said he didn't expect me to wear it but he was working on making those symbols of our new start together. I was excited to see what he could have sent me.

When I saw his gift I felt 16 again. Picturing him giving me this gift back then, it was a heart necklace with "Dee" printed on it and flowers in the background. It was so cute, and I couldn't wait to figure out what I would do with it. I understood what he meant by it being something you would give a young girl and thought, "I'll take it to Lisa's and see what we can come up with." I put it up on a shelf in my bedroom where it was displayed in its box.

Here is the note that came with the gifts:

HI DEE, ED & STEVE,

JUST A FEW THINGS TO LET YOU GUYS KNOW I'M THINKING OF YOU.

ED... LOOKING FORWARD TO A FISHIN' TRIP SOMETIME SOON! KEEP UP THE GREAT WEB-SITE WORK!!

STEVE... GOOD LUCK WITH YOUR NEW DIGS, JOB, ETC. HOPE YOU CAN WEAR THE SHIRT.

DEB... YOU KNOW HOW I FEEL, CAN'T WAIT TO SEE YOU!!

LUV, - STAN -

I missed him so much, but life was beginning to get a bit hectic for the both of us. My oldest son, Steven, was moving out into his first apartment. The thought of my boys leaving home left me seriously thinking about my future and where I would go. It would only be a few years and Ed would be moving out and leaving me alone. The thought of being alone without my sons, while knowing Stan was going to be my future, left me with mixed emotions. I loved being with my boys all the time, but spending every moment with Stan, wherever we ended up, brought such a warm and happy feeling to me. I did have a future to look forward to for once in my life. And what perfect timing, each of us raised our sons and they were ready to move on. It would finally be our turn.

Stan was making arrangements and trips to help his middle son Steve get settled in West Virginia for college. I could tell he was pushing it and trying to fit in too much in a short period of time. As much as I wanted to be with him, I was afraid of him over doing it and possibly getting sick. Of course, he denied it and kept up with his plans and travels for his sons. I knew he was busy, so I didn't push for too much time with him. We both figured we had plenty of time and wanted to make each time together as special as possible. We needed to get our personal lives settled and that was our sons.

----- Original Message -----
From: "Dee"
To: Stan
Sent: Tuesday, August 16, 2005 12:03 PM
Subject: I miss you

I hope you had a good trip to West Virginia. You're travels this month are starting to worry me especially when you talk about trying to fit me in. As much as I want to see you and be with you, your health is more of a concern to me not to mention the money you are spending on everything.

I'm getting very concerned you are pushing yourself, especially this month. Trying to fit me in before our September trip may not be feasible, not just time wise but the money also. We have to be realistic about this and not go overboard or broke trying to be together. I realize you have a busy schedule and do not expect you to drop everything to be with me nor do I want you to put off any tests for your health because you want to save the money to see me.

I guess I'm trying to say, we need to talk about the best way we can do this without it being a financial or physical burden to either of us. I cherish every moment we're together and even just talking on the phone may have to be enough for now. As long as we have some type of communication we'll be ok.

I love and miss you,
Dee

-----Original Message-----
From: Stan
Sent: Wednesday, August 17, 2005 6:53 PM
To: Dee
Subject: Re: I miss you

Hi my Cutie!!

Yes, the trip to WVU was pretty nice...it rained, but it was a lot cooler...just the low 70's. It's really beautiful up there in the mountains...yet another place you'd love. The orientation broke up at about four thirty and the trip one way is about 3 hours...not too bad. It was pretty exciting for both of us...Steve had to change his major from agriculture to exercise/physiology which is pretty much pre-med. He has to take organic chemistry, two biology courses and do an internship in the campus hospital. He's scared to death...not only about that, but also because he signed up for football. If he makes the cut, we may be seeing him on TV in seasons to come. There are 26,000 students there too, and he's pretty excited about the girl situation. I know he'll be a little homesick too though, but he'll get over it. Also, they moved up his move in date to tomorrow...so...it's "on the road again". We're madly packing tonight and hope to get up there by about two in the afternoon...have to wait until after my doctor's appointment.

You're right of course...about dropping everything for us to see each other...I don't expect you to do that either...very

- 162 -

sensible....but, where you're concerned, I find that sensibility takes a back seat. I want to see you. Don't worry, I won't sacrifice my health...that would defeat the purpose wouldn't it? And just to nag a bit....I expect you to start slowing down too and taking care of that bikini body of yours. We'll just have to play it by ear on the meetings. My main concern now is leave time...I want to make sure we have enough for September. I only have 3 days after the OBX trip, but I should be able to save 3 more days and with some creative work scheduling, I can stretch our time together to the week or so that we want. Money IS an issue, but not an insurmountable one...I don't think I'll go broke spending a few hundred for the chance to be with you

Anyhow...better grab a bite then get into the packing again. I'll talk to you soon.

Love and kisses...(all over :)

-Me-

Our phone conversations always began with talking about what we were having for dinner, comparing the main course and all of the dishes that would go along with it. Once a week, I would surprise him with a full menu that I was preparing, but most of the time, I would listen to what he was cooking, and then he would ask what I was having.

My response, I could tell, frustrated him. I would just be silent…. I always told him that I wouldn't lie to him, so I just said nothing instead of telling him what I really had. Most meals were fast salads or nothing. Whenever I said nothing to a question he asked, he knew the answer would be not what he wanted to hear. This drove him crazy and he'd tell me how worried he was that I wasn't eating right. As for answering questions about eating, my answer would always be that I was working on getting back into a bikini for him. We would spend at the least the first 15 minutes just talking about food ….

We both avoided discussing how much we missed each other and how frustrating it was that we weren't together

yet. It's funny how food became the first topic between us as it was with his job.

It was so depressing thinking it would be months before being in his arms again. I knew it was getting to him also and I could hear his frustration when the topic came up. We didn't want to go overboard and spend all the money we had. We figured it would be best to save it for the future.... We kept reminding each other that we had plenty of time.

We didn't realize we wouldn't see each other again until the end of September....

Chapter 10
The Months Apart
August 2005 until September 2005

After my plans falling through to go see my mom in May earlier that year, we discussed spending my birthday with my mom in New Jersey. We again discussed me to flying to DC and then driving up to see our parents together ... His mom and step dad still lived next door to my mom, so we could visit with all of them. I loved the idea of spending my birthday with him and visiting our parents together; I couldn't wait for the time to come.

Through all this time apart from Stan, Lisa was my savior. She listened to hours and hours of me moaning about how much I missed him. The true friend that she is, she just sat, listened and supported me throughout all of my insecurities.

Stan and I continued to correspond via emails and phone calls, giving as much time as possible to each other. I tried to keep him in my daily life. We tried to get together in late August, but it fell through due to money constraints. I could tell the frustration was getting to us both and wondered if maybe the stress of the distance was one reason for not hearing from Stan as often as I wanted.

He would tell me how much it hurt him to hear me upset. It left me conflicted, not knowing whether to tell him how much it was affecting me. Our time together was so important, and I wanted to make each moment as happy as possible.

Talking about being together became a very sensitive subject. We tried to discuss the good things that were going on and avoid that subject as much as we could. He always wanted to talk about the future and where we would live instead of how much we were missing each other.

The more Stan and I talked, we kept asking ourselves why we were waiting. I was looking for signs to see if I should just go for it and move up there with him. I wanted it to be done the right way and so did he. We didn't want to ever struggle financially, and he wanted me to be able to only work if I wanted to and not because I had to.

It was a hard decision, but I finally told him I couldn't make any permanent changes until he was divorced. I told him I'd gone to the doctors and got a diaphragm. We'd been using condoms for protection, and I thought it would be easier to keep up with.

He kept asking me if I was sure I didn't want another child. He promised he would be there for the whole thing, and the thought of having a child with me would make him very happy.

If only he was divorced, if only I didn't live so far away. Things could be so much easier.

My company announced it was doing some internal re-organizing, and it was looking like I would be finally getting a promotion. Maybe this was the sign I was right and should stay in Georgia for a while. I could save up more money and be able to really contribute to our life together.

I went to work that Monday morning, excited to hear the announcement. Unfortunately, the "internal reorganization" at the company did not end up shuffling me to the position I had hoped for. I read and reread the following announcement from my boss with disbelief. Not wanting to concern Stan, I downplayed the message and forwarded it on to Stan with a personal note:

From: Brian S
Sent: Mon 8/22/2005 4:31 PM
To: Everyone
Subject: Personnel Announcement

Personnel Announcement

This is to announce that effectively immediately Regina has assumed the role of Supervisor for the call center. In her new role, Regina will have overall responsibility for the day to day operations of the call center. Reporting to Regina will be: Jerone, Charles, Pam and Tony.

Dee will continue to report directly to me. Dee will continue to provide technical customer care support, data reporting and Goldmine support. She will also begin to provide additional QA support to Mike and his team on an as needed basis.

Please join me in congratulating Regina on her new role.

Brian W. S
VP General Manager

From: Dee
Sent: Wednesday, August 24, 2005 8:56 AM
To: Stan
Subject: hey stranger

After receiving that announcement on Monday about my "sort of" new position, it's been a running joke that everyone is asking me, so what's changed?

Have you heard anything from Steve? How's he liking WVU?

I feel like it's been forever since we've talked even though it's only been a few days. Sometimes I feel like forgetting it all down here and just coming to be with you. If only it could be that easy. I miss you. It's starting to feel like a dream... us being together. I guess because it's been so long. This time apart and distance between us makes it so hard to feel real. Maybe I just need a good hug and I'll feel better. You must be swamped... I'm having a time trying to reach you at home anymore. I hope you're feeling ok and it's nothing to do with your health. I'll talk to you soon, Love Dee

He called me that night and said he felt bad that my sort-of promotion really didn't mean any change to my job and felt it was a sign I should be up there with him instead.

He also explained he'd been just a bit tired lately and was sorry he missed my calls. Of course, he said it was nothing to worry about and he'd be back on track soon.

He blamed it on all the traveling he was doing for Steve and said after some good rest he'd be his old self again. I could tell he wasn't being totally honest with me about how he was feeling, and I worried as to why he would hold it back from me. Our communication was slipping, but he said it was nothing to worry about, just trying to get back into the swing of life. It took a little more out of him than he thought it would.

I was at Lisa's one Saturday, enjoying our craft time together when we started talking about me needing a recent picture of myself to send to Stan. Lisa decided to send him one while I was sitting there. She giggled and raised her finger to dramatically hit the send button.

----- Original Message -----
From: Lisa
To: Stan
Sent: Saturday, August 27, 2005 12:33 PM
Subject: Dee's Picture

Hey Stan Dee asked me to write and flirt with you. Hahahahahaha
Here is her best picture that she hates.
Enjoy
Lisa

----- Original Message -----
From: Stan S
To: Lisa
Sent: Sunday, August 28, 2005 10:09 PM
Subject: Re: Dee's Picture

Hi Lisa....so let's hear some flirting!!

Hey, thanks for the pic...I re-sent it to Dee, she says she looks old in it, I don't see it. In fact I think she looks cute in the hat. It was a little dark though. Anyway, I like it but Dee says I had better not print it. Speaking of pics, my son Matt wants equal time (haha), in other words, he'd like a pic of your daughter if you have one. Who knows, this matchmaking thing could work!!

- 168 -

Cheers, -Stan-

----- Original Message -----
From: Lisa
To: Stan S
Sent: Tuesday, August 30, 2005 2:44 AM
Subject: Re: Dee's Picture

Hey Stan I didn't forget to respond I just had to come up with
something witty to say. All I can say is sometimes words just aren't
enough........See attached. I can't send out Destiny's Pic.... it's top
secret ..... I guess you will just have to bring him down to meet her.
By the way we are all going to www.wildbillsatlanta.com this Saturday
(that's where Destiny hangs out) if you are in town we would love for
you to join us. I know it would make Dee's weekend, she is planning
on spending this long weekend scrubbing the boy's bathroom. At any
rate I am glad you liked the picture. Have a great one!!!!!!!!!!!!!
Hope to see you soon.
Lisa

----- Original Message -----
From: "Dee Keller"
To: Lisa; Stan
Sent: Tuesday, August 30, 2005 4:10 PM
Subject: Re: Fw: Dee's Picture

OK you two... I said flirting is fine but no telling on me Lisa :)
I had a feeling you two would gang up on me.

From: Lisa]
Sent: Tuesday, August 30, 2005 5:33 PM
To: Dee Keller
Subject: Re: Fw: Dee's Picture

What are you talking about? Telling on you? Never, I mean you would
never do anything wrong and me, I am as sweet as sugar......... I
would never gang up on you unless it was for your own good, like
putting the bug in Stan's ear about coming down so you will have a
good weekend and not one spent cleaning, or god forbid your lawn
needs cutting or let's see what other kind of mischief could you get
into? Oh yea Wild Bills sounds like a Saturday night to remember. Oh
guess who showed up there Saturday night and jammed and stayed
and partied with everyone? Ok I'll tell. Ted Nugent's band.
Destiny said she ended up shit-faced.
Gotta go get her. She is sick and can't get home from work. Call me
later laf

- 169 -

It was great seeing how relaxed Lisa felt in emailing Stan and of course, how she would later share it with me. It seemed like now Lisa's approval became as important to me as even that of my boys. I always respected her intuitions, and somehow, knew she could tell whether or not something was right.

It was driving us both crazy not seeing each other, and the end of September seemed so far away. We both consumed ourselves with our daily lives, just trying to make the time go faster. Even my co-workers commented on my mood, threatening to buy me a ticket to go see him if I didn't cheer up soon. At that point, I realized it was affecting a little more of my life than I had thought it would.

From: Stan S
Sent: Wednesday, September 14, 2005 8:05 PM
To: Dee
Subject: Hi

Just a line to let you know I'm thinking of you. Hope all is well at work...or at least tolerable...if not, well, it'll just make your visit that much more enjoyable. I've been working, sleeping or painting Dave's room...nothing earth shattering, just time consuming. Well, gotta get ready for work...talk to you soon!

Love, -Me-

Stan finally admitted that he hadn't been feeling very well. During our calls I could hear him coughing more and more each day. He'd been sanding down the walls in Dave's bedroom trying to get it ready to paint, and he must have inhaled some of the drywall dust. Of course, he didn't want to go to the doctor for such a trivial thing, and he brushed it off for weeks.

Finally, a few weeks before my trip to go see him, he told me about his eye hurting. Again, he brushed it off as nothing

and said he probably just got dust in it. I promised him that if it wasn't better by the time I got there, first thing on the agenda would be a doctor. I was beginning to see how stubborn he was about going to the doctor.

Stan called to tell me that the CIA was having an open house on September 17th and only family was invited. "Of course, you are family now, and I told them that you were my fiancée. I want to show you off."

It was such a shame the open house wasn't for the week I would be there. I could tell how disappointed he was that I couldn't get that time off also. The following weekend was "Poolesville Day" in his small town. They hosted a picnic for everyone, and he wanted me to go with him.

He said, "The timing just isn't right and I promise next year you will be by my side for both." Next year would be the year we would do everything together.

Stan had just started a special project at work in late August that changed his work hours to nights. It was hard for us to keep in touch with the mixed schedules, but we did our best. Emails became our main source of communication. We would occasionally talk before dinner and then he'd be off to work. We couldn't wait for my birthday week, and we both looked forward to it so much. It was going to be the longest period of time we'd spend together. He was having so much fun coming up with details for what we would do, but I kept insisting he needed to rest and recuperate. We finally decided that the trip to NJ would be enough to plan on, and the rest of the time we would just relax and be together.

I was getting so excited to see him again. It had been almost two months, and this time apart was the hardest and longest we'd had to deal to with.

Chapter 11
My September Trip
2005

It was a beautiful Sunday afternoon in Georgia. The day was finally here for my trip to see him. My son, Steven, drove me to the airport. He unloaded my luggage and turned to give me a hug. He said, "Have a great birthday and have a good time." It was nice to see that even the one short time he had with Stan was enough for him to approve of my being with him.

For the longest time after Billy and I had split up, Steven told me many times that he didn't want me to date again. I could tell he had my best interest at heart and didn't want to see me hurt again. From just these short months that Stan and I had been together, Steven could see the type of man he was and how different he was from Billy and his father.

The two hour flight seemed to take forever, and I tried to sleep to pass the time. My excitement got the best of me, and I got no sleep at all. The plane finally landed, and I walked to the baggage claim where we had discussed meeting, but I didn't see Stan anywhere. Disappointed, I decided to find the carousel, which would have my luggage. As I was walking down the hall way, he must have seen me walk by because after I got to my luggage and turned around, he was walking towards me with the biggest smile.

The first thing I noticed was his eye. It was a little swollen and red, and I could tell he was having problems seeing with it. I frowned and said, "You lied to me. Your eye looks awful."

He looked down at the ground and said, "It's not as bad as it was. You should have seen it a week ago. It's getting better and nothing to worry about."

He could tell how worried I was and took me in his arms. We kissed and hugged. I never wanted to let go.

His eye will be the first thing on my agenda to take care of during my stay. I didn't care that he wasn't feeling well while I was there; I could take care of him. It didn't matter if we couldn't do anything while I was there; I was there to be with him.

After giving me a kiss, he raised my left hand and looked at my fingers. He then raised my right hand. He was checking to see if I had my mother's ring on. Of course I did.

He said, "Why don't you wear it on your left hand?"

I responded, "When you're divorced it will move over immediately. But until then, it will be on my right hand every day." I loved my ring and let everyone who commented on it know that he cut the stone for me. I wore it with pride.

We drove to his house mostly in silence, a peaceful and happy silence. He held my hand the whole time and occasionally commented about memories that were sparked by a song on the radio. They were always about us.

As we approached the ferry, I was overwhelmed by the feeling of being taken to a different world again, his world.

That night, dinner again became the chore he loved. We stopped to pick up a few things at the grocery store on the way home, and I watched him in his element. While I was watching him cook, I looked around the kitchen to get to know the little touches that he put into his home.

I found his calendar on the pantry door. On the day I was arriving, he had a smiley face, and on the day I was leaving, he had a frown. I smiled.

I saw all the doctors' appointments and asked about each one. I could tell he didn't want me to worry and said they were just checkups. I asked which one was for his eye, and he just smiled. He was using my little trick of not saying anything instead of saying something he knew I didn't want to hear. Silence as a response was always bad news.

We spent the first evening at home watching TV. His favorite TV show was a comedy cartoon series called *American Dad*. It was about a family whose dad's name was Stan, and he worked for the CIA. The family even had a son named Steve, but his personality couldn't have been further from Stan's son's. He loved that show.

His other favorite, which he shared with Matt, was *Smallville*. It was about Superman's adventures as a teenager. It was nice to see the bond Matt and Stan had about these shows. They really enjoyed that time together.

He also spent a lot of time watching cooking shows. That was the only one that surprised me… but then again, I was sure that was a part of how he became so creative in the kitchen.

After we went to his room that night for the evening, Stan had gone into the bathroom and came out a few minutes later. I could see that something was wrong. He found my empty diaphragm case and asked me if I was using it.

I think this was the first time it really sunk in for him that I wouldn't have a child while things were the way they were with us. I told him the time just wasn't right. A child needed both parents, and with the distance between us, I just couldn't do it alone.

We agreed to put aside the topic and had the best evening together alone. We stayed up until 2 AM, which was rare for me. I so easily adjusted to his late nights just to be with him.

He told me that night that he'd been taking some sleeping pills called Ambien because of the cough and pain he was in from his eye. I was a little worried that he needed to take something to be able to sleep but I figured as long as he didn't use it for a long time, it would be okay.

On Sunday, we agreed to hang around the house because it was Steve's last day at home before leaving for college again.

We stayed up late the night before, and got up so early that we were both ready for a nap after breakfast. He fixed homemade blueberry pancakes. We decided that before things got crazy, we would take a little nap on the couch.

We were surprised at how our sleeping patterns mirrored each other. We napped every day I was there. He told me when he was with Shelley; she always went to bed early, while he was a night owl. I had always been like Shelley, mostly because I had to get up early for work the next day, but that week, it was nice to be on his schedule.

He kept saying, "This feels so right. Wouldn't you like to have this kind of life?"

As the afternoon approached, the house became hectic getting his clothes and things together. I could see the sadness in Stan as Steve was packing. His friends came in and out saying their goodbyes.

I wished he wasn't leaving; we didn't have any time to get to know each other better that trip.

Steve's ride arrived, and we watched him pack the car. He came back into the house, and we said our goodbyes.

Stan closed the door and walked into the other room.

I walked into the TV room, and Stan was on his computer. He was so cute trying to explain problems he'd had on it and how he fixed them all by himself.

He was trying to not think about Steve, while I could see he was proud thinking he just might be teaching me something, but I would just say "Oh, really" and he'd chuckle, knowing that I already knew the solution and was just humoring him.

We went back and forth about what to do about dinner that night, and no one really could agree. Stan, I could tell, was a bit concerned about money and at the same time, didn't have any meal planned. We finally decided to go to Stan and Matt's favorite seafood restaurant for dinner, the same place we went the first night I met Matt months ago. They both got the all-you-can-eat platters again, which took up almost the entire table, while I got again the salmon platter.

We had a great time sitting and talking and laughing, just getting to know each other. Seeing Matt and Stan together and how close they really were and how much they had in common made me think about my relationship with my sons. Being a woman, the relationship I have with my boys is different, not having the common male bonds that Stan and Matt have. It made me sad to think that my boys didn't have a father figure in their life and how much they missed out on. Stan felt the same anxieties about his boys not having a mother around during the last six years, their most important teenage years.

We spent the rest of the evening watching TV, and I took in all of the differences of a household mainly styled by a man.

Stan had to work for a bit the next day, so we attempted to go to bed early that night. I'm not sure how he made it in the next day since we still stayed up late talking and sharing our feelings and hopes and dreams. This became our topic of conversation each time we talked. He had so many dreams for the future, and I was always a part of them.

It was Monday morning, and Stan had an early meeting at 4AM and said he should be home by noon at the latest. He was so quiet getting ready it barely woke me up, but he kissed me goodbye before he left. I could see the smile on his face as he was leaving and he said, "This is the way I'd like to go to work each morning, after giving you a kiss and telling you I love you."

I smiled at him, curled up under the covers and fell fast asleep.

His job was fascinating to me, but I knew not to ask many questions. I always let him take the lead on any work conversations and knew he would tell me what he could. It never left me feeling like he was hiding anything; he didn't have a choice.

Stan had been on a special project the past few months. He was working nights and was not able to tell me any details of the project. The night shift was getting to him. Not just because of the conflicts of our schedules but also for his boys. He loved cooking them a big dinner, and most evenings he was leaving as they were coming home from work. This left a lot of days without him being able to be the chef that he so proudly was.

He was hoping that the meeting would give him an idea of how much longer the project would last and put him back on his normal day hours.

I struggled out of bed at about 8AM and saw he had made me coffee and left me a note to help myself to anything I wanted to eat. Being the undomesticated person I am, I stuck a half a bagel in the toaster and drowned it down with coffee.

I saw Dave was still home and thought I would wait to take my shower so I wasn't in there when he needed it. He walked into the kitchen about 9AM, and I made us a fresh pot of coffee.

It was nice to finally get to talk with Dave. He'd been out the other visits, so I didn't have time alone with him until that morning. We talked about school, and he opened up a little about the girl in his life. He talked to me like a friend, and I could tell he also accepted me in his dad's life. "My dad has been very happy since the two of you got back together."

"Your dad is very special to me." We talked for about an hour and then he had to get ready for school. He was going in late that day.

"It was nice getting to know you, Dee. I hope you are around a lot more." Dave said as he gave me a hug. He smiled and continued, "I better get ready for school or I'll be late."

"I hope to see you again before I leave." That was all I could get out before he was off to the shower.

Stan got home from work about noon and came in with a big smile. Luckily, I nagged him enough, and he finally made an appointment that afternoon for his eye. It was with his General Practitioner, so he said I didn't need to go with him.

I spent the time reading and even went for a long walk around his neighborhood. It was nice to be able to take a walk and not have to worry about anyone bothering me.

He got home about an hour later wearing another big smile. He said "I have two favors I need from you. First, is that the doctor gave me eye drops, and I need help putting them in. He also said if it didn't get any better by tomorrow to call an eye doctor." His regular doctor wasn't sure if he had gotten dust in his eye or if something else was wrong.

After I put the drops in his eyes, he went back into his room to put away the medicine. I kept thinking he said two favors and wondered what the other was. A few minutes later he came back into the TV room and I asked him, "So, what's the other favor?"

He grinned, looked over at Dave and said "I want you to fondle my balls." I must have turned five shades of red, and Dave burst out laughing. Apparently, Dave was in on the joke. Stan explained, he was making stuffed meat balls for dinner and wanted me to help make them, I actually think he just wanted to say that to me in front of Dave. He loved making little innuendos, especially when the boys would hear.

We made meat balls stuffed with cheddar cheese and fresh jalapeños grown from his garden. They turned out delicious. I'd never had anything like that before. He told me about all the other stuffed meatball recipes he'd come up with and would often improvise with new and unique stuffing's depending on the kind of mood he was in.

He kept asking me what I wanted for my birthday. I told him all I really wanted was an evening alone and maybe that he cook me dinner. I'd never had a man cook for me before Stan. It had always been my job, and I guess I lost my drive to cook when I really didn't have anyone to cook for anymore.

My son Ed and I had different schedules, so he normally grabbed something quick. I normally didn't eat dinner. It was refreshing to see a man enjoy the little things in life and to be with someone who took such pleasure in having people enjoy his cooking.

We spent a quiet evening at home just enjoying each other's company.

Tuesday was our first day totally alone. I kept checking on his eye, and it wasn't getting any better. He kept saying to give the medicine time, but I could see it was really bothering him. Finally, about 2:30 in the afternoon, he called the eye doctor. Unfortunately, they couldn't get him in that day but they stressed not to wait and wanted to see him the next day, which was my birthday. He kept resisting, not wanting to spend my birthday that way. It took some convincing, but he finally agreed to make the appointment. He was so sweet not wanting to ruin my birthday. I told him that if he wasn't feeling good tomorrow when he could have gone for help that would ruin it more.

That night, I went to bed before him to read a little and just relax.

I had been reading a book called "Natural Cures" each night. I was hoping to find something that would help him feel better. He was taking a lot of different medicine. I was shocked when I saw it in his bathroom. For the first time, it really hit me how sick he'd been. It broke my heart looking at everything in there.

I had to find something that he could take to feel better that wasn't a chemical. I shared everything I could find, and we both talked about how we would start a healthier life. We both had something to live for now.

He came into the bedroom around midnight with another big smile. He said he loved walking in his room to find me lying on his bed waiting for him. He couldn't wait until it was permanent. He made love to me three times that night. I didn't think I had it in me.

When we were lying there afterwards, he said, "Happy birthday. I wanted to be the first person to say it to you."

I slept so peacefully that night. In the morning, he made me a delicious breakfast, and we just sat around until it was time to go to the eye doctor. It was a late afternoon appointment, but he had his mind elsewhere. He was worried about cooking my birthday dinner. We had gone out the day before to pick up groceries for the dishes he was going to make, and he didn't want anything to get in the way.

On the drive home, I could tell he was having problems seeing, but he had insisted on driving anyway. The doctor said his eye was inflamed, and it could have ended in blindness if he had let it go much further. He had to put drops in his eyes every hour for the first week. I was glad I was there for him. It was so nice to be able to take care of him, but I worried that he wouldn't keep up with it once I was gone.

We got home after 6pm because of the traffic, and I could see his disappointment. He felt so bad that he wouldn't have the time to make all of the special dishes he had planned.

I knew it was going to be the best birthday, regardless of what we did, because we were together. That night, we had take-out Chinese. It was a great dinner, and I didn't mind putting off the steak dinner he planned.

Josh joined us for dinner, and it was nice to see him again. As always, he was very nice to me, and I could see how much he really cared for Stan and the boys. Josh looked up to Stan with all he'd accomplished in his life. He was a father figure to him and you could see the respect he had.

The next day, Stan asked what I felt like doing. Again, just being with him was enough. We stayed at the house for a while, and it as if we were kids playing house. We enjoyed every minute. I continued to put drops in his eyes each hour and kept a good watch on it to see if it was responding at all. The medicine seemed to be helping; the swelling was going down, and it wasn't as red as it had been when I first arrived. Stan was enjoying being taken care of, and each time after putting the drops in his eye, I gave him a kiss.

He said, "I want to take you to one of my favorite spots. Let's grab Buster and go for a ride." Stan picked up his keys and Buster's chain. Buster came alive and got excited. He knew where we were going.

We drove for about 10 to 15 minutes through the Maryland countryside. It was so beautiful. We stopped at this small park which had a tiny parking lot. It must have been a place only locals knew of and visited.

It had a small path that ran along the edge of the Potomac River. We walked up to the dock where people would launch their small boats and drift down the river. There was a path you could tell was used quite often but still very secluded. It was undeveloped land that had been; in its time, a popular place.

Time had taken its' toll on some of the small areas which had been used for camping. The old water pump was still there, but it had rusted so badly that no water would come out of it. Stan tried anyway.

We talked and walked and before we knew it, we passed the two mile marker. It was the three of us, Stan, Buster and me. No one else was there. We talked about our future together, getting married; where we'd like to live, but again I told him until he was divorced he really couldn't ask me or make any definite plans… For some reason, this time I had a heavy feeling that made me wish I didn't say that to him.

"Here it is." Stan said. We finally made it to his favorite spot. He led me off the main path towards the river. There was a small beach with huge rocks lying in the water close to the shore. I smiled thinking of our rock back home. It had been such a big part of our life back then. He took my hand, and we climbed onto the rocks.

It was a beautiful warm, breezy day as we sat on the rock, enjoying the peaceful sounds of the flowing river. Stan put his arm around me as I leaned on him. No words needed to be said. The view was extraordinary. The trees that lined the shore of the river were decorated with autumn colors. In the distance, you could see the old bridge we drove over to get here.

We did do a lot of talking about plans for the future and seeing if we both wanted the same things out of our life together. It was nice to see that both of us wanted so many of the same things. We had some differences, but he would always laugh and say we could work on it. The only substantial difference I saw between us was how we handled finances. We both were good but had different ways of how we handled certain items. Granted he made twice as much as I did, and it was a little easier for him to maintain his finances the way he did.

One of them was about carrying cash. I almost never did. I use my debit card everywhere which makes it so much easier to control what I spent, and I always felt safer not carrying cash. He, on the other hand, didn't have a card because he felt it could be stolen. He carried cash or checks.

I hadn't written a check in years. I paid my bills online, while he still did it the old fashioned way, mailing checks.

We sat there talking until Buster got bored and wanted to walk more. More than an hour had passed as we sat there enjoying the sounds of nature. We slowly walked back towards the car not wanting to leave.

On the ride home, he asked, "Can we talk about marriage?"

I looked at him and smiled, "Once your divorce is over."

He started asking other questions, avoiding the word marriage. He found other ways to ask.

He asked, "Would you take my name?

It made me grin and I responded, "Of course I would take your name if we got married."

After that response, the questions began with *"when we get married."*

"I really don't want to wait. Please quit your job and come live here with me." Stan made enough money to support us very nicely; that wasn't the issue. I couldn't make any commitment right then.

"After the holidays, I promise its first on my list. I don't want to ruin the boys' holidays. They know it's coming and accept it. It will be a sad subject for them." He smiled and added, "They love you and accept you. After the holidays, it will be easier to discuss."

"Let's talk about something else." He continued. "Wouldn't you love having a little girl, my little girl?"

I smiled, "I'm 46 years old and I'd be 64 before the child graduated from high school and went into college. Let's talk about something else."

Though we had some things to work out, we realized that it could really work between us, and just being with each other was all we needed. He didn't need to wine and dine me. He cooked for me each night and made me feel like I was his entire world.

Each night I was there it was such a joy to see the look in his eyes when I would dress for bed. His reaction was always the same. It was refreshing to see that no matter what I wore he was very attracted to me. He asked me, "What would you like to see me in? Anything special that would turn you on? I'm fortunate to love anything you wear or don't wear."

I just smiled, "Seeing the look in your eyes when you look at me is all you need to wear." I'd never been the flashy kind and could tell that even the simple things meant as much to him as they did to me. I did bring a couple of special outfits to wear for him at night. I could immediately tell what he was thinking when he looked at me.

It was my last day there. We went for a drive, and he showed me more of his favorite homes in the area. He would check my reactions to see which I liked. They were all beautiful and I loved the area. I felt safe there. The day seemed to fly by while we spent the afternoon relaxing at home.

Dinner was the quietest we'd been all week. Matt joined us.

After dinner was done we moved into the kitchen as Stan cleaned up after dinner. Matt and I sat at the kitchen table to talk, and he saw my ticket to go back home lying on the table. He picked it up and frowned when he saw the date, "I thought you were going to spend the weekend too."

I explained, "I have to work on Saturday, otherwise I would have stayed a lot longer." Matt looked sad to hear I was leaving the next day. Then he said, "Dad, can't you do something so she can stay longer."

"I wish I could. I want her to stay permanently." Stan said and winked at me.

That night we just held each other and drifted off to sleep. Neither one of us being able to say what we were really feeling. Each time I woke during the night, I would roll over and watch him sleep until I drifted off again.

I finally woke about five in the morning to find him staring at me. He smiled as he stroked my hair.

"Want some coffee?" I asked.

"Of course." He smiled.

I put on my robe and went into the kitchen. As I looked around the kitchen trying to wake up, I found this note taped to the exhaust fan above the stove from his son Matt:

DEE -

IT WAS REALLY
NICE HAVING YOU HERE.
YOU SEEMED TO HAVE PUT
EVERYONE IN A BETTER MOOD.
(☺) HAVE A SAFE
TRIP HOME AND TRY NOT
TO WEAR YOURSELF OUT
WORKIN TOO HARD!
SEE YA AGAIN SOON!

- MATT

His note brought tears to my eyes. I wanted to stay so much. I was home. Somehow, whether we were together there or even at my house, it just felt so right for the both of us. I finished making the coffee and brought it back to the bedroom with Matt's note.

I handed the note to Stan and watched as he read it. I could see how touched he was by it. I knew it meant lot to him to have his sons like me, but accepting and caring about me was more than he could have hoped for.

I finally felt like the missing link in my family was found, and felt myself glow with the idea of having all five boys together as a family.

Before we left for the airport, Stan packed me a little care package of his homemade barbeque sauce to take home with me. It was the best I'd ever had, and I couldn't wait to get home and try it out with my boys.

The drive to the airport was silent. This silence was different from the trip to his house. We were both at a loss for words, and I knew I would cry if we talked about our destination. I hated leaving and wanted to tell him to turn the car around and drive back home.

Chapter 12
The months apart again….
October thru November – 2005

The plane arrived in Atlanta, and I couldn't believe how much I missed him already and dreaded the thought that it might be months before seeing him again. Phone calls and emails were no longer enough, and I was beginning to wonder how we could get through this time apart.

I got to the baggage claim and called Lisa to see where she was, and unfortunately, she hadn't left her house yet. Knowing the time of day it was and how she'd hit rush hour to come get me, I decided to take the mass transit system home instead.

I knew with all the luggage I had it would be a struggle, but they were all on wheels, so I decided to take it anyway.

I got off Marta and struggled to make it down the massive stairway. Half way down the escalator I dropped my small luggage bag that had his barbeque sauce in it. Everyone around me watched me struggle, but no one stopped to help.

I knew that the jar was probably broken but didn't want to think about it. I had still had a long train ride and then a taxi ride before I would get home.

The train stopped close to my house but the journey was still not over. I struggled with my luggage again making my way to the parking lot. I found a cab waiting.

I settled in the cab and reluctantly checked the bag. Just as I feared, the jar had broken. Luckily, it was in a plastic bag, so the sauce didn't get onto anything else. The jar had shattered inside the bag, and I knew I couldn't save any of it. I was so disappointed. I called Stan while I was still in the cab to tell him I was home, but the sauce didn't survive the trip. He promised to send me more.

After watching Stan in his cooking element for an entire week, I decided my first night back I'd surprise my boys with making a special dinner and couldn't wait to tell Stan all about it.

From: Dee
To: 'Stanley S'
Sent: Sunday, October 02, 2005 6:45 PM

You would have been proud of me ... we had a delicious roast (off the grill) with baked potatoes and broccoli with cheese for dinner. Steven came over and it was real nice having dinner with just the three of us tonight, it's been a while. I guess I'll take tonight off and start with my studies again tomorrow. One more night of peace before the daily grind starts again. I'm going to have a tough time with this after last week. I will take time to for a shower and then relax for the night.

Love you,
Dee

From: Stanley S
Sent: Sunday, October 02, 2005 8:57 PM
To: Dee
Subject: Re:

Very Proud indeed!! Sounds delicious and I wish I was there to enjoy it with you. Looks like some of me rubbed off on ya (ha, ha) in more ways than one. It hasn't been the same here without you, and only a small bit of that has to do with dinners. I haven't cooked since you left by the way... I forget what I had on Friday, frozen lasagna last night, and pizza tonight. Yes...last week was wonderful, and it just strengthened my desire to be with you. The boys have really taken to you too, I think you got that from Matt, but Dave likes you too.

Not much happening here this weekend...housecleaning yesterday, and of course football today (your favorite TV right?). Your Dad tried to call twice...saw the caller ID., but I must have been folding clothes or something. I've been medicating my eye regularly...no, really I have! I think it's slowly getting better, but it still gets a bit swollen overnight. Hopefully it'll be cured by my next appointment.

Well, back to the laundry...

I love you honey!

-Stan-

p.s. Buster says "wooooooo"

From: Dee
Sent: Monday, October 03, 2005 3:20 PM
To: stanley.s@verizon.net
Subject: my dad

I talked to Karen to see what my dad wanted and he said just to say
hi. He called me last night also and wanted to make sure everything
was ok between us. It was, as usual, a strange conversation and he
did want to verify your phone number ... sorry. He had it on caller id
and asked me last night for it. He kinda put me on the spot and I'm
sorry. Hopefully he just wants to chat. I told him you are working
night's right now and will be a little hard to reach. :) Love you, Dee

Stan was still on the special project working nights. He
still had no idea how long he would be working on this
project.

We would send each other a lot of jokes, but after time, I
had to avoid certain types. I'm not sure if it was because of
something that had happened with his wife or maybe not
knowing my sense of humor or if he felt it was my way of
sending some strange hints to him.

From: Dee Keller
To: Stan
Sent: Wednesday, October 05, 2005 9:37 AM
Subject: FW: Words Women Use (very helpful information)

Words Women Use

Fine - This is the word women use to end an argument when they are
right and you need to shut up.

Five Minutes - If she is getting dressed, this is half an hour. Five
minutes is only five minutes if you have just been given 5 more
minutes to watch the game before helping around the house.

Nothing - This is the calm before the storm. This means "something"

- 191 -

and you should be on your toes. Arguments that begin with "nothing" usually end in "fine".

Go Ahead- This is a dare, not permission, DON'T DO IT!

Loud Sigh - Although not actually a word, the loud sigh is often misunderstood by men. A "Loud Sigh" means she thinks you are an idiot and wonders why she is wasting her time standing here and arguing with you over "Nothing".

That's Okay - This is one of the most dangerous statements that woman can make to a man. "That's Okay" means that she wants to think long and hard before deciding how and when you will pay for your mistake.

Thanks - This is the least used of all words in the female vocabulary. If a woman is thanking you, do not question it, just say you're welcome and back out of the room slowly.

This was his response:

From: Stanley S
Sent: Wed 10/5/2005 4:33 PM
To: Dee Keller
Subject: Re: Words Women Use (very helpful information)

(laughing...nervously) I'll keep those words in mind.

Love ya....

Stan was still on the eye drops and would be for several weeks. I was concerned, but he had promised me he would keep up with the drops and his appointments.

From: Dee Keller
To: Stan
Sent: Wednesday, October 05, 2005 7:09 AM
Subject: good luck at the doctors today

Let me know what she says.... how is the eye doing? Keeping up with your drops?
Love Dee

From: Stanley
Sent: Wed 10/5/2005 4:28 PM
To: Dee Keller
Subject: Re: good luck at the doctors today

Hi Cutie,

Just got back from the doctors in fact, and she said it looks good but
she said the case was so severe that it's going to take a while for it go
away completely. She reduced the drops to six times a day this week
and 4 times a day next week. My next appointment is the 17th. I just
hope insurance won't give me a hard time about it. The doc seemed
concerned or perhaps scientifically interested in why this happened.
She kept asking me if I had a tick bite or if I have arthritis. She never
saw a first time case of this that was as severe as mine. She also
wants blood work done at some point. Personally, I think it's the
chemo I had...it has some strange side effects. No, I chickened out on
asking the doctor's assistant if she was single for Matt. Other than
that, nothing new. I hope you're doing ok...have you been taking your
pills?

Love you and miss you...
-Stan-

On weekends, I would go to Lisa's and work in her
craft shop. I had been working on two wood boxes for him
since August and finally would be able have them ready the
day after his birthday. I had his named "STAN" engraved on
the outside of the larger box by Lisa's husband, Kevin. On
the inside, it had a medallion that said "It doesn't matter
where you are; it's who's next to you that counts."

I wanted to give it to him personally but had to settle
with shipping it to him. My timing, of course, was off and I
hated that it didn't get there until the day after his birthday.
He emailed me that night.

From: Stanley S
Sent: Tuesday, October 11, 2005 4:10 PM
To: Dee
Subject: I'm Awed....

Dee,

I don't know what to say! I'm so touched by your gift ... I'm speechless. I received the box you made me today and it is absolutely gorgeous! To know that you made that for me...it has your soul in it...I'll treasure it always my love.

Love You,

-Stan-

Life was getting hectic again, and I was busy with work and everything at home. I was still working two jobs, just trying to keep my head above water.

Ed was ready to start practicing driving, and the only thing I knew I'd have trouble teaching him was parallel parking. Again, I drafted the help of Kevin, and he patiently spent hours with Ed one Sunday showing him exactly the formula to park straight each time.

Kevin's office was about 10 minutes from my house, and the back parking lot was perfect for his training. Kevin set up the back lot so we could come and practice anytime we wanted.

Time again began to pass as the daily chores and work took over our lives. I wanted to see him again and began trying to think of ways or events to invite him to. Even Lisa did her part of coming up with ways to get Stan back down here. Lisa's birthday was at the end of the month, and we were planning on having some type of gathering. Of course, we had Stan in mind.

I was looking for any reason for him to come down and visit. Stan was very receptive to coming for Lisa's party but couldn't make any definite plans just in case something came up with work.

It was driving me crazy that I couldn't get him to commit to any time right now, but I also understood he was still going crazy with the travels for his son to college, not to mention his eye wasn't fully healed. It was so hard knowing he needed his rest and he didn't need to drive but at the same time wanting to see him again.

From: "Dee Keller"
To: Lisa
Sent: Tuesday, October 18, 2005 4:00 PM
Subject: Re: Re: girls night

Hey... have you decided when your birthday bash will be? Stan maybe coming up the 5th and wanted to check with ya.... Matt should be coming with him

----- *Original Message* -----
From: Lisa
Sent: Tuesday, October 18, 2005 5:24 PM
To: Dee Keller
Subject: Re: Re: girls night

looks like it will be the 5th

It was early afternoon, and I got home from a long day at work. Ed was in his room working on his latest project. His door was open, and he smiled and waved. His room was off the kitchen, and I could see he had his headphones on enjoying his techno music. I sat down my purse and study books on the kitchen table as my phone rang.

"Dee, this is Matt. I hope you don't mind me calling you but dad is in the hospital with an apparent heart attack. I wanted to be sure you had the information. Here is the number for his room."

I wrote down the number and said, "Thank you so much for calling me Matt. I will call him right now and if I find out anything I will let you know."

"Thanks, Dee. I'm here if you need me."

My heart was racing as I called Stan's hospital room. He answered the phone and sounded very weak, "Hello."

"Hey Stan, its Dee. How are you?"

"Hi honey. I'm sorry I haven't called."

"Never mind that. What is going on?"

"I'd been getting bad chest pains since you left and had another serious attack at work today. They called an ambulance and rushed me to the hospital."

"Was it a heart attack? Should I come up?" My heart was racing, and all I wanted was to go up there and be with him.

Ed could see that something was wrong and came out of his room.

He said, "I'll be fine. It was just a scare. I don't want you to use your vacation time for this. Save it for the holidays when I'm better. They did testing on my heart, and so far everything is fine. They said that's not what my pain was."

"What was it then?"

"They said it was my stomach and complications from my cancer operation a few years ago. The doctors had warned me it could be like this."

I looked at Ed and said, "Stan said is ok, he's in the hospital for stomach pains."

"Tell him I said to get better. Let me know later what is happening." Ed said, and then he walked back into his room.

"Stan, this makes me worried. You're still married, and if something was too happen to you, they will call Shelly, not me. Legally the hospital couldn't release any information to me. No one would even talk to me knowing you have a wife."

I could hear some rustling in the phone and then him talking to someone, "Even though my records say I'm married, we are separated. The woman on the phone is my fiancée, Dee. If she calls, I want her questions answered."

Stan handed the phone to the male nurse, "Hello Dee, nice to meet you. My name is Doug. Call and ask for me anytime you want an update."

"Thank you Doug. I'm very worried and live in Georgia. I can't come up there right now, but if you could call me if I need to, I would appreciate it." I gave him my phone number, and he promised he would call me first.

Stan came back on the phone, "Does that make you feel better?"

"It does for this instance, but what happens if you go back in again? Are you sure I shouldn't come up?"

"No, save the vacation days, I promise that this was nothing, and I will be fine. I should be going home tomorrow anyway. Talking to you is enough, just knowing you want to be here."

It made me feel better that he did want me to be there. We talked for over two hours that night, and it was quite amusing. He was on morphine and I could tell he wasn't totally with it, but we talked anyway. He wanted someone there.

I wanted to go and just hold his hand. He kept talking about our future and then asked me what I thought about North Dakota as a place to live. He told me about this house he'd found on the internet that was a mansion, and we could get it for next to nothing. I loved the mountains, but the thought of being so far away from everyone was a bit scary. I teased him, saying that it was the drugs talking but could also tell he was very serious about moving there if I were to give the go-ahead. I laughed so much at him during this conversation and told him he'd better watch what he said. I would remember every word, but he might not.

After my talk with Stan, I called his boys to let them know how he was doing and to check on them. I knew they were very upset, especially after all they'd been through with his cancer.

The next morning, I called the hospital four times to check on him, but he was still in the middle of all the tests to be sure his heart was okay.

Each time, Doug was very nice to me and told me everything that was going on each time I called.

I finally got Stan on the phone around noon, and he said he was okay to go home. We talked about our conversation from yesterday, and I was surprised how much he really did remember and how much he meant of everything he'd said.

The nurse came in to release him, and he said he would call me when he got home.

He was getting a ride from one of his friends at work. His car was still at the job, and he needed to bring it home.

I had promised Matt the night before that I would call to let him know what was going on, but Stan insisted that he would call Matt so I didn't.

Matt called my cell phone that afternoon on my way home from work and was very upset. He couldn't find Stan, and no one had called the house to let them know what was happening. Stan didn't have a cell phone, and there was no way for them to contact him. It really bothered me that Stan promised he would call but didn't.

I let Matt know that he was going to work to get his car and should be home soon. We both agreed the delay was probably a stop at the grocery store. I promised Matt that I would never let him worry again and would always let him know what was going on regardless of what Stan said.

Stan finally got home, and after being yelled at by Matt, he called me.

"You are going to laugh at why I was late."

"Somehow I don't think so. Everyone has been so worried about you."

"Well, when I walked through our security gate, the alarms went off. Apparently, the tests they give you for your heart have radium in them. The level was so high, I was just about glowing." He laughed so hard.

He didn't seem to be worried about the chest pains, but I wanted him to find out what was causing them. He kept insisting that he didn't want to be in the hospital during the holidays, and he would go for a follow-up first thing in January.

After this episode, I emailed Matt to let him know how to reach me immediately just in case.

Stan insisted on putting off going to the doctors to see the cause of his chest pains and instead decided to play a little doctor himself. He kept saying that he didn't want to ruin the holidays by being in the hospital and would take other precautions instead. He spent time reading up on all the medications he was taking to see if any of them could be the cause.

At the same time, both Kevin and his daughter were having their own health issues, and I felt torn about wanting to go up there to be with Stan, but knowing Lisa needed my emotional support also. Kevin had been rushed to the hospital with a collapsed lung while her daughter, Destiny, was being scheduled for surgery the following week for the problems she was having. Lisa was going through her own rough times but still had time for me and listening to my sorrows about Stan.

I was torn with who I should be with while knowing Stan would want me to wait to come up when he was better.

From: Stanley S
Sent: Friday, October 28, 2005 3:14 PM
To: Dee
Subject: Health Report...

Hi Dee, first off how are Kevin and Destiny doing? on the mend I hope.

I saw where you called last night...me and Matt had both dozed off, and of course the ringers were turned off. I'll give ya a buzz tonight if I can stay awake.

I think I have my "heart attack" figured out...I'm running an experiment over the weekend and so far, it looks like I'm right:
For years I've been using Rogaine on a small balding spot on the top of my head. 2% or 5% solution. Whatever was on sale at the time...never had a problem. Now, about six or seven weeks ago, I started work on Dave's room...breathed in some dust and got a bronchial infection. It cleared up. Also about 2 months ago I ran out of Rogaine and never bought more. After the infection cleared, I almost immediately got that eye infection and was put on antibiotics and steroids to treat it. When you went back to Georgia, I started using the Rogaine again...5% solution. Within a couple of days as I recall, I started getting chest pains. Mild at first, then severe, and thought it was muscle strain. Then last Wednesday happened and I got cleared of just about all major reasons for the pain. So far, we're up to date.... This past Wednesday, I was reviewing all the meds and vitamins I was taking and lo and behold it said on the Rogaine bottle that a side effect is "chest pain and a rapid heartbeat". I had used it that Wednesday before I read the label and had bad pain all day...I stopped it on Thursday, and today I hardly have any pain at all.

Soooo, what I think happened is that the Rogaine reacted with the steroids and antibiotics and THAT produced the side effects listed on the bottle. If the pain is completely gone by Monday, I'm going to use the stuff once to see if the pain starts to come back and that will prove my theory...after that, I guess I'll just have to go bald!! Also I got my lab results back today from the Doctor...everything is near perfect...my cholesterol total is 210 which is down from 234, so the Niacin, alfalfa, garlic and grapefruit juice are all working...just not as fast as prescription meds. And the bad cholesterol (LDL) is only 12 points high. No Lime disease, no cancer cells and no enzymes that would indicate heart damage.

Now you know as much as I do...anyhow, I'll talk to you soon!!

Love ya, -Me-

From: Dee
Sent: Friday, October 28, 2005 5:44 PM
To: 'Stanley S'
Subject: RE: Health Report...

You know…. It's not the hair I'm after ☺
I really hope you're right on the cause of your chest pain, as much as I love your hair, if that's the cause then stop now. It won't change how I feel. Besides, you said it was a "spot" you were correcting and I've already seen you totally bald via pictures. If that's the worst I have to deal with I'd rather you feeling better. Maybe then I won't be so self-conscience about some of my flaws. We all have them and hopefully you'll accept mine too.

I love and miss you,
Dee

From: Dee
Sent: Friday, October 28, 2005 7:04 PM
To: 'Stanley S'
Subject: RE: Health Report…

Btw… why are we turning the ringers off…. Now what if I needed to contact you for an emergency? How would I get thru?
You're gonna make me think it's me your avoiding
☺

As the time went past, I wanted more and more to see him and would send him messages every once in a while about a good flight deal. We talked about meeting half way again, and he said he was afraid about driving any distance alone with how he was feeling. I tried to see about going up there instead, but he wanted to save time for the holidays.

From: Dee
Sent: Monday, November 14, 2005 6:39 PM
To: 'Stanley S'
Subject:

This could be my flight… all you have to do is come see me

I really want to be with you for new years and it doesn't matter if you come down here or I come up there… with all the time I have off during that period it really would be nice to spend it with you.
I love you,
Dee

The holidays were coming, and I had saved enough vacation time at least a week off for both Christmas and Thanksgiving. Stan's schedule with his sons was so hectic we realized we wouldn't be able to see each other for Thanksgiving. I decided to only take off from Wednesday till Sunday and save the extra days for Christmas.

Stan's son Steve was home from college for the long break, but Stan had to drive him back on Sunday. I could hear the exhaustion in his voice. He'd picked Steve up from West Virginia University just a few days before.

I tried to convince him to meet me in Virginia and could hear his frustration. I know he wanted to see me, but he didn't know how he could possibly fit it in with having to drive Steve back. I told him I understood and that we'd try for something in the beginning of December.

I tried to convince him of just one night to meet, but with the schedule he had between getting Steve back to college, it just didn't work out.

He said he still wasn't feeling good and down played how he was really feeling. I could tell there was something wrong. I was hearing from him less frequently. He told me about not feeling well but always said it would pass and to not worry. We discussed him flying down instead so he wouldn't be traveling alone.

From: Dee Keller
To: Stanley S
Sent: Monday, November 28, 2005 1:03 PM
Subject: hey you

I checked with Steven and he said he could pick you up so go for the best prices if it's still possible for you to come...... I'll figure out what I can do to sneak out of here.
love you
Dee

From: Stanley S
Sent: Monday, November 28, 2005 2:12 PM
To: Dee Keller
Subject: Re: hey you

Hi Dee....sounds good....hope we still recognize each other. (Steve and me that is)

Had my visit with the cardiologist today...he wants me to go to the hospital to get an amigo or catheter exam within the next couple of weeks...tried to postpone it until February, but he wouldn't go for it. Anyway, it's a simple one day, in and out procedure, so it shouldn't affect any visit plans...which I'm still trying to figure out.

My Steve is back in school...trip for Matt and Dave was horrible...in the rain, bad traffic...took 5 hours to go what should take less than 2 hours. Dave didn't even have enough time to really see the campus, which is the reason he went along (reluctantly), so he's pissed at me for making him go. He did at least see the dorm and some of the buildings. Oh well.

Anyhow...I'll talk to you soon!!

Love, -Stan-

p.s. Almost had a win for the Jets...but no cigar!!

----- Original Message -----
From: Dee Keller
To: Stanley S
Sent: Monday, November 28, 2005 2:20 PM
Subject: RE: hey you

Wait a minute... I thought all the tests were negative when you were in the hospital. What is he looking for? Don't push yourself and if these trips are too much please tell me. We'll figure something out. Maybe I should come up there for New Years instead.... your health is more important. Besides, we could always pray for a snow storm and the airports closing :) - not much chance of that happening down here.

love you,
Dee

From: Stanley S
Sent: Mon 11/28/2005 2:55 PM
To: Dee Keller
Subject: Re: hey you

I wouldn't bet on it not snowing us in...even down there. This is a strange year for weather.

Yes, the initial tests in the ER were negative, but according to the cardiologist I saw today, they weren't complete or detailed enough to rule out a problem in there. Not only that, but he wants me to go to the heart center in DC....another hassle, because Matt will have to drive me there and back and it takes all day beginning at 6am. Anyway, either I go there and do it, or I go to a closer hospital and have some of it done now, and some later....I'd rather get it all done at once. Once this is ruled out, then I can schedule something with the gastroenterologist to see if I have any post-operative adhesions or something....but I'll put that off until February at least and just deal with the pain...it's manageable anyway. The main concern is to rule out anything that needs immediate attention so we can figure out the next steps to take.

As to the visit over New Year's...I still plan on coming down there...it's only the visits in between that we'll have to try and plan day by day....but I'm determined for us to get together even if I have to get there by ambulance (he, he).

I told the doc about Rogaine....did you know it was originally developed as a blood pressure medicine? It didn't work, but people got hairy...that's how it came to be an anti-baldness drug used topically. It used to be taken in pill form. Also, it caused "Angina" whose symptoms include chest pain.

Anyway, don't sweat things...I'm ok, and I'll let you in on any news good or bad as it occurs.

Love You!!
-Me-

I wanted so badly to be able to get together before Christmas, especially when things didn't work out for Thanksgiving. Keeping myself occupied during that time was pretty easy for me. I was still working two jobs and getting ready for the holidays.

I started making plans for his boys' Christmas presents and spent a lot of time thinking of each of them and what would be the perfect gift that they would remember. I wanted to put my personal touch on each gift. Stan and I spent time on the phone, and he gave me a list of what each of the boys liked and what they had specifically asked for.

We tried to see about Stan coming down for a long weekend in early December, and a lot of it depended upon how he was feeling. I knew he was still having chest pains and had gone to the doctors, but he still insisted he was going to put off any procedures until after the holidays. He was so afraid if he went to the doctors they would put him in the hospital during the holidays, and he wanted nothing to do with it.

Chapter 13
Getting to Know His Wife
December 2005

We started making plans for the Christmas and New Year's holidays. I had enough vacation time to take off between the two holidays, giving me 11 days off. I had from December 23rd until January 2nd off.

The main plan was to spend as much time with Stan as possible. We discussed which days were the most important and both agreed that Christmas day we would stay at our own homes with our boys and then the rest of the time we would spend together. We decided he would drive down on December 26th.

He mentioned that he still didn't know what Shelley's plans were for the holidays yet, and he knew she wanted to spend some time with their boys. He said that when Shelly was up there, he would spend that time with me, and we began making our arrangements. I was excited we had a plan for the holidays, and I knew when we would be together.

Shelley called Stan the next day saying she had decided she was coming up to visit December 26th through the 30th.

Stan called me that night, "Honey, I'm sorry but the plans have changed. Shelley is coming up and I won't be able to come down until the 30th."

I was devastated; instead of seven days together, we would only have 3. The phone call ended in Stan trying to assure me that there was nothing between him and Shelley.

My last statement was to him was "It seems it is more important to be with Shelley than me. Maybe we should call the whole trip off and forget about any plans for being together for the holidays." The hurt consumed me so much that I knew I was talking out of anger and had to get off the phone before I said anything else I would be sorry for.

He tried to call me a few days later but I was still so upset that I didn't feel I could talk to him yet and didn't answer the phone. I was too upset and needed to cool off first so I wouldn't say anything else I didn't mean. I decided to email him instead.

----- Original Message -----
From: Dee Keller
To: Stanley S
Sent: Monday, December 05, 2005 11:27 AM

I got the message you called last night and you probably haven't noticed but I haven't tried to contact you since our last talk. You said you would call me last Thursday after you talked with Shelley about the holidays but you didn't so I can only assume your holiday plans with her are set.

You know, we spoke about what time I had off just days before she called you and I thought we had made plans for that time. From how I see things, you had 2 choices when she called, you could have told her it was a bad time to come up because you were going to spend the time with me but, instead you called ME to say you're going to spend the time with her.

I'd be lying if I said this didn't hurt because it does more than you will ever know. I have been so upset since our talk last week and I'm not sure what to do or say at this point.

I love you but I can't fight a battle that I have no control over. I feel like I'm fighting a battle I can never win. Did you ever hear the saying "Actions speak louder than words"? Well, you say one thing to me but your actions are telling me something totally different.

From: Stanley S
Sent: Mon 12/5/2005 3:24 PM
To: Dee Keller
Subject: Re: And By the Way...

What can I say? you won't believe it anyhow...believe I'm a liar if you want...Shelley will be here on the 26th and staying until the 30th TO SEE THE BOYS. I would have been home here while she was here for 2 days. I was calling you last night to tell you what I thought would be good news, that we would have 6 days to spend together...so how is that putting her first? Now it seems I won't be coming down at all. If YOU want to leave me alone, that's your decision. I just can't make

- 208 -

you understand that I don't like to make plans because they always seem to fall through...I don't DECIDE to cancel...you expect me to have control over things that I don't. Now you turn around the phone call thing...it wouldn't be a discussion...you would accuse me, and guilt me. Once again, when we talked about me coming down...as I recall it was two visits, one before Christmas and one during the time you would be off...you indicated that you wanted mostly just to spend time together and that over New Year's would be great...I misunderstood your work and time off schedule thinking you could shift around the time you had to use or lose, and made the (false) assumption that Christmas Day itself wasn't a priority. And, I thought you understood why the other visit did not appear possible. I am what I am...if you want me, I'm here...believe me or not...be patient or not...love me or not...

I'm pissed, but I love you more than anything... always will...and this is breaking my heart because we can't seem to make it work....I don't know what else to say, I'm tapped, and I probably am saying things now because I'm upset and depressed...I'm sorry

From: Stanley S
Sent: Monday, December 05, 2005 12:26 PM
To: Dee Keller
Subject: Re: And By the Way...

Shelley told me she had her lawyer's office draw up divorce papers...guess you don't care about that now...

From: Dee Keller
To: Stanley S
Sent: Monday, December 05, 2005 12:36 PM
Subject: RE: And By the Way...

I've always cared, I just didn't think you did. You were the one who said you didn't want to do it right now. I don't want to get into a battle over who said what. I was trying to explain how frustrated I am over this situation. You keep canceling coming down here and when you called saying she was coming up there during the time I thought we would be together, it hurt really bad. I guess telling you how I feel wasn't anything you wanted to hear. You shouldn't have to keep defending yourself but it just seems like you keep putting her ahead of me. If you avoid calling because you don't want to discuss things or hear that I'm upset then there is nothing I can do. I'm sorry and will leave you alone.

----- Original Message -----
From: Dee Keller
To: Stanley S
Sent: Monday, December 05, 2005 8:00 PM

Subject: RE: And By the Way...

Call me if you want to talk and work this out. I think we're both feeling the frustrations of everything, I guess me more than you. I do love you.

From: Stanley S
Sent: Monday, December 05, 2005 10:34 PM
To: Dee Keller
Subject: Re: And By the Way...

Dee,

I think it's time you talked directly to Shelley. I talked to her tonight and she chastised me...she wants to talk to you and give you her perspective and assurances. She has your e-mail, but would rather call...I said I would have to ask your permission before giving her your number. Let me know. Yes, I'd like to talk to you...but not when I'm upset....you get quiet when you're upset...I do too...it happens for a reason.

Love, -Stan-

From: Dee Keller
Sent: Tue 12/6/2005 8:15 AM
To: 'Stanley S'
Subject: RE: And By the Way...

I'm glad you decided not to call last night... you are right in us needing a little time before we talk, maybe in a few days or weeks after all has cooled down we can discuss things. It gave me time to re-read your message to try and see things from your perspective.

I never said anything about Christmas day.... I'm sorry if you got that impression. I thought we both agreed it was important to spend that day with our own boys. As for the other time, I've been trying to get as much time with you before tax season starts.... I've told you how busy it is for me during that time. I work pretty much straight thru from January until April 15th, nights and weekends. The timing, for now, just isn't with us and it won't be any better in the coming months. I guess I was just trying to fit in as much time as possible and I'm sorry for the pressure.

Having you as pissed off as you are because I wanted to spend time together shows I am pushing you too hard for your time. I guess it was the lack of communication that made me wonder but now I understand the reasons for you not calling. Love Dee

- 210 -

I was beginning to think that maybe our relationship wasn't what I originally thought. His relationship with Shelley was starting to bother me and his lack of total understanding of how I was feeling and that he thought me talking to Shelley would be the fix to our strained relationship frustrated me. Our problems really weren't with her. They were between us, and bringing in an outside factor could only make things more frustrating.

I received an email from Shelley saying how happy she was for us and that she had actually been praying for me to come into his life. She had felt so guilty through the years since she left and only wanted him to find happiness, especially after all he went through with his cancer.

From: Shelley
Sent: Tuesday, December 06, 2005 2:38 PM
To: Dee Keller
Subject: Hi Dee

Hi Dee:
I hope you don't get angry with me for contacting you. I have had your e-mail for a long time from a joke that I had saved that Stan had sent or forwarded. I really need to speak with you. You see, I talked to Stan the other night and he was really down in the dumps about the two of you. I feel responsible and I would like you to give me the opportunity to clear things up if you will let me. If he knew I contacted you he would probably stroke out but I really feel like you need to hear it from me. So I ask that you will please listen and hopefully you will forgive any ill words that were said. Stan has a tendency to say stupid things when he gets backed in a corner and becomes defensive and I hope to clear the air.

Firstly, I want you to know that I am tickled to death that you both have been seeing each other. I know all this seems very strange to you and perhaps you are confused about this whole thing. But I promise you, I can clear up any misunderstanding if you give me the chance. I spent hours thinking last night how I would approach you and then another hour this morning writing you a letter to send. I want you to know from my heart that I have no intention of "popping" back in

Stan's life as a significant other and I want to get a divorce as quick as possible.

So if you will let me, I would at least like to speak with you person to person or send you an e-mail and I really would like to be your friend or at least on speaking terms. My kids adore you and I really would like to get to know you better. After all, we both live in Georgia. I told Stan a while back that I would be happy to pick you up in Atlanta and would welcome the travel companionship if you would like to travel with me to Maryland. I would stay somewhere else if it makes you uncomfortable. Think about it.

I look forward to hearing from you. Contact me at home (***) ***-**** or work (***) ***-**** or by e-mail Shelley@mail.com. Stan loves you and I would hate to be the cause of any ill feelings so I ask you to help me out.

From: Dee Keller
Sent: Tue 12/6/2005 3:32 PM
To: 'Shelley A. S'
Subject: RE: Hi Dee

Shelley,
Stan had actually suggested we talk so I don't foresee any stroke on his part. I have no ill feelings towards you or about you going up there. Those are your boys and you deserve as much time with them as you want and can get. They are great. I cherish all of the time I have gotten to spend with them and they have made me feel so welcome.

I've tried to explain to Stan how his distance and unwillingness to discuss things with me has given me the wrong impression. We'll never have the communication between us that I thought we did but then again, nothing is ever as it seems. You aren't the cause of any of our problems.... communication is. I would love to talk and want you to know that you aren't the problem and I do see that. I'm sorry he felt the need to involve you but at least you have the type of relationship where you can talk about anything. It does make it easier during a separation and divorce, I know mine was a nightmare and I don't have the same type of relationship with my ex as you two have. It is important, especially for the kids, mine unfortunately have grown up with just me and I do see the effect it's had on them. I should be home tonight if you'd like to talk.... my number is ***-***-****.

And again, you have no reason to feel responsible for any of our problems and I really hope he didn't give you that impression.

Dee Keller

Shelley called me that evening. We spent close to two hours on the phone. It was a little strange at first, but she was very talkative and I could tell wanted to share with me exactly how she felt about Stan. She told me about their split and what parts she took the blame for. Both of their versions were similar. She really didn't blame him for their problems. As with him, she felt they both contributed to the lack of communication and lack of trying. I guess in time they both grew apart.

We talked about the Christmas plans, and she offered to pick me up and have me join her for the trip again. The thought of it scared me a bit. I didn't know if I could handle seeing the two of them together and seeing what type of relationship they really had.

From: Shelley
Sent: Tuesday, December 06, 2005 10:28 PM
To: Dee
Subject: Great Talking With You, Dee

Dee,
I just wanted to say how nice it was to talk with you. We have a lot more in common than you probably realize. I called and talked with Stan briefly as he was getting ready for bed. I told him he needed to call you and set things right and he said he was going to call you but I told him you were talking with your friend and he said he would call you tomorrow.

I told him he needed to be more understanding and quit being such a horse's ass. He laughed and knew I was right. One thing I meant to mention and it slipped my feeble mind, Dee, is Stan isn't much of a talker. If he doesn't have anything important to say he doesn't pick up the phone. Don't take it to heart he's just always been that way. He would rather have a meaningful conversation than talk about the price of celery in the supermarket. (My mom used to call me to discuss the price of celery so I thought it was a good analogy). I told him if he doesn't feel like talking, rather than being short and making you feel like you are taking up time, or talking to yourself, he could at least send an e-mail and say, "hey Babe, thinking of you, love ya, etc.".

Short sweet and to the point. Men are not very creative are they? ha ha. I mean how hard would that be? Just call me Cupid. ha ha.

Anyways, I told him he needs to work on the communication department because right now he is getting a "D" in that department and if he ever expects to have a relationship with anyone that his communication skills need to improve. He realizes he lacks in that area and said he will try to be more understanding and not so short.

Please give him a chance, Dee. I think things will really start to improve.

Take care.
Shelley

Stan called me the next evening and we talked things out. He suggested I come up with Shelley on the 26th and then he and I could drive back together on the 28th. He would stay at my place until January 2nd.

I still wasn't sure if I could handle going up there. I continued to be uncomfortable with the idea, despite Shelley's attempts to make me feel at ease. I was also concerned about how his boys would feel. It was one thing knowing I existed in his life but to have both his mom and me in the same house at the same time might make them uncomfortable also. I asked Stan to please ask the boys how they felt and that would determine my answer. It took a couple of weeks before Stan told me about how the boys felt, but it seemed like the idea was a good one to them also.

From: Stanley
Sent: Sun 12/11/2005 1:35 AM
To: Dee Keller
Subject: la, la,la

Getting the house ready for ya...if you plan to come up with Shelley that is.. Counting the days baby :)
Love, -Me-

I got such a chuckle from his message…. He was trying so hard to convince me to come up, hoping that seeing them together would finally put my mind at ease. I decided to just not think about it, but of course, Stan continually consumed my thoughts.

I would email him at least once a day to check in and let him know that I loved him. I could see he was trying to make an effort to work on his communication, and I started hearing from him a little more. He gave me every way I could contact him, any hour—day or night—which did relieve some of my anxieties as I counted the days until Christmas.

During this time, Shelley and I started corresponding everyday about everything and nothing. Whenever I didn't hear from Stan, I would ask her if she had. Or even when I did hear from him, I would ask if she had talked to him that day. I know she called frequently to speak with the boys, and occasionally Stan would get on the phone and talk. It was a little strange talking to his wife about our relationship, but she seemed to be very supportive of it.

When I talked to him the weekend before Christmas, he didn't sound like himself. Normally, when I called, no matter his mood, he would always cheer up. That time he didn't, and I wondered why. He'd said he hadn't been feeling very well and blamed it on all the traveling he'd been doing back and forth to West Virginia to either pick up Steve at college or drop him back off.

I was so worried and couldn't wait for the day we were together again.

Shelley shared many things with me about not only her relationship with Stan but also her current relationship. It made me wonder if she was confiding in Stan about her current relationship problems also. It worried me because she was unhappy about some of the same things I was, like lack of communication and if somehow he was taking the trip as a possibility that Shelley would come back home.

Shelley tried very hard to be friends, but I was still a bit apprehensive about it. I knew we could be friends but there would be a limit as to how much I could really share with her. After all, she was still married to Stan, so I didn't share a lot of the details about us, especially things like our plans for getting married or him wanting to have a child with me. I just wasn't comfortable coming out and sharing that with her.

From: Dee Keller
Sent: Monday, December 19, 2005 11:32 AM
To: Shelley A. S
Subject:

Did you talk to Stan at all this weekend? We spoke last night and he sounded really depressed. Not his usual self.

> **From:** Shelley A. S
> **Sent:** Monday, December 19, 2005 12:25 PM
> **To:** Dee Keller
> **Subject:** RE:
>
> I talked with him yesterday. He was exhausted from shopping and maybe a little down. He had to go pick up Steven Saturday. Says he feels like he is in a whirlwind with everything he still needs to do. Maybe that was just it. Knowing him, he probably ate too much and was in agony.

From: Dee
Sent: Monday, December 19, 2005 12:25 PM
To: Shelley A. S
Subject: RE:

You're probably right.... he was pressuring me to give him an answer about coming up there but I didn't want to say anything yet. I know he's really worried about the chest pains... if he would just go and get it checked out. He's thinking the worst and I'm really hoping it's not. He really thinks that whatever it is will lay him up for weeks. He can be so stubborn.

> **From:** Shelley A. S
> **Sent:** Monday, December 19, 2005 12:30 PM
> **To:** Dee Keller
> **Subject:** RE:

- 216 -

I told you so! Stubborn is his middle name.

From: Dee
Sent: Monday, December 19, 2005 12:41 PM
To: Shelley A. S
Subject: RE:

He'll just need to get over that...I've gotten pretty stubborn in my old age so he's in for a real battle

> **From:** Shelley A. S
> **Sent:** Monday, December 19, 2005 12:47 PM
> **To:** Dee Keller
> **Subject:** RE:
>
> You and me both. I have gotten to be such a witch. I am sick of being shit on, not paid attention to, and picking up after men.

From: Dee Keller
Sent: Monday, December 19, 2005 12:47 PM
To: Shelley A. S
Subject: RE:

Tell ya what.... when we get up there, first thing I'm going to do is slap the back of his head
Talk about no attention.... that's my biggest complaint about him, makes me wonder if this is what I'm in for if we did get together

---

It seemed I had more communication with Shelley during this time than with Stan. It was starting to get to me a bit, and letting him know that it still bothered me to see how close he and Shelley were was hard to explain to him. It was another major difference between us. While he forgave her for leaving, when someone hurt me, I had a hard time forgiving them. It made me wonder how he could so easily forgive her. It made me wonder if his forgiving her was perhaps to let her know that the door was still open for her to return.

It seemed like every time I tried to get time with him anymore, it didn't seem as important to him as it was to me. I tried to see how far we could stretch the time together during

- 217 -

the holidays. I was starting to worry about my time off from my part-time job and didn't want to work at all during our time together.

From: Shelley A. S
Sent: Thursday, December 22, 2005 8:28 AM
To: Dee Keller
Subject: RE: hey woman

I am getting so excited. We are going to have such a blast! I know people must think we all have the most crazy relationship going. I don't care. My way of thinking is why do people have to be at each other's throats just because something didn't work out.

P.S. do you think it would be bad timing for me to present Stan with divorce papers to sign or do you think I should wait until after the 1st? :) I am eager to get this over with. I don't think I need a summons if I am presenting it to him in person, and since everything is agreeable I don't even know why I need a lawyer's signature on it anyways. Can't I just act as myself? Now let's see, I get Stan to sign the agreement first and then I guess we file everything. Right?

From: Dee Keller
Sent: Thu 12/22/2005 8:37 AM
To: 'Shelley A. S'
Subject: RE: hey woman

I know about what you're saying, everyone here thinks I'm crazy. About the only person that understands this relationship is my mom, she thinks it's great. One of my buddy's here wants Stan's email address to let him know how nuts he is getting us together. I'm the same way, if it can be handled without bullshit, why bring it in. No reason everyone can't get along. It's a shame I don't have the same relationship with my ex. I sort of do, we can talk but he does get on my nerves especially when he calls drunk. That's when he gets all sentimental and talking about how we should have tried harder and all the crap.

On the papers, to be honest, I'd rather not be there when you give them to him. Even though it was the right thing for me to do, I do remember how it affected me. That might work out better if just the two of you were there. I have a feeling he is going to have a rough time with it regardless of what he's saying. It's only natural, I was

- 218 -

pretty upset myself even knowing I had to do it. But, It is up to you and I understand you wanting to get it over with.

After the papers are all done, Stan just has to sign them in front of a notary and then you make a court date. It's pretty easy actually.

With Shelley finally mentioning the divorce, I was surprised she wanted my advice on it. I felt uncomfortable being there when she gave him the papers. I'd remembered my divorce. Even though it was the right thing to do, it still upset me. My ex and I had dinner the night we got divorced and talked about what went wrong. It had actually been a good conversation, and we were both surprised at how well we got along now that we were no longer a couple.

Shelley was already counting on me going with her to Maryland, even though I was still had not made a decision. ·

Hearing for the first time that the papers were all drawn up, I was starting to feel a little more at ease about his relationship with Shelley. Hearing that she couldn't wait for it to happen and that she would finally be able to marry her boyfriend of the past six years was definitely the news I wanted to hear, but hearing she would have the divorce papers with her made me even more apprehensive about going.

Shelley and I continued to correspond every day, and I could sense her frustration with me each time I showed any apprehension about going with her. It was a long drive to Maryland, and if I joined her, she would have some company for 10 hours of her 14 hour ride. I kept arguing that I didn't want to get in the way of her time with her boys, but she insisted that her time with them would be after Stan and I left and that we could share the time with them while I was there. It was nice to see she wanted me to have a relationship with her boys, knowing I wasn't trying to replace her in their lives; I would only replace her in Stan's.

When my ex remarried, I wanted it to be like that, but his new wife didn't want a relationship with my boys. I was very glad Shelley felt no jealousy about me having a relationship with her sons. They were so important to Stan, which made them important to me, and I could feel that Stan felt the same towards my sons.

The closer the time came to her departure, the more I wanted to go with her. Besides missing him terribly, I was also afraid with the way he'd been feeling that if I didn't go up there, he might not have the strength to drive all the way down to Georgia by himself. I was worried something might happen during the trip, and he really needed someone to be with him and possibly share some of the driving.

I was so torn by wanting to see him but at the same time feeling guilty for being asked to be a part of their family time together. I was bothered by their closeness and didn't know quite how to handle the situation.

I knew that my past with Billy had a lot to do with my feelings. The fact that it took Billy so long to finally get his divorce fueled my fears that the same would happen with Stan. I dreaded going through that again, even though Stan promised he was going to get the divorce, and Shelley confided to me that it was her deepest desire to make the divorce happen. I'd been told so many excuses before in my life that I had learned to mistrust words until they were followed through with action. I knew deep down that I could never really compare Stan with Billy, but the divorce issue continued to be my stumbling block.

It was driving Stan crazy that I wouldn't commit to coming up with Shelley, and I was beginning to really believe that they did want me to go. Every time we talked, all he would go on about was me coming up with her, and I could feel the excitement he was feeling. He'd told me that it had been a long time since they'd had any type of "Norman Rockwell" holiday and having me there would bring it back.

I was still worried about how his boys would handle it. Having Shelley and I there together would only be a validation that they would be getting a divorce. I hated that it was me that was causing the divorce to finally happen while at the same time I wanted nothing more than for the divorce to be finalized.

He'd told me that I was the catalyst that was causing the divorce, even though he would never take her back. He kept assuring me that it was a good thing and not bad. I wasn't the cause of their split but would be the reason for their divorce.

Chapter 14
The Christmas Holiday Trip
December 26th – January 2nd

I didn't make a final decision until the day we were to leave. Talking with Shelley on the phone and emails were one thing, but being face-to-face was another. I wondered what she looked like and if seeing the two of us next to each other would make him possibly change his mind about us. I suddenly realized how insecure I was with our relationship, and how much I didn't like how I was feeling.

Wanting to be with him again became more important than my apprehension about seeing them together. Shelley got to my house about 10AM to pick me up for the long drive to Maryland. As soon as she got there, I went outside to greet her, and she gave me a big hug. I felt at ease with her right away and saw how happy she was to finally meet me in person. I could tell immediately that the trip would be fine. She made me feel so welcome, and I knew all the talking between the emails and phone calls were really how she felt about me, and it wasn't just an act. Everyone I had told about us traveling together thought it might be a strained situation, but our personalities clicked so much that I really felt we would have a good time and possibly a good friendship that could last.

The drive was 10 hours and the only part that was a bit strained was that she didn't smoke. I've always been very respectful to those who don't and felt uncomfortable smoking in front of others that didn't. I didn't even smoke in my own home because my sons didn't like it.

We talked the entire ride up, and I got to know her pretty well. It was good to see how well we really got along, and it made the ride up there fly by.

I called Stan when we were about 45 minutes from the house just to give him some warning about when we would arrive. It was the only time in months that when I got off the phone, I didn't end it with "I love you". Somehow I just didn't feel it was appropriate yet. I could tell he felt the same, he didn't say it to me either, but instead he said, "I'm so excited you're almost here. I can't wait to see you."

We pulled into the driveway. Shelley tooted the horn, and his middle son Steve came outside immediately to great us. Here it was, the end of December in Maryland and freezing outside, but he came out with only shorts on. I chuckled and said, "You are crazy, get back in the house dressed like that." He smiled and gave both Shelley and I a hug. Steve grabbed the largest pieces of luggage, and we walked to the house hands full.

When I walked into the house, Stan greeted us at the top of the stairs. He gave me that look he always did and smiled and gave me a big hug and kiss. Matt and Dave then came out to greet us, and it was so nice to see that they really didn't mind Shelley and me coming up together and were embracing the relationship between Stan and I with open arms.

The first thing I wanted to do was go have a cigarette, so I took my things to Stan's bedroom and sat for a smoke and to freshen up a bit from the long ride. After I was done, I went out into the kitchen and found Stan cooking dinner for us. I could see he was crying. He smiled at me and said, "I didn't realize until I saw you again how much I'd really missed being with you." He looked so tired, and I could see the physical pain he was feeling in his eyes. He had put up such a front that the pain wasn't that bad, but I could tell he wasn't doing well when I finally saw him in person. After his heart attack scare, he was so adamant about waiting to go to the doctors that it caused some tension between us. I just wanted to know what was wrong.

I walked over to him and we embraced. I could tell he didn't want to let me go. It was a strange knowing that his wife was in the next room, but when she walked into the kitchen, I could tell by the look on her face, it didn't bother

her at all. It was so strange that Stan and I were uncomfortable but Shelley seemed at ease when she saw the two of us together. I think it finally gave her a relief to the guilt she had been feeling all these years for the way she left.

Stan had gone to great lengths to make us a wonderful dinner that evening. He made lamb chops with two vegetable dishes, potatoes and even an appetizer. Dinner was delicious as usual. I was amazed at how upbeat his boys were, and I knew a lot of it had to do with how well Shelley and I were getting along. They could see that there was no animosity between us, and we had actually become pretty good friends.

After dinner we adjourned to the downstairs where he had his tree set up. I originally told him that we could exchange our gifts to each other when we were alone, but I could tell he couldn't wait for me to open my presents. I had only brought one gift for him, deciding I wanted to have something for him when we got back to my house. Out of all the gifts I bought him, I decided to give him the cordless phone while I was up there.

I sat back and let them take the lead on how the gifts would be distributed. I didn't know what their traditions were and thought I would just go with the flow.

Stan and his boys had a private Christmas together on Christmas day, but he saved some presents to give to them while Shelley and I were there. When I got downstairs and saw all the unopened presents, I could see they wanted to have everyone there for most of the unwrapping. Stan had given his boys their big gifts and left just the little ones and the stockings for our time.

Stan handed out all of the presents to everyone and then everyone, at the same time everyone started opening the gifts. I sat back a little bit and watched the boys because I wanted to see their reactions to my gifts. Inside of each gift I gave them, I wrote a special note to each of them and signed them *"Santa from Atlanta, Love Dee"*.

Dave was the first to find and open my gift. I gave him a clock from his favorite football team, and the note to him said: *Every "time" the Falcons beat the Panthers you'll think of me.* He smiled and said, "Ah Dee, this is great." The Falcons are the Atlanta football team, and between the Jets and the Panthers, we had a little battle of the territories going on during the football season.

For Steve, I made him a box and inside had Dallas Cowboy Cheerleader playing cards. The note to him said: *Someday the "girls" will be cheering for you.* He smiled at me and said, "Thanks, these are great."

For Matt, I made him a box that he could put his art supplies in. It was just the right size for his paint brushes and pencils. I also gave Matt a pair of lounge pants that I got from the Jets website. The Jets were his favorite team. He smiled and said, "These are perfect. Thank you Dee."

I knew how much all of them loved football and wanted to give them something they didn't have already. I loved seeing the look in their eyes when they opened my gifts. They made me feel so loved and welcomed in their lives.

I started with opening the gifts I got from Shelley. She had gotten me the same thing I got her: candles! When I opened her gift, it made me feel better that I not only included her in my gift-giving but also that she thought enough to get me something.

It was then time to open Stan's gifts to me. He not only got me quite a few gifts, he even stuffed a stocking for me with a lot of little things.

The first gifts I opened were two books, both of which were about the CIA. The first one was a cookbook/history book on the CIA. It was written by different CIA agents and had a lot of recipes that they shared from all of the travels in different countries they had visited. The other book was about the women who were married to CIA agents and even some stories about women that were agents themselves. I could tell Stan wanted me to learn as much as possible and maybe get an understanding of what his life had been like since the years we were together so long ago.

Inside of my stocking were two little boxes. He stopped me before I opened them and said, "One of them is kind of a joke gift, and the other is from my heart."

I opened the joke one first, it was a magnet for my refrigerator that was a small computer and when you hit the little button on it, it said, *"You've got mail."*

I then knew the second little box wasn't the joke, and I couldn't wait to see what it was. It was in a tiny box, and I gently opened it. Inside was a beautiful heart necklace that had an amethyst stone with a diamond on the side. I was so surprised and he could tell how much I liked it. I put it down beside me and decided to wait until we were alone to put it on.

I continued to open my presents and the next big one he gave me was a knick-knack that is a bit hard to describe, but I will do my best. The shape was kind of odd; sort of like an egg, but on the outside it had a beautiful decoration of a woman and when I shook it you could tell there was something inside. Stan explained, "They are called Nesting Dolls." He showed me how to open it and it turned out to really be five separate pieces. Each one had the same shape but a little smaller than the other so it would fit inside the other. All of them were decorated very similar but when looking at the details, each was unique. It was so different than anything I'd seen before and couldn't wait to find the perfect place in my house for it.

Stan finally got to my present, and I sat in anticipation to see his reaction. After all the hounding I had done about calling me, I wasn't sure how he would take me getting him a cordless phone. He smiled when he opened it and said, "Now I'm sure there's a hidden meaning somewhere for this." I told him the main reason was so he didn't have to stretch the phone cord to let me hear Matt and Dave playing their guitars. I was surprised that he actually really liked it.

There was only one big present left to open and that was from Shelley to Stan. I wondered what it could be, especially because of the size of the box. When he opened it and heard his reaction, I was a bit disappointed. He had this bathrobe that he loved but it was very worn out. It looked like a magician's robe with the stars and moons all over it. Shelley said that she was tired of seeing him wear the old worn out one, so she got on EBay and found the exact same robe. He was so excited. I was disappointed because I also had bought him a robe and was very glad I didn't bring that gift with me, I even thought about not giving it to him at all after seeing his reaction to hers. I figured I would decide whether or not to give it to him once we got to my house.

After all the presents were opened, Matt got up and asked Stan, "Is it time?" Stan said, "Yes".

Matt left the room and came back a moment later handing both Shelley and I paintings he had made especially for us. Both paintings were of hummingbirds, and they were gorgeous.

Stan had told me weeks ago that Matt was making me something for Christmas, and knowing how talented he was, I couldn't wait to see what he was creating for me. His gift touched me so much. I knew I had to find a place that would display it for everyone who visited my home. It brought tears to my eyes, and I tried not to show it; again, I didn't want to overshadow any reactions that Shelley might have for hers.

This was so difficult; my reaction to his gift would have been so different if she hadn't been there. I wanted so much to just jump up and give him the biggest hug and let him know how special that gift really was to me. He told me that Stan made the frame for it. Now, I had something special from the both of them that I could keep forever.

After the gifts were all opened and we said our thank you's to each other, everyone went to their own space.

When we got to Stan's room, the first thing I did was ask him to put the necklace on me. I loved it, and the stone was my favorite color. I could see how happy he was that I wanted to put it on right away. I told him I would never take it off.

That night we were both a little uneasy about doing anything while Shelley was only a few doors down the hall, so we spent the time talking and holding each other. It felt so good to be in his arms again.

On Tuesday morning, I got up a little earlier than Stan and went out to the kitchen to have some coffee. Shelley was up already, and we sat and talked until Stan got up.

He made us a late breakfast, and then he started on the big Christmas dinner he had planned. He was making a turducken, or should I say his version of a turducken? He stuffed a duck with a goose, instead of the traditional duck inside a turkey. I'd never had it before and had such fun watching him prepare it.

We then took our showers, and he wanted to go shopping. For the first time, it wasn't just for food. We first went to this novelty-type food store that had a lot of different things from other countries. He'd said it was one of his favorite stores. I picked up some cooking oil that had garlic in it and a couple of Christmas stuffed animals. I had warned Stan that I had one obnoxious Christmas habit; I have a collection of over 50 stuffed animals, all with a Christmas theme to them. That is how I decorate my house for the holidays. I'd started the collection over 15 years ago and each year right after Christmas; I would buy a couple of them. I could never justify the cost of them before the holiday, but the few days after, they are sold for practically nothing. He chuckled when I picked them out, and I told him, "Just wait till you see the rest of them."

We then went shopping for Ed's present. Stan wasn't sure what to get him and wanted my opinion. As soon as we walked into the store, we saw this really nice leather chair that I knew Ed would love. Stan said, "Let's keep looking in case there's another one we like better." After trying out every chair in the store, we went back to the first one we saw and got it for him. Stan put it in the back of his SUV, and we decided we'd just leave it there until we got to Georgia. I couldn't wait for Ed to see the chair.

Stan had already ordered Steven's gift and was proud at what he'd come up with. With just the short period of time getting to know my son, he'd decided to get him some steaks from *Omaha Steaks* and had them delivered to his house. I knew that would be a great gift, so my present to Steven was a *George Forman Grill* for his new apartment. Since he'd moved out, that was the one thing he missed the most, grilling steaks. I knew both would be the perfect combination gift for Steven.

Dinner that evening was, again, delicious. I watched him prepare all of the dishes, and he occasionally asked for help just to get me involved. It was so nice being able to enjoy dinner with all of them, and even the boys seemed to be in the greatest of moods.

On Wednesday morning, as we prepared to leave for Georgia, his boys came out to say goodbye. I was touched that they made the effort to get up early and help us pack the car. They each gave me a hug and told me to come back anytime, that they enjoyed my visits and especially the great mood it put Stan in.

On the drive back south, Stan and I drove down to Virginia to the area where we met the second weekend we had spent together for our last minute rendezvous, and we decided to try out another hotel this time. He was feeling really bad that day, so we just had a small dinner and sat in the room talking for hours. I could see how disappointed he was that he wasn't feeling very well and how much he just wanted to hold me. I kept telling him it was okay. "Being with you again was all I needed. We have plenty of time for sex and doing things together in the future. Let's just spend this time enjoying being here alone."

It started snowing as we arrived at the hotel. It was a beautiful quiet evening as the snow fell.

Stan was in more pain tonight and I was afraid of him driving any further. I was beginning to wonder if we should just head back to his house so he was closer to his doctors but Stan wanted to hear nothing about it. He wanted to go see my boys and get to know them better, and he didn't want to put off visiting them anymore.

He made love to me that night, but I could tell it took everything he had to keep the pain he was feeling from getting in the way. He said, "I can never imagine not wanting you. You make my whole body come alive again and for many years after Shelley left I didn't think I would ever feel this way again about anyone."

We stayed overnight in Virginia to keep the amount of driving limited and not put any further strain on how Stan was feeling. This also allowed us to be alone for the night. I could tell he wasn't doing well, though he did try to put up a good front. He avoided eating as much as possible because he'd said that food seemed to enhance the pain in his chest. I was hoping that meant the cause was possibly some type of stomach issue instead of anything more serious, like his heart.

The next morning we continued our drive to Georgia.

We tried to avoid the subject of how he was feeling so Stan asked, "Did you develop the slides I left my last trip?" On my first visit to his house, he gave me negatives of pictures he had taken of me when I was 16.

I smiled and said, "You ruined one of my surprises."

I had purposely left them home so I had something to give him when we were alone.

"I can't wait to see them." He said.

- 231 -

I was looking forward to see his reaction when he did see them.

Occasionally I would ask if he wanted me to drive some, but he would respond that he was concerned that it would be too much for my back and he was doing fine.

We arrived at my house in the early afternoon Thursday. When I first walked in the door, I noticed a new Christmas stuffed animal that was sitting on the steps. Ed came down the stairs, and I asked him where it came from.

He said, "I'm assuming Steven got it for you. When I got up and came downstairs it was here." Steven was so sweet to remember my collection, and he knew each of them had a special meaning. I had three new ones for that year that I would really cherish.

Ed gave me a hug and shook Stan's hand. Stan smiled and gave him a big hug too.

Stan and I had the luggage out of the car when we came in except for Ed's chair. Stan said to him, "Hey Ed, there's one piece of luggage left in the car, would you go get it for me?" We followed him outside, and he smiled when he saw the chair. It was exactly what he had wanted.

"It's exactly what I was looking for! Thank you." Ed gave me another hug and then brought his new chair up to his room.

Once all the luggage and packages were taken upstairs, we decided to find a place for Matt's painting. Stan found the perfect place on the wall in my living room and hung it for me.

I then looked around for a place for the knick-knack Stan had gotten me. With all the Christmas decorations consuming my living room, I figured I would find a temporary place for it until the decorations came down.

Since Stan's last visit my older son Steven had moved out, so I had invited him over for dinner that first night.

Steven came into the house like he still lived there and said, "I'm here, we can open the presents now."

We were in the kitchen and he walked down the hallway to find us. I was at the stove getting dinner ready while Stan and Ed were at the table talking.

"Presents will wait until after dinner, it's almost done." I said.

The three of them proceeded to have their own conversation as I tended to dinner.

I left the kitchen for a moment to be sure everything was set for our Christmas celebration afterwards. Everything looked perfect, and I walked back into the kitchen to find Steven standing in front of the stove, with his arms crossed over his chest, and the most serious look on his face. He said to Stan "So, what's the plan? What are your intentions with my mother?"

I stopped in my tracks.

To my shock and surprise, Stan smiled, winked at me, and said, "My plan is to marry your mother."

I could tell the boys were very surprised at his answer, but it seemed to break the ice with them.

That evening, Stan and my boys each sat and had a long talk about where they were and what they wanted out of their futures. Stan talked to them about joining the CIA and how they could go about it. I could tell he got both of their interests. Knowing how different my boys were from each other, Stan was able to show them the different areas they could get into.

After dinner, we finished exchanging gifts. Stan gave Steven his present, and then I gave Stan the other presents I'd got for him.

The one gift I was worried about giving him was the Jets bathrobe. After seeing his reaction towards Shelley's robe, I was apprehensive about giving it to him. I handed him the box and told him before he opened it, "I'll understand if it's not what you wanted."

When he saw it, the smile on his face showed me exactly how he felt. He'd said, "I'd always wanted one but couldn't spend that kind of money on myself; I love it." He put it on immediately.

The next gift I had gave him was a DVD of an old soap opera about vampires from the late '60's and '70's. It was a show called *Dark Shadows* and was a big hit with everyone back then.

Stan and I had talked about the series a few months back, and I'd remembered how much he said he loved the show. We both had been hooked on the show when we were young. We had talked about how different that show had been from any other of its time and how much it consumed both of us when we were young. I was surprised he when he said "Do you want to watch some this evening?"

I responded, "Ed, do you want to join us?"

Ed said, "What's it about?"

"It's a soup opera from the '70s about vampires. It was a big hit back when we were young. Try it." Stan said.

"Ok, sounds interesting. I'll watch some." Ed agreed.

Being a show from the '60's, it did have a lot to be desired. No editing, all the mistakes were there, and it was in black and white. Ed made it through the first episode but took off after that.

Stan asked, "Do you want to watch more?" We ended up staying up till three in the morning watching the first DVD; there were four DVDs, four hours each. We both got hooked all over again.

We decided we were going to cook at home every day this trip. He was looking at the supplies I had, especially my spices. I had to laugh and ask him, "Do they expire?"

When he asked why, I told him I hadn't bought any spices since I purchased my house over five years ago. The look on his face was priceless... We went food shopping and he said he was going to fix me right up. He picked out all the spices I needed and a variety of sauces for marinating meats. He picked out a pepper grinder and tried to find me a coffee grinder. "There are just some things you cannot skimp on," he said.

When we returned to my house, he took out all of my old spices and opened the oregano first. He took a small pinch of the old container into the palm of his hand and then a small pinch of the new container. He said, "Now taste a little from each."

I had to laugh because just looking at them I could see the difference. The old was brown and had no taste. While the new was green and had a nice aroma that you could almost taste before you put it into your mouth.

I enjoyed watching him trying to teach me. He would get so excited when he'd talk about what he wanted to cook for me and how he would fatten me up.

We had originally made plans to go out two nights during his visit, but I could see he wasn't up to it so I cancelled both of them.

On Friday night, he had a very serious attack, and I could tell he was in a great deal of pain. It scared me. We argued about getting him to the hospital, but he said it would pass and just give it a little time. It took until the next morning before he was feeling any better. I suggested we go back to Maryland and spend New Year's there, but he kept saying everything was fine.

On New Year's Eve, we went food shopping again. Each time we went shopping, we'd fight over who would pay when we got to the register. I let him pack the groceries and then I'd sneak in and run my card through the machine before he had a chance to take out his money. I could see how bad he felt, but I was very adamant that I should pay while he was visiting me because he always paid when I visited him.

As we were shopping, I could see Stan believed in all of the traditions for New Year's. He made a list of all the "good luck" items you must have to bring in a new year. We got champagne and pickled herring for midnight and then the black eyed peas and collard greens for New Year's dinner.

We had trouble finding the pickled herring in the regular grocery store, so we went to a specialty store that I knew about but had only been there once. He was certain we'd find it there.

When we got there he was like a kid in a candy store. It took us about two minutes to find the herring, but with all the fresh meat in the store, we ended up staying a half hour just so he could see all they had. He explained all the differences between the types of meat to me and said he couldn't wait to shop there again.

It was the first New Year's I'd ever had these *"good luck"* items. I never followed many traditions through the years. I was surprised that Stan even convinced Ed to join us for the champagne and pickled herring at the stroke of midnight. I was hoping this would mean that the coming year would be the best year of my life. It was definitely starting out the right way.

We had a great time that night. My neighbors had fireworks going off from about 11:30 until close to 1 AM. Stan had never seen such a display in his area; they were illegal. Last year, had been the first year Georgia legalized smaller fireworks, and you could tell that everyone stocked up for the celebration.

Stan, Ed and I stayed outside watching the celebration. I was so glad that the evening had turned out this way and that we didn't need to leave the house for entertainment. After Friday night's episode, I was afraid to take Stan anywhere in case the pain returned.

We watched the fireworks for about 30 minutes until we decided to settle in for the night. Again, we watched a DVD of Dark Shadows. I could see he wasn't feeling very well and was having difficulty sleeping. This was such a nice way to sit and spend the time together. We watched about five episodes that night because of the late start.

New Year's Day was, unfortunately, a reminder that we didn't have much time left for this visit. I could see it was bothering Stan, and he'd gone upstairs a couple of times and just sat alone. One time when I went to go find him, he'd been crying. He said, "I just don't want to leave you." This was the second time I'd found him crying this week, and it was so out of character for him. He'd always been the tough one that didn't get emotional. He'd say the words, but it never got him to tears before.

We sat and talked about our future, and Stan promised we'd start seeing more of each other after he found out what was causing his pain. We talked about selling our homes and finding "our place". He said, "Once Dave graduates high school in June, I'm going to start the ball rolling and put my house up for sale."

I received an email from Stan's mom while he was visiting, and it made me feel guilty about taking him away from his family during the holidays. She said that she wanted to see him and the boys for the holidays and only seeing them during that time of the year just wasn't enough. I showed the message to Stan and could tell from his silence that he felt bad about not going to see her. He said, "I'm just going to have to fit it in before I take Steve back to college." This worried me that he was pushing himself too much. He really needed to just take some time and get better.

We spend that evening watching the rest of the second DVD and then finished the third. Neither one of us wanted to go to sleep. Sleep only meant for the morning to come faster, and he would be leaving.

I asked him if he would leave me the last DVD we hadn't watched and I would ship it up to him. Of course, he said yes and handed it to me.

The morning of January 2nd, as he was getting ready to leave, I felt such a sense of loss that I couldn't stand it. He had planned on leaving by 9am but stayed until 11:30 to visit a little more.

I wanted to ask him to stay but knew that he had promised we'd never go more than a month between visits again. I stood at my front door and watched him pull out of my driveway. I had the strangest feeling that this was the last time I would ever see him.

I was so sad that I spent the afternoon thinking of him and watching the last DVD of Dark Shadows. I promised I would ship it to him and wanted to send it up as fast as possible. I don't think I could have managed to do anything else that day. I was so torn about him leaving and wanting to go with him. My heart was breaking every moment we were apart.

Stan had promised he wouldn't drive the entire way home that day, and he called me when he got to the hotel that we stayed at. He didn't have a lot of minutes left on the cell phone, so we made it a quick call.

Later, as I was settling down for the night, I decided to call him at the hotel. I could hear the surprise in his voice when he answered the phone. He said, "I was sitting on this big bed just wishing you were here. Nothing seems right anymore without you in my life and by my side." I wanted to jump in my car and drive up to be with him. Knowing I had to go back to work the next day, I had to accept it wouldn't be a good idea. Besides, we would have plenty of time for visits in the future.

Chapter 15
The Plans We Made
January 2006

When Stan got home he made plans to go see his mom the following weekend. I was so worried about his health. He was pushing himself too hard. He left on Friday to go see his mom in New Jersey, and on Sunday, Stan drove Steve back to West Virginia in time for college to get back into session.

Stan drove back from West Virginia by himself and called me when he got home. I could hear in his voice how exhausted he was, and I kept telling him he needed to stay home for a while or at least until we heard what was causing the pain he was in. He promised me he'd make an appointment with a doctor immediately.

During this time, Shelley and I were still corresponding almost every day. What I didn't get from him, at least she was able to get. He seemed to be confiding in her a little more about how he was feeling. I'd wished he would share it with me, but I also knew he didn't want to upset me. I got this message from Shelley the day he left for New Jersey.

From: Shelley S
Date: 2006/01/06 Fri AM 05:52:04 EST

Stan is really really down in the dumps. Please call him. A good friend of ours from Australia died of cancer. She was only a little older than Stan. He is really getting frightened now about this pain in his chest.

From: Dee
Sent: Fri 1/6/2006 8:52 AM
To: Shelley S
I'm really sorry to hear about your friend.... Stan has talked about her before. It's a shame I didn't know last night, I would have called but with him going up to NJ this weekend I guess I'll have to wait . He's told me that he doesn't like to call me when he's down so I guess I'll wait for him to be ready to talk. I hate it but I have to respect his wishes. I'm glad you were able to be there for him, I'm sure it helped his mood and at least he does have someone to talk to about it.

Talk to you soon,
Dee

    Stan called when he returned from his trip, and he told me
about his friend's passing. They had gotten word a few
months prior that she'd been told she had cancer, and he so
hoped that her outcome would have been like his, a full
recovery. It depressed him thinking about losing her and
made him start thinking fearfully about how his own health. I
could tell he was sorry he'd waited. He was beginning to get
a little scared. I asked him if he wanted me to come up there,
and he promised it wouldn't be more than a few more weeks
before we'd get together again.

    Our phone conversations became more about cooking,
and it seemed to be turning into a little contest between us.
We both tried to lighten the conversations to only good
things. Whenever I'd make a special dinner, I always sent
him the details.

From: Dee
Sent: Wednesday, January 04, 2006 7:03 PM
To: 'Stanley S'
Subject: Hey you

Well dinner was a success.... it was great and even Ed really liked it....
I made the salmon of course, with white rice and sliced tomatoes. I put
that oil I bought up there on them with a little salt and pepper.... see
what you're doing to me :)

Ed even said he was open to trying new stuff, I guess you got to him
too. I miss you so much. Keep me posted on the docs....

Love ya,
Dee

    My life was getting a bit unsettling during the past
months, and I tried as much as possible to keep it from Stan.
He had so much on his plate already. It started with someone

trying to break into my house, and then I started getting collection calls for Billy again.

Since Stan and I got back together, I'd received quite a few calls from companies looking for Billy. Most went away after I told them he hadn't lived there in years, but for some reason these new people wouldn't stop. I started asking them when he opened the accounts, and all of them were new accounts within the past year. I feared I would start hearing from Billy again. The calls were getting more and more harassing as the days went on. I called the local police to see if there was anything I could do, but unfortunately, they said there really wasn't except for what I'd been doing.

They said he could use my address and phone number all he wanted, since that wasn't against the law, but if he lied about anything that would have included me, then that might be something illegal. One of the calls I received informed me that Billy had used my house loan as a reference and also had told them that I was his wife. This scared me knowing there might actually be something out there that I wasn't aware of and could possibly become responsible for.

I found that Billy's mom was also still using my address for her car insurance, and the police said if I didn't inform the insurance company it might make me an accessory. Taking their advice, I called her insurance company and told them to stop sending the bills to my address. I'd been marking the bills "return to sender" for over a year, and they still continued to send the bills to my house.

I wanted to get my new life started with Stan. Having an old relationship come back to haunt me was getting to be more than I could stand. It was as if something was holding me back from moving towards our future together, even though I knew my old life was not what I wanted any more.

I didn't want Stan to know about all this, not wanting him to worry about me, but Lisa was becoming very worried, and she decided Stan needed to know.

Hey Stan It's me Lisa, Hope all is well with you and the boys.
I don't usually get involved with Dee's life but this is one time I feel you need to be aware of a situation. I was talking to her tonight and could hear the fear in her voice and she feels you have too much going on to bother you with it so I will. I will preface this with an apology if I am stepping over the line of friendship but I care about her and her well-being. I don't know all the details but I know her old boyfriend has apparently used her name and home address for getting credit cards and god only knows what else, he has somehow used her house as collateral (again I don't know all the details, you might be able to get more from her.) His mother has been using her address for her auto insurance and Dee called the insurance Company today and they are canceling the policy and she called the police last night to make a report. She is scared to death that he & his family (who have a long history of breaking the law and who knows what else) will come after her. I know you can't do anything more than I can but I think she will feel better if you know. She is really scared.
I will tell her I have sent this to you ....tomorrow might be
a good time...yea I am a chicken.... no I'll call her in a few minutes and confess, she's gonna be pissed but what done is done.
Talk to you soon.
Lisa

Stan called me the next day, and we talked. He commented that if it had been just five years ago, this situation would be taken care of. I was so relieved there really wasn't anything he could do; this was something I felt I needed to take care of myself.

He said, "If anything starts, get in your car and get up here immediately." Knowing how stubborn I could be, he knew I'd stay and take care of things myself.

To change the subject I said, "How are the boys?"

"Steve was playing football a few Sundays ago and collided with another player. Unfortunately, Steve's knee took the brunt of the damage which delayed him being able to try out for the football team at college."

Stan was very worried about him and also about all the bills that were accumulating from the effects of the accident.

I talked to Steven yesterday. His leg is doing better. He is now talking about playing rugby. He says they are hounding him to death to play. My son will always be a sport player or he will die.

Talked to Stan too. He is still having pains and I told him to get on that phone and call the doctor and DEMAND an appointment. He said if he is told he has to live with this pain the rest of his life he is going to put a bullet in his head. He means it too. That man worries me.

Well, that's it from my neck of the woods. Have a good one.
Shelley S

I knew Stan didn't need this extra stress of Steve being hurt and could tell that him being distant was due to his health. I was beginning to worry more about him. He finally answered Lisa and that gave us a little relief.

Hi Lisa,

Sorry for the delay in getting back to you. Dee had told me pretty much all that you did and from the sound of things, she's more than covered legally. It's the illegal possibilities that are worrisome. I think for you and I the worst part of this is the feeling of helplessness...if it was a few years ago, I may have taken more direct action, but as of this moment all I can do is offer a safe haven for Ed and her if it comes down to that. I know she cares about her house, job and possessions, but safety is most important I think you'll agree.

Anyway, don't worry too much about contacting me...I for one am glad you did and Dee knows the level of your friendship... so don't hesitate to keep in touch.

How is your daughter doing? And how is Kevin recovering? I hope all is well down there...and your holidays were great!

Talk to you soon, -Stan-

Stan finally made an appointment to see the doctor, and I couldn't wait to hear what was going on. I had to keep positive, thinking this is something that would pass and be something the doctors would fix. I dreaded thinking anything else. I wanted him to know that I would be here for him and on the first plane if he needed me there.

At the same time, I started having a few health problems of my own, which he'd been after me to go to the doctors for. I didn't feel it was really anything to worry about, just some old stuff coming back.

I'd been diagnosed with acid reflux about four years earlier, and it was starting to bother me again. I figured it was the stress I was under and would pass. With the bout of cancer he'd had, he was getting increasingly worried that I might come down with the same type and wanted me to go get checked out again just in case.

From: Stanley
Sent: Sunday, January 22, 2006 5:03 AM
To: Dee
Subject: Hi

Hi Dee,

Just checking in...been in pretty bad shape since Friday, but don't feel too bad right at this moment Basically, none of the pain stuff was working on Friday night...when I was finally able to go to bed...I just stayed there...took some sleeping pills and didn't get out of bed until about 10pm on Saturday night.

Can't wait until Monday is over...I just hope the doc can find something he can fix...I don't know what I'll do if he says he can't do anything about the pain.

So how's things with you? Better I hope.

It's 5am..gonna try going back to bed for awhile.

LY ME

From: Dee
Sent: Sunday, January 22, 2006 2:16 PM
To: 'Stanley S'
Subject: RE: Hi

I'm sorry your still feeling really bad, I was hoping the pills would have helped. I hope all goes well tomorrow and they find out what it is. LY

I worried about his appointment and hoped he would contact me immediately after. When I didn't hear anything, I reached out to Shelly.

From: Dee Keller
Sent: Monday, January 23, 2006 9:40 AM
To: Shelley A. S
Subject: RE: FW: Hey there

So... have you heard from Stan?

> From: Shelley A. S
> Sent: Monday, January 23, 2006 9:49 AM
> To: Dee Keller
> Subject: RE: FW: Hey there
>
> I called yesterday. He was in bed all day Saturday because he was in agony from the pain. He took 2 sleeping pills and he didn't eat because he hates to eat now because of the pain. So say a little prayer for him today that whatever is ailing him will be fixed (they said if it is a stricture, they can go in with a balloon during the endoscope and enlarge it. I am afraid that if they can't fix him or find out what is wrong with him.

From: Stan

- 247 -

Sent: Wednesday, January 25, 2006 7:51 AM
To: Dee Keller; Dee
Subject: Status

Hi Honey,

Just an update and a check on you. I'm feeling a bit better today, not
nearly as much pain, kind of like going back in time to about early
December. I had lamb chops and rice-a-roni last night with a v-8 and
only had moderate pain...not to get my hopes too high, but it looks like
I'm on the mend.

Now...how did your appointment with the GP go yesterday? Were you
able to get a referral for an endoscopy? Did he put you on any meds?
Be sure you follow up...it's important to me as much as you.

Anyway, love you lots!!

-Stan-

From: Dee
Sent: Wednesday, January 25, 2006 9:52 AM
To: Stan
Subject: RE: My Mistake?

My appointment's today at 1:30... I'm a little nervous cause some of
the symptoms have gotten worse and hopefully they will let me know
something. I woke up yesterday and my left eye really hurt and today
it's all swollen so I have a feeling they'll be looking at that too. Kinda
looks like what yours did but it's mostly swollen on the outside. Just
falling apart here. Love you too and I'll let you know what happens.
Dee

    I was hoping when I opened my email in the morning
there would be a note from Stan. Instead, there was one
from Shelly.

From: Shelley A. S
Sent: Thursday, January 26, 2006 8:43 AM
To: Dee Keller
Subject: Hey Woman

How did your appointment go yesterday? I see you were out of the office. You took off all day?

> From: Dee Keller
> Sent: Thursday, January 26, 2006 8:45 AM
> To: Shelley A. S
> Subject: RE: Hey Woman
>
> I really shouldn't have taken the whole day but I was feeling pretty rough....
> It was with a GP so he really couldn't tell me much. He said it could be an ulcer, hernia or cancer amongst other things. I have to go for both a colonoscopy and endoscope. My next appointment is on the 31st.
> fun fun fun

From: Shelley A. S
Sent: Thursday, January 26, 2006 8:49 AM
To: Dee Keller
Subject: RE: Hey Woman

Ouch. Well I will keep you in my prayers, Girlfriend.

Chapter 16
The Strange Phone Call
January 29th 2006

It was a beautiful Sunday afternoon, and I had the music playing in the background as I was doing my house cleaning.

In the distance, I hear my phone ringing and walk to find it.

It was Stan... he was crying. "I spent the afternoon copying my old family VHS tapes to DVDs using the new burner Shelley gave me for Christmas. Looking at the old family videos made me sad. I was thinking about the good times we had and how things would never be the same again. It was overwhelming." He paused, "Then I started thinking of you and realized how much I miss you and wished you were here."

I'd never heard him so upset, but at the same time, it was the most he'd talked about us being together and our plans for the future in a few weeks.

We spent an hour on the phone, making plans for our next visit and how soon we could make it. He wanted to wait until after his February 13th appointment, and then we would set a date to meet in Virginia. Neither one of us could wait for February 13th to come.

While we were talking, he'd mentioned that he finally moved the cordless phone upstairs and was using it. I mentioned that it also was a speaker phone, and I talked him through how to use that part. He was so thrilled. He put me on speaker and as loud as he could, he said "I love you and want the world to know". He was so out of character that day, and I loved how he was talking. It had been a while since he openly discussed missing each other so much, and it felt good.

He said he'd been spending a lot of time on the internet trying to find that special place for us to go for at least a two-week vacation that year. I asked him what the boys wanted to do; he said, "I'll worry about what the boys want to do later in the year. I want to plan our vacation first."

His time off was a bit harder to accumulate than mine. I got four weeks off automatically each year, while he had to earn hours off by working. I was never sure how exactly it worked for him. He tried to explain that for 40 hours of work he'd get four hours vacation/time off. I was worried that with how sick he'd been, the time off wouldn't be as easy for him to accumulate.

He said he was seriously thinking of selling his house and wanted to get the little things done that would make a difference in what he could get for it.

He made me promise that I would go see a doctor and get any procedures done that they felt were needed. After our conversation, I'd wondered if Shelley had spoken with Stan and if possibly she'd prompted his call to me.

From: Dee Keller
Sent: Monday, January 30, 2006 9:35 AM
To: Shelley A. S
Subject: RE: Morning....

so tell me... did you have a little talk with Stan about me this weekend? :)

> From: Shelley A. S
> Sent: Monday, January 30, 2006 9:41 AM
> To: Dee Keller
> Subject: RE: Morning....
>
> No, I didn't talk to him this weekend.

From: Dee Keller
Sent: Monday, January 30, 2006 9:46 AM
To: Shelley A. S
Subject: RE: Morning....

thought maybe you did from the call I got from him yesterday. wonder what prompted the call if you didn't call him - just a strange conversation

From: Shelley A. S
Sent: Monday, January 30, 2006 9:55 AM
To: Dee Keller
Subject: RE: Morning....

Nope, I can promise you I did not talk to him or call him this weekend. I didn't have anything to say. ha ha.

-----Original Message-----
From: Dee Keller
Sent: Monday, January 30, 2006 10:07 AM
To: Shelley A. S
Subject: RE: Morning....

wonder where the phone call came from then - hard to believe he all of a sudden started missing me :)
oh well... maybe he's feeling a little better

> From: Shelley A. S
> Sent: Monday, January 30, 2006 10:25 AM
> To: Dee Keller
> Subject: RE: Morning....

You don't give him enough credit nor yourself. Maybe he IS feeling better. I told you, when he is in pain, he doesn't feel like talking. Personally, I would rather not hear from him if he is going to be in a freaking grumpy mood. Just really brings you down. I would rather hear from him when he is more chipper.

From: Dee Keller
Sent: Monday, January 30, 2006 11:04 AM
To: Shelley A. S
Subject: RE: Morning....

I'm just hoping whatever they find is wrong with me can be dealt with pills.... I can't take any time off right now and am really thinking of putting this off until after tax season

> From: Shelley A. S
> Sent: Monday, January 30, 2006 1:22 PM
> To: Dee Keller
> Subject: RE: Morning....

YOU HAD BETTER NOT PUT ANYTHING OFF UNTIL AFTER TAX SEASON!!!!! GET IT DONE NOW before it is too late.

- 253 -

From: Dee Keller
Sent: Monday, January 30, 2006 1:29 PM
To: Shelley A. S
Subject: RE: Morning....

ok ok... had this argument yesterday
He made me promise to go to my appointment tomorrow but we'll see about the next step
Just not sure if I could handle any bad news right now
Besides, I don't think it's that bad, after all, I'm still going strong, well sort of

> From: Shelley A. S
> Sent: Monday, January 30, 2006 1:33 PM
> To: Dee Keller
> Subject: RE: Morning....
>
> Don't make me get out my can of WHOOP ASS!

From: Dee Keller
Sent: Monday, January 30, 2006 1:36 PM
To: Shelley A. S
Subject: RE: Morning....

It's just not good timing.... especially if I need to take time off
I'm already behind and cannot afford this right now
Believe me, I would prefer to get it over with but I'm worried about where it will put me financially
I don't have anything to fall back on and really am afraid of possibly losing my house or job

> From: Shelley A. S
> Sent: Monday, January 30, 2006 1:52 PM
> To: Dee Keller
> Subject: RE: Morning....
>
> I know, but if there is something that requires surgery, chances are they will probably wait a little while anyways. Besides, doesn't your company offer you short term disability? Just don't worry about that right now. You need to go get this checked out.

From: Dee Keller
Sent: Monday, January 30, 2006 2:13 PM
To: Shelley A. S
Subject: RE: Morning....

I will.... I have disability but thing is my other boss Neil, my part-time job doesn't pay if I don't show up... I'm more worried about his money than my full time job

> From: Shelley A. S
> Sent: Monday, January 30, 2006 2:17 PM
> To: Dee Keller
> Subject: RE: Morning....
>
> Well, he will just have to float you a loan.

> From: Dee Keller
> Sent: Monday, January 30, 2006 2:16 PM
> To: 'Shelley A. S'
> Subject: RE: Morning....
>
> He just did... that's what worries me

Neil had always paid me in advance, 40 hours at a time. Once I worked off the hours, he would pay me for another 40. The job was a part-time job on Saturdays about 4-5 hours so it took a while to work off 40 hours. I never wanted to get any further in debt to him than that.

I called Stan on Monday, and he immediately brought up the subject of my doctor's appointments. I teased him saying, "I only promised to go see the doctor; I didn't promise to get the procedures." This was the first time I think he ever got short with me. Even when we had argued in the past, it was always civil.

This time he raised his voice at me, "You promised you would find out what was wrong with you. It's only semantics, and you're messing with OUR future if you don't go for the tests."

I'd never heard him so upset and promised him I would go for the procedures. I told him I had my first appointment

- 255 -

on Tuesday to see a gastro doctor about my stomach and the blood I was seeing.

He stressed how much I needed to go and how worried he about was about me.

When I talked to Shelley the next day, she told me Stan told her that he loved me to death but was so worried about my tests.

Chapter 17
My Doctors appointment
January 31st

Stan didn't call the day of my appointment, and I wondered if he even remembered. After all the fuss he'd made about me going, it was strange he didn't call to check how it went. I heard from Shelley instead.

From: Dee Keller
Sent: Tuesday, January 31, 2006 8:44 AM
To: Shelley A. S
Subject: almost time to go

Hope you're having a good morning... I'll be leaving in about 15 minutes for the doctors...

> From: Shelley A. S
> Sent: Tuesday, January 31, 2006 8:56 AM
> To: Dee Keller
> Subject: RE: almost time to go
>
> My prayers are with you.

From: Dee Keller
Sent: Tuesday, January 31, 2006 12:18 PM
To: Shelley A. S
Subject: RE: almost time to go

I'm back.... got both procedures scheduled and he put me on new medicine

> From: Shelley A. S
> Sent: Tuesday, January 31, 2006 12:42 PM
> To: Dee Keller
> Subject: RE: almost time to go
>
> For when did you get them scheduled?

From: Dee Keller
Sent: Tuesday, January 31, 2006 12:42 PM
To: Shelley A. S
Subject: RE: almost time to go

This Thursday is the endoscope and the 22nd is the colonoscopy

From: Shelley A. S
Sent: Tuesday, January 31, 2006 12:56 PM
To: Dee Keller
Subject: RE: almost time to go

I am glad you scheduled the more important one first. That is the utmost priority to determine what might be going on. I will say lots of prayers for you this week that everything will be okay.

I decided to email Stan about the fight we had over my doctor's appointments. I wanted to give him a chance to see if he did remember or at least if he was still mad over our conversation.

From: Dee
To: Stanley
Sent: Tuesday, January 31, 2006 1:21 PM
Subject: ok both are scheduled...

Sorry if I upset you a bit last night... that's not why I called
LY ME

From: Stanley [mailto:stanley@verizon.net]
Sent: Tuesday, January 31, 2006 2:22 PM
To: Dee
Subject: Re: ok both are scheduled...

That's what we're here for honey. I can't say it enough....if we didn't care, we wouldn't nag. So, both appointments are scheduled now?

Keep me informed,

LY ME

He'd stressed so much for me to go to the appointment but hadn't called me to see what was going on. I was hoping that Shelley didn't tell him what was happening. I was worried his reason for not calling was because of his own health. Finally, he emailed.

-----Original Message-----
From: Stanley S
Sent: Thursday, February 02, 2006 3:15 PM
To: Dee
Subject: Fw: Fwd:

Hi Dee,
How is every little thing with you? Past few days have been rough for me....new type pain and I had to take off today. I've been thinking of pleading with the doctor to move up my next surgery...this pain is bad...keeps me from lying on my side.

Anyway, not much else is going on...talk to you soon.

LY ME

I called him on Friday night to let him know what was happening with my appointments.

"Hi honey, how are you feeling?" I asked.

He said, "Wednesday and Thursday I experienced the worst pain I'd been in since all of this started. The pain had moved from the middle of my chest and was now off to the side a little. The pain was so bad I could barely get out of bed."

I felt guilty for being upset with him for not calling and promised him I'd keep my appointments. He promised that if the pain didn't go away by Monday, he was going to knock down the doors to the doctor's office and demand an immediate appointment.

He asked how my appointment went. "Unfortunately, my scope didn't give me results right away. My doctor called today and said what he saw was mostly from the acid reflux, but he'd taken some cultures which would be back the following week."

On Saturday, his mom sent me this message which I forwarded to Stan. I felt it said so much about the people in my life and thought of him as my Life Time relationship.

-----Original Message-----
From: Dee
Sent: Saturday, February 04, 2006 4:22 PM
To: 'stanley.s@verizon.net'
Subject: FW: [Fwd: Fwd: Re: People come in your life for a reason]

PEOPLE COME INTO YOUR LIFE FOR A REASON

People come into your life for a reason, a season or a lifetime. When you know which one it is, you will know what to do for that person. When someone is in your life for a REASON, it is usually to meet a need you have expressed. They have come to assist you through a difficulty, to provide you with guidance and support, to aid you physically, emotionally or spiritually. They may seem like a godsend and they are. They are there for the reason you need them to be. Then, without any wrongdoing on your part or at an inconvenient time, this person will say or do something to bring the relationship to an end. Sometimes they die. Sometimes they walk away. Sometimes they act up and force you to take a stand. What we must realize is that our need has been met, our desire fulfilled, their work is done. The prayer you sent up has been answered and now it is time to move on.

Some people come into your life for a SEASON, because your turn has come to share, grow or learn. They bring you an experience of peace or make you laugh. They may teach you something you have never done. They usually give you an unbelievable amount of joy. Believe it, it is real. But only for a season!

LIFETIME relationships teach you lifetime lessons, things you must build upon in order to have a solid emotional foundation. Your job is to accept the lesson, love the person and put what you have learned to use in all other relationships and areas of your life. It is said that love is blind but friendship is clairvoyant.

Thank you for being a part of my life, whether you were a reason, a season or a lifetime.

From: Stanley S
Sent: Saturday, February 04, 2006 11:45 PM
To: Dee
Subject: Read: [Fwd: Fwd: Re: People come in your life for a reason]

This is a receipt for the mail you sent to at 2/4/2006 4:21 PM

This receipt verifies that the message has been displayed on the recipient's computer at 2/4/2006 11:45 PM

I only got a read receipt back from him.

Chapter 18
The Morning I'll Never Forget
February 6th 2006

I didn't hear from Stan all weekend and believed it was because he wasn't feeling good. It was Super Bowl weekend, and I knew how much he loved watching the game with the boys. I figured I would let him enjoy the game with the boys and call him Monday evening to see how he was feeling. For the first time, I watched the entire game. It would give us something to talk about the next night.

I got up Monday morning wanting to just stay in bed. I somehow found the energy and got ready for work. Something just didn't seem right. I had an overwhelming feeling to call Stan and not wait until tonight.

I brushed off the feeling and went to work. It was a rainy and chilly day. I sat down to get into the day's activities, and time seemed to fly by.

I looked at the clock and it said 11:26am. The morning went fast and I decided it was break time. I went outside to have a cigarette and it started snowing, snowing these big beautiful snowflakes, snowflakes that were the size of a silver dollar. Silence except for the falling snow surrounded me and I felt a wave of peace go through me.

I was reminded of our trip to Virginia during the holidays, how as soon as we got there it started snowing. I missed Stan and wondered if it was snowing where he was. How lucky I picked that time to take a break.

It lasted about five minutes and when it was done the ground showed no signs that anything had fallen. It rarely snows in Atlanta, but when it does, it melts by the time it hits the ground.

I went back inside and as I walked past my buddy Gregg's desk I said, "It was just snowing outside."

He got up to look, and of course it had stopped with no sign of a flake on the ground. He smiled and said, "Yeah sure, Dee."

Shelley and I were talking via email as usual all morning, and I wanted to see if she'd heard from Stan during the weekend.

From: Dee Keller
Sent: Monday, February 06, 2006 9:23 AM
To: Shelley A. S
Subject: RE: G'Day Girlfriend

So how was your weekend? You and Mark do anything?

> From: Shelley A. S
> Sent: Monday, February 06, 2006 9:34 AM
> To: Dee Keller
> Subject: RE: G'Day Girlfriend
>
> Don't even go there. If he's not careful, I am going to trade him in for 2 20s. ha ha.

From: Dee Keller
Sent: Monday, February 06, 2006 9:34 AM
To: Shelley A. S
Subject: RE: G'Day Girlfriend

Sounds like how I feel about Stan

> From: Shelley A. S
> Sent: Monday, February 06, 2006 9:47 AM
> To: Dee Keller
> Subject: RE: G'Day Girlfriend
>
> Yeah, but you are 800+ miles apart. I live with Mark in the same house. Big difference!

From: Dee Keller
Sent: Monday, February 06, 2006 9:55 AM
To: Shelley A. S
Subject: RE: G'Day Girlfriend

With the distance and time apart, you'd think I'd get a little attention. I guess I'm just disappointed in him about last week.

We had a fight on Sunday about me going to the doctors and how he was nagging me to get it all taken care of and must have said at least 3 times, he would call me to see what happened on Tuesday. But, he finally got around to calling me on Friday. I guess he wasn't that worried about it.

> From: Shelley A. S]
> Sent: Monday, February 06, 2006 10:03 AM
> To: Dee Keller
> Subject: RE: G'Day Girlfriend
>
> Well, I wish I had the answers but I don't. I haven't talked to him. I know that the medication that he takes is making him do some really weird shit. Like taking all the bottles out of the liquor cabinet and taking shots and he doesn't even remember it (which is dangerous to take sleeping pills, this medication, AND drinking), like going into the kitchen and eating dry cereal and making a mess then blaming it on the kids and not remembering it the next morning. Weird stuff. He told me once it gives him short term memory loss. Hell, I don't know why he continues to take that crap. Other than that, I don't know what to tell you. You know how men are; their version of support is certainly not the same as my version of support. They are definitely from another planet, no doubt about it.

From: Dee Keller
Sent: Monday, February 06, 2006 10:08 AM
To: Shelley A. S
Subject: RE: G'Day Girlfriend

If it had been just this time, I would let it go but he did the same thing the when I went for my surgery last year. Nagged me to go and then never called to see what happened or how I was doing, I had to call him. Of course, he was getting ready for vacation that week so maybe that's what distracted him last time.

I guess things just aren't turning out as I thought they would and now with all I'm going thru it would have been nice to have someone to lean on a little. Again, asking too much. I wonder how he would react if I wasn't there worried about him. He probably wouldn't even notice and would enjoy not being bothered.

Aren't we a pair.... at this point in my life, I'm over the games and just thought I could find someone that would want to be with me as much as I do with them. But then again, it might be a gender thing and what I'm looking for isn't out there.

- 265 -

From: Shelley A. S
Sent: Monday, February 06, 2006 11:05 AM
To: Dee Keller
Subject: RE: G'Day Girlfriend

Oh I think he would notice. Like I said, maybe we both
need to just not depend on men so much to make us
happy. A wise person once told me, you have to be
happy with yourself. Only you can make yourself
happy. I am beginning to realize that. I am trying to
teach myself not to depend on Mark to make me happy
because I will be disappointed every time because he is
a MAN!

From: Dee Keller
Sent: Monday, February 06, 2006 11:06 AM
To: Shelley A. S
Subject: RE: G'Day Girlfriend

How true that is....
Now to just get him to stop nagging me about going to the docs
I'm just not going to tell him anything anymore

From: Shelley A. S
Sent: Monday, February 06, 2006 11:22 AM
To: Dee Keller
Subject: RE: G'Day Girlfriend

Just nag him about going to the docs. Give him a dose
of his own medicine. Besides, you know yourself you
are just like him about going to the docs. Someone has
to nag nag nag you. :) It's because we love you and
don't want anything to happen to you.

From: Dee Keller
Sent: Monday, February 06, 2006 11:34 AM
To: Shelley A. S
Subject: RE: G'Day Girlfriend

My reasons for putting it off are very different from his.... I can't
afford to take any time right now
Don't know what I'm going to do, I'm getting very frustrated over
all of this and feeling like we're drifting further and further apart. I
appreciate your concern.

God, I'm sounding so depressing. I hate this, it's just not me.

- 266 -

I hated sharing my insecurities with anyone, especially her, but she knew him very well, and I was hoping for some type of reinforcement. I was also wondering at the same time if some of the things she'd said to me were adding to my insecurities. I knew I should keep in mind that her relationship with him was different than ours, and his reasons for not keeping in touch with me as much must have been a good reason. The more I talked with Shelley, the more I was beginning to wonder. I'd been worried about my health problems and hoped he would be there to talk to, but again, I didn't want to worry him and downplayed most of what I was going through. I knew he had enough on his mind, and I just couldn't add to it.

I was planning to call him that night and decided to go out and have nice lunch with one of my friends to take my mind off of things. I was worried and upset at the same time, not knowing if it was just my insecurities or my increasing concern about my health.

When I returned from lunch, I got this message:

From: Shelley A. S
Sent: Monday, February 06, 2006 1:16 PM
To: Dee Keller
Subject: **Call me immediately ***-***-****

I called her immediately. She was crying and hard to understand at first, but I fell apart at the same time when she said "Stan is dead". I went numb not hearing or feeling anything. This can't be true.

She went on, "Stan fell in the hallway this morning and Dave dragged him back into bed. Dave left the room to get help because Stan refused to go. When Dave returned a few minutes later, he found Stan on the floor again, but this time, he knew he was gone. There was no reaction to anything he did. He called 911, and they worked on him for about 45 minutes between his house and the hospital but got no response out of anything they tried. He was gone."

"Dee, I'm leaving within the hour and will pick you up on my way to Maryland. We will need each other for the drive."

"I'll be ready." I responded, and hung up the phone.

Standing in my cubicle, I could barely get my thoughts together. I stood there not knowing what to do but knowing at the same time I had to get up to Maryland as soon as possible. It was as if my mind and body weren't communicating, and I couldn't move.

My friends gathered around my desk and were concerned that I shouldn't drive. I insisted I would be fine. Gregg grabbed my purse and keys, put his arm around my shoulders and walked me to my car. My body was numb, and I could barely focus.

Somehow I made it home, crying the entire way. I don't remember the drive. I was in another world. I longed to talk to Stan. I needed him.

As I pulled into the garage, Steven pulled in behind me. I had called him on my way home.

He had been at work also but left so he could meet me. He ran to my car, and I collapsed in his arms. I had never felt such a heart wrenching feeling of emptiness inside. The one thing in my life I had to look forward to was gone. The true happiness I'd felt in my life was gone.

I asked Steven to call Lisa. He did, and she rushed over to be with me. When she arrived, I was sitting in my bedroom trying to pack for the trip, still not believing what was happening. The shock of hearing he was gone was tearing my heart apart, and it was all I could do to even talk. As we sat in my room, I told Lisa about the last message Stan had left me on my answering machine that previous Friday. She asked if she could hear it. He said, "Hey, it's just me, baby. It's about 6:30. I just wanted to hear your voice a little bit. Oh well, talk to you later. Bye."

With tears streaming down my face, I said to Lisa, "All I ever wanted was for him to call me." As I finished my sentence, the phone rang, just once. Lisa asked Steven and Ed if they had picked up one of the other extensions and both of them had said no.

The three of them stayed with me until Shelley arrived. Steven told me they would come up for the services. Both of my boys wanted to be there for me and wished they could drive up with me right away but couldn't because of their work schedules. Stan had even touched them that much that they wanted to be there. I knew then the strength my boys would give me and how much I needed them to be there. I knew I would never get through it without them.

Shelley arrived at my house around 7:30PM. We immediately packed her car with my luggage and started the long ride to be with Stan's sons. It was raining and cold for the entire ride. The closer we got to Maryland, the rain turned into a light snow. During the drive, I listened to Shelley and her feelings on Stan's passing, not knowing exactly how much of Stan and my relationship she really knew about. I could hear how torn she was; knowing she had her life down in Georgia but at the same time knowing the boys would need her to be with them.

The only memory I shared with her was the ring Stan had given me. I told her that Stan had saved it for 30 years and gave it back to me last year, all for me to lose it just a few weeks later. She looked at me in shock and said, "I never knew anything about a ring." I could tell by her reaction that Stan hadn't told her everything about us. Her reaction of shock and that she'd never known about the ring told me how little he really did share with her.

I kept quiet for most of the ride and let her do most of the talking. I chose not to share our plans of marriage later this year. Somehow I knew this was not the time, somehow I knew my place was not going to be as Stan's true love, that our relationship was not going to be recognized as serious as it really was. I knew this time going to his house was not going to be the same as it had been while he was there.

We arrived at Stan's house by 6 AM to find Dave still awake in the kitchen. He hadn't been able to sleep since Stan died. We talked for a while, and Shelley and I finally convinced Dave to try to get some sleep.

I wanted to go to Stan's room alone and was uncomfortable just going. After a little time, I finally got the courage and asked Shelley's permission. It was awful. It hurt thinking of my last trip here, how I would just walk in there and make myself at home. Now, I was asking for permission to go there.

I walked slowly down his long hallway and into the room. I stood by the doorway and looked around. I wanted him to walk out of the bathroom and say it was a big mistake. I wanted to feel his presence; I wanted to see a sign of how much I meant to him. Looking around his room, it didn't take long to find something.

I discovered his ticket stub from the comedy show we had seen together the first weekend we got together after all those years. I picked up the ticket and sunk to the floor. I had been in shock still up until that point and finally broke down and cried long and hard. Seeing the ticket stub placed purposefully on top of the basket hanging by his bed finally broke the gates of a grief. All the weight of the previous 30 years of separation between us came crashing down around me, and the full realization of what could have been and that now it really was too late, irreversibly too late was too much to handle.

I had been lost in my frustration at wanting to be together, rather than remembering what I knew to be true – that we were both hopeless romantics who didn't always show it on the outside. I knew I had meant every bit as much to him all these years. And now, I finally was getting that reassurance I'd needed. Looking around his room, I began to notice the mementos of our time together were all around me: the ticket stubs, the photos of us from both recent and distant past, the DVDs of Dark Shadows propped up on his dresser, displayed as if they were the center piece of his world.

As I stumbled around Stan's room in a sobbing stupor, I hoped no one would walk in and see me. I felt so vulnerable, like the 16-year-old I thought I'd left behind all these years ago. Only then, it felt much worse. When I was 16, I had hopes and dreams… Now much of my life was behind me. I always knew he was out there somewhere… There was always a glimmer of hope in the back of my mind that there was a fairytale ending out there for us; even if it never happened, it was within the realms of possibility, and that was always a comfort to me. Equally, it was a comfort just knowing that Stan existed, knowing he was alive and being his wonderful self in the world. Now, it was all gone… Stan had left, and any hopes and dreams and comforts went with him.

I know I had been in there at least an hour when I heard a soft knock on the door, and it slowly opened.

I was sitting on the floor beside the bed staring at the ticket stub.

Matt came over and sat next to me. He took my hand and said, "Dee, it's time to get something to eat. Come with me."

I looked up and gave him the best smile I could. He stood up and extended his hand to help me up. We walked out together in silence.

Matt and Dave later told me that Stan hadn't been avoiding me at all. It wasn't that he didn't want to talk to me like Shelley had said; he just didn't want me to know how bad he really had been feeling. When he was in a lot of pain, he wouldn't answer the phone. Some of the times when I'd called, he'd been asleep, and they couldn't wake him up; he'd been so tired.

I finally understood why he'd been so distant. He was trying to protect me from knowing how bad he really was feeling just as I was keeping from him how I was feeling.

Dave told me he'd overheard our conversation that previous Monday. Stan had been very upset by what I had said. Dave was concerned; he had never heard Stan upset with me like that before. When he asked me what had upset Stan so much, I told how I had teased him about refusing to get the procedures done.

Dave immediately asked, "Did you get the procedures done yet?"

I looked at the ground and he knew the answer.

"I'm very disappointed to hear you had cancelled your appointment. I understand it was because of Dad but you need to reschedule them as soon as possible."

"I will."

I had been up since Monday morning and could not get myself to sleep or eat. Tuesday went by like I was watching someone else's life go by. Every time I lay down, thoughts of Stan filled my head. I tried and tried but couldn't sleep. All I could do was lie there wishing Stan would come out and greet me with his warm smile and embrace.

It was Wednesday morning, and the sun was shining, giving you the impression of a beautiful day outside, the coldness of the day hidden behind the protective walls of his home. Stan's mom and step-dad arrived and greeted me with a warm hug.

I went with Shelley and Stan's mom to make all the funeral arrangements, and everyone agreed that Stan had wanted to be cremated. No one could remember where he wanted his ashes thrown, and even though I remembered, I could tell no one was welcome to the idea.

He had told me that he'd like to have his ashes thrown either in his property up in New Jersey next to his mom's house or at the state park where he'd worked in our home town, so long ago, the state park we'd visited so many times during our time together 30 years ago. They decided the boys would keep his ashes at the home.

It was hard watching Shelley make the arrangements as his wife, sitting there in control of making the decisions. I could tell it was uncomfortable for all three of us. Shelley was introduced as his wife while I was introduced as a friend of the family.

How life seems to repeat itself. My dear friend who had passed when I was young never had the woman he really cared for by his side when he passed. And now I had to accept that this was also my place.

When it came time to write the obituary, Shelley listed all of his family and even herself as his wife. She asked Matt, "Did I forget anyone?"

Matt immediately said, "How about Dee?"

Shelley responded, "I didn't want to make your dad sound bad by saying survived by his wife and girlfriend. How can we word it?"

She finally decided to remove the titles and just said, "Survived by Shelley and Dee" at the closing of his obituary.

The day of his services was Thursday, and I still hadn't been able to sleep or eat. I was barely able to hold myself together. The family was arriving, and the more people who showed up, the more I could tell how little about us had really been known. I always knew Stan kept to himself and now saw the details of his life that he had shared.

No one really knew the details of his life. No one really knew what happened between him and Shelley; no one knew the hurt he'd been through because of her leaving. No one knew the recent happy details of his life that his boys and I seemed to know. As more and more people came by, I could see that Shelley was being treated as his widow, while I stood in the background watching and not being able to share with them the true happiness that Stan and I had found in the past months.

As the time came for the services, the tension was building, and I could feel how unwelcome my presence was becoming to the family. I could sense the desire to not tarnish Stan's name by having his wife and girlfriend at the services was becoming an issue.

Luckily, Steven kept up with Stan's boys, and we were able to follow them to the services.

Very few people knew who I was at the services, and I spent my time as close to Stan as possible. I was there to say goodbye to him and had barely noticed the very large crowd that gathered at the funeral home.

There was a small couch across from Stan's casket, and I sat looking at him and saying goodbye in silence. I knew this was my last chance to see him, be with him, and I had so much I wanted to say.

Only his very close friends from work actually knew how serious our relationship was. His acquaintances looked at Shelley as being the widow. Stan never told anyone about their split, he was such a private person, and I could see that our relationship was not known by many, including his family. Only his boys and close friends had known how important Stan and I were to each other. My heart ached knowing that no one knew that Stan did have someone who truly loved him and wanted to be with him for the rest of his life. I hated to think that he died with everyone feeling he died alone, not knowing the true happiness we'd found together again.

As I was sitting in front of him, one of Stan's best friends from work came over and held my hand.

"You're Dee aren't you?"

I looked up and smiled.

He told me so many nice things about how much I'd changed Stan's life. How his close friends noticed that since we'd gotten back together, it was the happiest they'd seen him in years. He joked how he always knew when Stan had seen me, "He'd have this jump to his walk and smile on his face that we all knew meant he'd been with you."

I tried to show how much I appreciated what he was saying, and I knew he was trying to make me feel better, but nothing could help. I was so overwhelmed, and my sons could see it. They each took an arm and walked me outside.

Stan's services were beautiful, and you could see all the people he'd touched. It was overwhelming to see the number of people who came to say their final goodbye to such a great caring man.

Steven and Ed never left my side during the entire time we were there. They could see and feel the uneasiness around us and made me feel like I wasn't alone and never would be as long as they were around. For the first time in my life, my boys took care of me and guided me through this difficult time.

I hadn't slept or eaten since I'd received the news, and I felt as if I was walking around in a fog. I don't know what I would have done if they hadn't been there.

Before we returned home, I asked Matt, his oldest son, if I could have a few of Stan's personal items. I wanted things that would remind me of him, things I could cherish forever.

I knew before I asked exactly what items I wanted. First, was his Jets blanket he slept with every night. Stan passed away on his bed, and that was one of the last things he touched when he was alive. The next item I asked for was his calendar from last year where he wrote down each trip we'd spent together, recording it for his memories. The last item I asked for was one of his shirts. I took his favorite t-shirt that had the name of his home town on it. It was worn but still his favorite. I knew these items would fill me with his presence whenever I'd look at or touch them.

When I returned home from the services, I sent his boys this message.

Matt, Steve and Dave,

I wanted to send you a note that I'm thinking of you and wished so much I was there to help give you the comfort and hugs you need to get thru this. I'm sick with worry about all of you and am here if you need anything.

I keep thinking about all your dad and I talked about and you boys were always the number one topic. One of the first things I noticed when I came up there was how each time, either coming home or leaving, you gave him a hug. That little gesture spoke volumes to him and he so looked forward to each one. He was so proud of all of you and had such a special but different relationship with each of you. He loved telling me about the special bonds you each had with him and what made each of you so unique and special to him.

Matt... Your dad wanted so much for you to do something with your artistic talents and I pray you won't let that go. You are so talented and your dad wanted so much for you to share your talents with others. Keeping up with your painting and other art projects will help keep your father's memory alive in each piece you make because that's what he wanted you to do. He wanted you to find something that would not only be the job you love but one you could be so proud of. I would love to help get you started in any way possible. Maybe get that website going to display what you could sell. You are so talented and have a special gift that is very rare. Someday, maybe you could make a sketch of him for me and I would cherish it always. Just remember, each time you are painting or working on one of your other projects, he'll be smiling down at you.

Dave... with you, your music gave him such pleasure. Every time we were talking and you were playing in your room, he tried so hard to let me listen. I pictured him stretching that phone cord as far as possible. You know, that's the main reason I got him the cordless phone. Know that when you play now, he'll be listening and you will be letting him know how much he is missed. He was so proud of how you are doing in school, even with that note he left you. He mentioned that you had thought about going into the service and how scared of it he was because of everything that's going on right now over in Iraq. At the same time, he was so proud of you even thinking of it, to carry on the tradition. He wanted you to go to college and get the best education as possible so you never have to struggle. The times you came to him for emotional support meant so much to him. He realized you weren't as open as Steve and Matt but it really touched him when you would go to him for comfort. Please know that I will be there for you also.

Steve... all I keep thinking about is how much he enjoyed watching you play sports and the way you are with the girls. He teased me about how you got it from him and then would say "if only". You were the athlete he loved to watch the most and so looked forward to you going "pro" in the future. He had absolutely no doubt you would make it someday. He used to tell me how it would be when he would finally get season tickets to a team. I know, in time, whatever team it was, they would overshadow the Jets in his heart. He knew you were struggling with school but also had no doubt that you would get thru it. These next few months will be hard to concentrate but if you keep him in your heart, which I know you will, he will help you get thru it.

Sharing memories and talking about your dad will help us all heal. He was such a special part of my life and I so looked forward to the future we would have had. We talked so much about the five boys we have and how proud of all of you we were. You three were the most important people in his life which makes you very important in mine. I can never take the place of your father but hopefully I can help fill some of the tremendous void he left in our lives. I would never dream of trying to take the place of your mother either but I feel I can also help you thru this in a different way. Your father and I had a very special relationship which I will never be able to replace. You staying in touch with me will help me get thru my pain and emptiness and also help keep him as a part of my life always. Hopefully I will be able to do the same for you and will be there if you need anything, anytime.

Love Dee

We had been so happy to find each other again, and it felt like that happiness would last forever. I would always wonder if I could have or would have handled things differently had I known we really didn't have plenty of time.

Chapter 19
Life after Stan

I returned to work immediately and tried to continue on with my life. The numbness was still overwhelming, and the physical aches would not subside. I was devastated and lost. What will be my future now without him? Everything I looked forward to was gone. Even communication with Stan's boys drew down to nothing. I hadn't heard from them in months, even with my attempts to keep in touch.

When I returned to work after his funeral, I met a new employee at my office, Natacha. She became my savior during these months and tried everything she could to keep me from sitting home alone wanting desperately to join Stan. She became my main distraction, and I know she had no idea how devastated I really was when we first met. The nights she wasn't around were spent talking to him, asking him why he left me so quickly. I was slowly withdrawing into a shell, not wanting anyone to come in. She would drag me out to listen to music and have drinks with her friends, anything to distract me.

My mom tried everything she could to be there for me and demanded I still come up for her birthday in May. She knew I needed a distraction and hoped that I could visit the one and only place that Stan and I had a strong connection. We'd spent so much time at our rock so many years ago, and we both couldn't wait to visit it together again.

On the three month anniversary of his death, I went to visit our rock. It was the day we planned to visit there together.

I worried I wouldn't be able to find it on my own, it had been 30 years since I'd looked for it, and I knew the woods would be overgrown and look very different. More than that, I was worried about how I would feel once I found it. I was drawn to going there; nothing would have stopped me.

There had been no communication with his family in these months. I felt strange and almost like I was trespassing on his property. When I first arrived at my mom's, I snuck in and tried to find the rock. I didn't go very far into the property, being afraid I'd be caught and my presence wouldn't be welcome. I quickly returned to my mom's house, very disappointed. My sister, Sue, came over later that evening, and we took my mom out to dinner. After a few glasses of wine, Sue and I got liquid courage and decided to try to find it again. This time, we snuck in a different way so we wouldn't be seen, and when I saw the rock, I immediately knew it was the right place. All those feelings from many years ago overwhelmed me, and I felt Stan's presence was around me. It was a solemn feeling and a place that will forever be dear to my heart.

I would have spent hours there but knew it wasn't a good idea. Sue took a picture of me sitting on the rock, trying to sit in the same poise of the picture he'd taken of me so many years ago.

That afternoon, I took quite a few pictures of the rock and woods around it and said my goodbyes to Stan.

Life went on without Stan, but each day seemed to still be filled with thoughts of him. I clung to all the mementos of our time together and continued to mourn the lost ring. It was the one thing that had marked our 30 years of caring for each other, and the loss of that broke my heart even more now that he was gone.

My mother told me about a bracelet that she had lost a few years ago and about how she gave up looking for it and decided to replace it with another and within a month, she found the original one. I decided I would try it, desperately hoping that it would bring back my ring. I went online and looked for another ring just like the one Stan had given me. I found one almost exactly like it and purchased it. I knew it would never replace the ring he gave me, but it would be something that would always remind me of him.

I needed to put what I had of our time together and make something special. I found the special items I brought back from Stan's house and carefully put together a shadow box that displayed our memories together. I placed his blanket on my bed and slept with it each night.

Natacha and I quickly became close friends. We'd only known each other a little over two months, but I felt I could share more with her. If it hadn't been for her and her insistence on getting me out of the house and back into the real world, I'm not sure how I would have made it through those first few months. I was consumed with just wanting to join Stan. She was so sensitive about my feelings and all I was going through.

After three months had passed, Natacha insisted that I do something to help brighten my life, and the first place to start was my home. The months had gone by so fast, and my house had suffered from the depression I was feeling. Cleaning or decorating became a chore that I wanted nothing to do with. Everything began to fall apart. I had no desire to go on, and knowing how I felt, she took over immediately.

The weekend after what would have been the one year anniversary of getting back together, Natacha came over to my house and insisted we brighten up the place a little more.

I loved her ideas and was ready to get started. Maybe that was what I needed to help cheer me up? She made a list of everything we would do and let me know that there was no backing out. I couldn't argue with her. I knew her intentions had my best interest at heart, and I was really hoping it would help.

She decided we would start in the bathroom, and one of my tasks before she came over was to clear everything out of it. I had become a pack rat during the past months and had accumulated a bunch of junk that was never being used. For some reason, I had a burst of energy and the excitement of making the house look better was definitely the driving factor. Purging my old junk was a great idea, and getting organized again was definitely something I needed.

I looked at the clock and realized that it would be over an hour before she was to get there, so I kept working. The first thing I did was take everything out of the bathroom, including everything in the tub, vanity and medicine cabinet. The next step, after cleaning the bathroom, was to repaint the trim and vanity. I started with the trim and was very happy with how it was looking. After the trim was done, I sat down on the floor in front of the vanity to begin painting. Out of nowhere, I became overwhelmed with a sadness which worsened the more I worked on the vanity, a sadness that was all too familiar, the sadness of not having Stan in my life anymore. I don't know how or even why I was feeling this way, but through the tears I forced myself to finish painting the vanity.

Natacha arrived to find the vanity painted and drying and me in a collapsed heap of sobbing. It had been four months, and the pain hadn't lessened any. I felt so bad that she was coming over to cheer me up and brighten my life all to have a silly thing like painting my vanity to affect me so much. We talked and she slowly got me back into the mood of moving on with our plans.

She decided we needed to go shopping to get a few things to spruce up the place a bit. Shopping was just what I needed to get myself in a better mood and we proceeded back to the house for a light dinner, some wine, and then back to work.

Natacha made a rule that if I couldn't remember when I bought something or even used it, to the garbage it went. Knowing she meant it and being afraid that there might be something I wanted that I knew she'd disagree with me keeping, we went through the junk together piece by piece. It became quite comical digging through each "priceless" keepsake that ended up in the bottom of the box in the vanity in the bathroom. That seemed to be the catch-all place for anything that served no purpose that I just couldn't throw away. What a pack rat I'd become, and I could tell by her reactions that this was something very foreign to her. We laughed about it and were enjoying the time together.

We were sitting on the floor in front of the last box of junk to go through and I was finally reaching the bottom of the box. I picked up one last item and underneath, at the bottom of the box I saw something that made my heart stop, and I could barely move. My hand started shaking and my heart was racing as I said, "There it is!"

Natacha glanced inside the box and saw this mangled piece of metal that showed no sign of what it really was. She said, "Is that the ring?"

As tears fell from my eyes, I took off the ring I'd purchased just a month ago and handed to Natacha, as I said, "I don't need this one anymore." I carefully picked up the ring in its mangled form and asked Natacha if she would come downstairs with me to watch the video I had explaining how to put it back together. It took us about 20 minutes, but we got it back in one piece.

I would never have found the ring if I hadn't followed Natacha's rules. Going through each item and deciding whether or not I should keep it made me carefully pull each item out of the box. If she hadn't been there watching each step, I probably would have dumped the box into the garbage or just stored the contents in another area in my house, never to have found the ring.

Having the ring back in my life has left me with a peace, a peace of knowing it was real between us, a peace of knowing the type of love that can last forever, the peace of knowing that someday, we'll be together again. Even though life and death had come between us, my ring had come back to me. Stan will always be with me.

Chapter 20
Epilogue

I began writing this story to help remember the greatest part of my life, to remember the fairy tale that I was once a part of. I was afraid the details would fade after time. No one can say it's for the best that things turned out like they did, nor can any of us tell what happy endings are in store for us before we reach our end of the road, but I do know for certain that my life has been and will always be enchanted by Stan.

Perhaps my struggles defined too much of who I was and who I am now. Perhaps, like Romeo and Juliet, our story is all the more meaningful for ending how it did; no one would ever remember poor Romeo and Juliet if there'd been no family conflict to pull them apart and no angst-ridden tragic ending. Maybe my happily ever after didn't turn out the way I expected it to and hoped it would, but hopefully this story will live on and perhaps, just perhaps, my story does not end here.

The five boys were my incentive to write this book, to show the kind of man Stan was, the caring person he was and how special everyone in his life was to him. He can never be replaced in any of our lives, especially mine.

My world changed forever for me that day; just as it began that fateful day the spring of 1976 when Stan entered my life; just as mysteriously and suddenly as when he arrived to swing my world into a different orbit, so he departed leaving me swinging out there in space without a solar axis. He always told me, just look up into the stars, and we'd be together. I still do... and I feel his presence with me.

Knowing now how our story has ended brings to me a world of questions left unanswered. Would I have been so insistent about not making changes until he was divorced? Would I have moved up there to be with him when he asked? Would I have had the child he'd wanted so badly? Would I have stopped him from asking me to marry him until the divorce was final?

If I were not so life-wrenchingly shattered, I might understand why I ever doubted his feelings for me. It made sense, the pushing me away for my own protection – it was the courageous thing for him to do, as each day marched him inevitably towards his end. It was the Stan thing to do; like a brave soldier putting a front on his pain to protect the perfect love at the other end of the phone line, the email, the solar system.

I suppose my lesson in this is to err instead on the side of optimism while I'm alive, to give the final boot to my insecurities and believe in the love I know is there at any moment, to believe without having to touch it, hear it, see it at every moment, to believe like any foolish romantic, to be led with my heart without losing my head. But wisdom does not allow for easy transformation, and experience can never fully roll over and hold its peace in the face of the kind of love that makes you feel young and silly and full of hope again. And would we want to become naïve again, for the thrill of making those mistakes and heartaches for the first time again? No, I confide to myself; I keep my mistakes and heartaches close as an apron of knowledge, but I also allow the leap of faith, wind in the face that shines its wisdom through everything that happens, reminding us that all things are possible.

I will always love and cherish what Stan and I had and somehow hope to find the reason for him being taken from me so quickly. I will wear his ring and necklace each day to remind me of the special bond and love we had for each other. I hope his boys will see that I truly loved their father and always will. He's been a part of my life for so long, it will be hard to go on without him again but somehow I must.

I hope the story of Stan and I can help the five boys we've cared about most, to help them follow their hearts and learn from our struggles, to go for it now, because you never know how many tomorrows you'll have. I don't know whether these stubborn old bones of mine will ever be able to act on the beautiful and horrible lesson Stan's departure from life has taught me, but I hope with all my heart that our five boys will take our story with them and let it inspire their future for the better.

I never wanted anything from Stan other than his love. The few items I have from him I will cherish forever. He always said he would leave me something, and the one gift he left was our story, our beautiful love story that lasted over 30 years. He left me this book. I would never have had this experience and memories without him being in my life. No other man has given me the gift of love as he did. Thank you, Stan, for my memories. I dedicate this book to you.

I am hoping this book will help my heart heal. I hope that someday I will be able to have a full and joyous life without him. Knowing that he will never again be a part of my life is the hardest thing I must deal with. I will always keep him in my heart. Our love lives on…. And hopefully now I can move on.

This is not goodbye, Stan, because I know we will meet again. I can, however, let you go in peace, though your shadow walks always by my side. True love never dies.

I want to send a special thank you to those who supported me emotionally and stood behind encouraging me to write this book. I would be here forever if I mentioned every person who touched my life during this time and for those who I have not mentioned, know that in my heart, your love and support got me through this time of my life and you mean no less to me than those who I have made a special mention.

To my best friend Lisa, who supported me for over 12 years and got me through my lifetime of challenges. Thank you for being my friend.

To my mom, who has not only been my inspiration but my friend, I couldn't have made it as far as I had in my life without your guidance.

To my sister Sue, who after all the years of being apart from each other to come back into my life during the time I needed your friendship the most.

To my sister Karen, who listened to me for hours and hours of complaining and hardships.

To Zoe and Neil, my special friends who not only helped edit this book but also provided the incentive to keep writing during the times I felt I couldn't go on. Your guidance and input on the book have helped make it what it is and I couldn't have done it without you.

To Natacha, my dear friend, for bringing me back into the world of the living again and giving me something to look forward to, you came into my life when I needed your friendship the most. You helped remind me to keep living during the time I had lost all hope. I wouldn't have made it through this time without you.

To my special friends where I worked, who put up with my bad moods and times of sorrow; thank you all for being there for me.

To Shelby, for your encouragement to finally finish the book, I will always be grateful to you for getting me to pick it up again. I will always be grateful for your hours of editing.

And to my Father, thank you for being who you are, it made me the strong woman I am today.

Thanks to all of you for being there and supporting me and giving me the encouragement to continue living.

Made in the USA
Charleston, SC
21 May 2014